Winner of

The Flannery O'Connor Award

for Short Fiction

Silent Retreats

Stories by Philip F. Deaver

The University of Georgia Press

Athens and London

Paperback edition published in 2008 by
The University of Georgia Press
Athens, Georgia 30602
© 1988 by Philip F. Deaver

Set in Linotron 10 on 13 Trump Mediaeval

Printed digitally in the United States of America

The Library of Congress has cataloged the
hardcover edition of this book as follows:

Library of Congress Cataloging-in-Publication Data
Deaver, Philip F.
Silent retreats : stories / by Philip F. Deaver.
229 p. ; 23 cm.
ISBN 0-8203-0981-8 (alk. paper)
I. Title
PS3554.E1756S55 1988
813'.54—dc 19
87-14313

Paperback ISBN-13: 978-0-8203-3066-2
     ISBN-10: 0-8203-3066-3

British Library Cataloging-in-Publication Data available

"Silent Retreats" was first published in *Puerto del Sol;*
"Fiona's Rooms" in the *South Dakota Review;* "Arcola
Girls" in the *New England Review and Bread Loaf
Quarterly;* "Wilbur Gray Falls in Love with an Idea" in
the *Florida Review;* and "Long Pine" in *Sou'Wester.*

www.ugapress.org

This work is dedicated,

with great love and respect,

to John Groppe and James Kenny,

St. Joseph's College,

Rensselaer, Indiana.

Contents

Silent Retreats

Silent Retreats

One Monday morning on the way to work, the traffic pausing behind school buses, Martin Wolf was suddenly struck by the circularity of life and began to sob. Or maybe it wasn't the circularity but something made him sob and he thought that was it. The air, autumn cool, and the clear sky, the nostalgia of the changing trees, the cars with their small rising trails of exhaust, all conspired to give him existential doubt. He pulled onto a narrow shoulder along Roosevelt Road, two hundred feet from the big intersection at Glen Elyn Pike, slumped in his seat, and let himself go.

He'd gotten up too early that morning, reacting childishly to the muddled rejections of his wife. In the dim light of the kitchen, he poached an egg, half listening to the radio tuned to whatever station he inherited when he turned it on. To keep from bothering her, he'd hit the shower in the dark—strange experience: in the shower was a handbrush and as he scrubbed his hands with it he was swept away with a recollection of watching his father scrubbing for surgery back when he was in high school. At that time it was presumed Martin would be a doctor too someday. Now he felt the bristles reddening his hands, and he brushed all the way to the elbows to sustain the recollection. He dressed mostly in the available light of a blue dawn—whatever of it could find its way past the pulled drapes of the master bedroom. Then he'd read a while, sitting near the woodstove in the den. Melissa Manchester and Jackson Browne were on WLS, their love songs, their road songs. Martin pouted through the final routines of tying his tie and finding his watch and keys, finally stepping out the back door around 7:30. The vinyl of his car seat was stiff with the morning chill. He worked as systems analyst at Argon Labs, a short commute. From the narrow shoulder on Roosevelt Road, he watched the cars go by and slowly turned the dial on the car radio, searching for the one station whose wave length he was already on. He looked intentionally into the passing cars. The drivers were looking ahead only as far as the back bumper of the car ahead of them, or, in extreme cases of foresight, as far as the Glen Elyn Pike crossroad. Stopped at the light, the men would pull the morning paper up out of the seat next to them and prop it on the steering wheel, take a sip of coffee from the cup balanced on the console; the women would sit perfectly still, waiting, or they would pull down their sunglasses—all the women wore sunglasses—they would pull them down and check their makeup, cocking the rearview mirror toward themselves, cocking it back.

And all the while he watched, he couldn't stop crying. He sank deeper and deeper into his seat, the warmth and humidity of his tears steaming the car windows until the idling migration on Roosevelt Road finally became nothing but fog around him.

Maybe he fell asleep a few minutes—at least he lost touch. Presently he realized there was a car very close to his, stopped next to him, and he wiped a hand over the fogged-up window to look out. It was a woman, leaning from her driver's seat all the way across to the window on the passenger side, which was already down. Martin rolled down his window, trying to clear himself.

"Hello," she said, "is everything okay?" She had to talk loudly over the traffic.

"Right," Martin said. "Fine." He was trying to think if he knew her. He didn't.

"Are you sure? I have a CB here—I can make a call."

"I'm fine, thanks."

She looked right at him. "I have the feeling something's wrong—are you sure?"

"No," Martin said, answering the wrong question, rolling his window up again, "I mean yes, I'm sure," slumping down in his seat. When he looked back, she'd driven on.

He dropped a dime in the booth, and had to open the door again to bend down and pick it up. There were watermelon seeds, gravel bits, butts, brown stains in the corners. He heard his phone call go through.

"St. Michael's rectory." The voice spoke quickly but also seemed casual, a young man; the voice was deep, resonant, accustomed to speaking from the pulpit in modestly didactic sorties on the values of suburbanites.

"Hello." Martin was staring up the long street. From the booth, there was a gradual slope upward toward the outer suburbs presenting a linear retreating panorama of plastic franchise signs and the high-mounted signs of car dealers. The Radio Shack sign and the far off Dunkin' Donuts sign were turning; the tasteful bank sign, with gold bank logo on black, was giving digital readouts on the time, temperature, and interest rates, interspersed with ads and announcements.

"Anybody there?" the priest said. With the Chicago accent, he sounded like a cross between a LaSalle Street speculator and an Irish city cop: the practiced tone of an urban populist.

"I'm here. Yes. Sorry," Martin said.

"Don't apologize," the priest said. "It's just . . . you called me so you have to talk." There was a smile in the voice.

"Sorry," Martin said, then winced that he'd apologized again. But the priest was silent.

"Listen, Father, you don't know me," Martin said, conscious of the halting way he was speaking. "I'm actually not a Catholic anymore. I work out at the labs."

"Lots of Catholics survive working at the lab, pal. Are you in a booth?"

"Right," Martin said. A Triumph and a Camaro were doing a ritual revving at the stoplight, intersection of Roosevelt and U.S. 54.

"Sounds like the Daytona 500 out there. Roosevelt Road, right?"

"You got it," Martin said.

"Why not drop by if you have time. You know where we are? I've got some iced tea." The cars tore away from the mark. The Camaro left the Triumph after first gear, catching rubber in all four. "Mercy," the priest said when the noise relented.

"Sorry," Martin said.

"You know the Heiss family? Rick Heiss? Out at the labs?" Martin caught a sunbeam off a car bumper and it went all the way through his brain. "Heiss has a lovely family," the priest said. "He was a seminarian for a while, you know. They come to St. Mike's."

Martin was squinting, looking around through the grimy windows of the phone booth. "Look here, Father, I'm sorry to bother you this morning, but I'm on the way to work and I started wondering if . . ." He paused. Call a person "Father," it made you seem like the child, it made you seem innocent and the father all-knowing, like in the old days. It made life seem solid instead of liquid and gas. Intervention was possible; solutions existed and were only as far away as a rosary, a confessional, holy water. The tears were in his eyes. "I'm wondering if they still have silent retreats like they used to. I went on one with the Knights of Columbus once, when I was seventeen. Down around St. Louis someplace. I figured you guys might know if they still have things like that."

It was quiet on the other end. There was clicking in their connection.

"Hello? You there?"

"Well, usually they aren't silent anymore, to the best of my knowledge. But they do still have retreats. We've got marriage encounters and renewals, held at the old Maryknoll convent, you know? And the diocese has a retreat consultant come through from time to time, usually in conjunction with special diocese-level initiatives." The priest sighed. "The stress these days is on community. I guess the silent retreat stuff— they used to have retreats like that all the time—I guess the silent ones are considered self-indulgent. These days, in keeping with the community thing, community of the faith, of the faithful so to speak, these days at retreats they get in small groups, you know, and share perceptions, building a sense of community, you might say. That's the idea."

"Well, I'd like to go to a silent retreat," Martin said.

"I understand. You know, the new thinking, you see—I know you know what you want and pointing this out is a pain, but the new thinking is that silence like in those old retreats is a kind of self-indulgence—part of the problem, you get me?"

"Well." Martin felt a huge swell in his throat and chest, the fear of tears, the need for them to come on. "I don't know," he said. "I'll say this. I don't want to spend a week sitting around in small groups sharing, if that's what you're talking about, sharing perceptions and everybody getting a warm feeling inside. I know about that stuff and it's a big goddamned joke." He tried to wrestle himself back.

"Look," the priest said. "I've got some time this morning—why don't you drop by the rectory? You know where we are?"

"Nah, thanks. I only wanted to check on retreats, maybe get a schedule. I thought you could tell me if there are still the silent ones. I've gotta get to work."

It was cool in the booth and Martin's headache felt vaguely like hangovers he'd had.

"If you want, I could meet you over at the confessional or something. Keep it anonymous. No problem—whatever you want. You upset?"

"They think silence is self-indulgent? I'd be interested to know what they think of the Trappists. There's some real hedonistic guys. I swear," Martin said, and found his hand-kerchief. The tears were flowing freely and it was a relief for him not to have to hide it from the man on the phone.

"Look. Would you do something? Would you get out of the phone booth and drop by? I'm free all morning—we could just sit around and talk."

"Nah, I'm fine. I've been crying all morning, is all." Martin looked down the road. He could remember when he was a little boy. When he felt like this, there was someone who could make him feel better. "I appreciate your concern, Father, but . . ." Right then Martin noticed the turning bank sign. "Jesus! Nine o'clock! I've got to get to work." He wiped his eyes, almost laughing. "I can't do this all day—I don't have the energy. Excuse me a minute," he said, and clanked down the phone. He opened the door to the booth and blew his nose. "I'm coming apart here," he mumbled to himself away from the phone. He leaned back in and picked up the receiver.

"What's that?" the priest said.

"I'm sayin', I just wanted to get some information. Thanks for your help."

"What's so great about a silent retreat? They've got retreats for execs, they've got 'em for young marrieds and old marrieds and singles and psychologists. They've even got 'em for cod fishermen and neurotic priests." The priest laughed, tried to bring Martin along with his laugh. "No kidding. Retreats are still with us, it's just the silent ones that you don't see much."

"I understand."

"They even have retreats on educational TV. Do you have cable?"

"We're talking about two different things, Father. Are you aware of that? You're not talking about the kind of thing a person can go to and think."

There was no response from the priest. Martin decided he was a Franciscan. The Dominicans were parish priests, acculturated; Martin was thinking this guy sounded slightly more missionary, defying gravity with faith, so to speak. Suddenly, over the phone, Martin could hear the rectory doorbell.

"Hold on a minute," the priest said. "Seriously, hold on and maybe we can chat a little longer. I've got to get the door. While I'm up, I'll try to find the number for the Jebbie retreat house in Des Plaines."

Martin heard the priest go to the door. "Have a seat," he heard him say to someone, "I've got somebody on the phone. He's asking about retreats—you know the Jesuit place out north? Know anything about it?" The priest was talking to someone he knew well, someone who didn't know anything about the Des Plaines retreat house. Then Martin could hear pages turning. Then the priest was back. "Here we go. Call Father Hollins—661-3428. Gotta pen? 661-3428—no, wait a minute, that's the business office, hold it. Here we go: 661-3477. I think I know that Hollins guy—from Catholic Charities or something. Anyway, give him a call, ask him if he's got something in the way of silent retreats. Just tell him you don't want a bunch of sharing, you never can tell. That's all I can suggest."

"Thanks," Martin said. He didn't have a pen.

"I have to tell you, though," the priest said with something in his tone that indicated to Martin he wanted to level with him, "if you aren't going to mass and taking the sacraments, a retreat won't help."

"Help what?" Martin said.

"Help."

"Well." Martin stared up the road. Traffic was relenting. "Thanks a lot for the numbers, Father."

"You see, a retreat might take some pressure off you, but what have you done for the Almighty lately, is my point." Martin had the feeling the priest was playing to the audience, this somebody who had come to the door and was now at least partially listening to the other end of the conversation while waiting. Martin pictured the rectory, holy water founts and gaudy sacred-heart renderings, crucifixes everywhere with small painted elaborations of Christ's blood and pain. "You see what I'm saying?" the priest said.

"I get it."

"I mean you can retreat all the way to Milwaukee and back, you get me? But if you aren't going to mass, if you aren't with the program, you aren't pointed in the right direction to solve anything."

"I get it. I said I get it and I get it." Martin clawed at his tie, getting it loose.

"You ought to start coming to mass. Do you have children?"

"What's this, the pitch? Right here on the telephone?"

"It's all we've got, you and me. Sorry."

"Don't apologize," Martin said, and before he could quite control it he popped the phone back onto its cradle, the bell inside it singing from the impact. "Think about it, you jerk,"

Martin said to himself, and left the booth, stuffing his handkerchief in his back pocket.

He pulled up in front of the school. He was self-conscious because the windows on this side of the building provided him with a cross section of all elementary grades in the school, each of which was partly distracted by him when he pulled up and parked in the drop-off zone. He was trying to remember his son's teacher's name, Solomon, Lamb, Kennedy, something like that.

The school was low-slung, brick and windows. He walked in the north end, hoping that as he walked by the classrooms a name would hit him. The teachers' names were in little frames on the blond classroom doors. He wanted to see his little boy through the narrow windows, watch him a minute just to watch. The long, narrow yellow-tile hall depressed him even worse, Bauhaus education. Gone the bell tower and the tower clock and the small teacher-student ratio of his own Catholic elementary school days. Back to basics, walls and halls, floors and doors. Cut-out autumn leaves were taped to the blond bricks. Each leaf had a name on it, scrawled in a hopeful hand. He heard a child coughing as he passed one room, low murmur of the teacher as he passed another. His child, Jeff—pressed into this mass process. This was where he learned reading and writing, and, out on the playground, the recently unveiled revision of "Yankee Doodle" (". . . stuck a feather up his butt and called it . . ."). Martin noticed a sign on a door. Mrs. Rudolph, that was it, his son's teacher.

He peered through the window, and all he could see were the backs of children's heads as they bent over their seat work in the beige light. Despite all the windows, at nearly noon on this clear day the whole idea of the out-of-doors seemed to evaporate in this building. The teacher at the rear of the classroom was grading papers at her desk. Occasionally a child would lean over to sneak a comment to a friend across the aisle. There was Daren, his son's friend, and there was his son, blond boy, blessed. Martin watched him, and the tears were there again, unexplainable.

"Excuse me," somebody said from behind. "Have you been to the office yet?"

It was a little lady with dark gray hair, tightly bound. "You have to go to the office and check in—it's right down there, take a left." She smiled.

"I have to what?" Martin said, hastily. They were talking just above a whisper.

"To check in," she answered. "Down there." She turned and pointed down the hall. "My sister-in-law has allergies, too," she said, observant.

"I was hoping to . . . my son wasn't feeling well this morning and I thought I'd just look in on him," Martin said. "I don't want to bother him in class . . . I just wanted to lay my eyes on him, you know?"

"Of course," she said. "They have an intercom in the office."

"No need for any of that," he said.

She stood there insistently as he went back to peering in the window. He sensed that she was impatient with him. "Listen," he said, "you seem like a pleasant enough lady. Why don't I just break the rules and take a look at my boy for about another thirty seconds, and then I'll head out the same door I just walked in, no problem."

"This, sir, is a city school here. We have to control who comes and goes. Besides they have a visitor's packet for you in the office, and they can call your son from there, on the intercom. Or you could wait," she said. "In a few minutes, they'll be coming to the gymnasium for lunch." She was still smil-

ing, perhaps a little more forcibly. Martin wanted to punch
her in her soft little jaw. "The PTA worked very hard on the
packet. It's got their newsletter and the financial report."

"Please," he said. "I don't want the PTA newsletter. I want a
moment's peace here, looking at my little boy. I don't want to
mess over school policy, but this is a little thing, not big. I'll
be out of here in a minute." Martin leaned down to whisper
something in the lady's ear. "I'm just not in the mood for the
visitor's packet. Frankly," he said, still talking in a loud whisper, and he winked, "I'm afraid it will piss me off." He stood
back and looked at her, his arms up. "I might go berserk right
there in the principal's office."

The woman turned and hurried down the hall to tattle. She
wore matronly black-heeled shoes that clacked as she went. At
one point as she hurried, she looked back over her shoulder.

A wave of restlessness seemed to sweep through the school.
The big round clocks were signaling to everyone that the
morning segment of confinement was close to over. Then
Martin noticed another lady coming down the hall, approach-
ing somehow warily but with a big smile.

"Good morning," she said. "Can I help you? I'm Dr. Cousins—Alberta Cousins—I'm the principal here. Is your boy in
this room?"

"Yes," Martin said, looking through the window. "I was just
looking at him."

"Which child is it?" She came close to look through the
same small window as he pointed.

"The white-haired boy with the pencil in his mouth.
Chews the erasers."

"I hear you just encountered our librarian, Mrs. Redding."

"Yes." Martin continued to look through the window.

"She probably seems like an old biddy to you, but she's a
real pro in the classroom, I can tell you."

"That's good," Martin said. "Very loyal of you to mention it."

"Want me to get your boy out here?—it's no problem at all." Before he could answer, she ducked past him and opened the door. She signaled to Mrs. Rudolph, a very tall, made-up woman, straight-backed, perhaps forty-five. "Jeff's father has come to see him—could we have him a moment?"

Then Jeff was out in the hall, a little bewildered. He grinned up at his dad, cheeky face, eyes like his mom. "Hey," Martin said to him.

"Hey," the boy said back.

"If you don't mind," the principal said to Martin, "would you take your walk out the north door? In four minutes the halls will be filled with masses of children, marginally controlled and very hungry." She smiled warmly. "And," she said, "I don't know whether our librarian mentioned it, but when you're finished we have a visitor's register for you to sign and a packet of materials for you, in the office."

"She mentioned it."

The lady faded off, back down the hall.

"How you doin'?" Martin said to Jeff when they were alone. Jeff was in the first grade.

"Fine," he said. As they walked toward the north door, they were holding hands, both looking at the floor. Martin was fighting another swell of emotion. "We goin' home now?" Jeff asked.

"What're you studying in there?" Martin said in a low voice.

"Nothin'."

"C'mon."

"Vegetables."

"Vegetables, great. Which ones?"

"We had to write our favorite ones."

"That must have been tough. Which ones are your favorites?"

"Carrots, root beer, and grape juice."

"Real good, fresh produce. I saw Daren—he's almost as tall as you are now."

"We had a army guy today." They arrived at the north door.

"Yeah? A real one?"

"He let us sit in his jeep. Army guys aren't to kill people—they under-arrest 'em."

"Did you sign up?"

"Sign up for what?" Jeff said.

"Hey, Jeffrey. I just thought of something." They were sitting on the north step in warm sunlight. "Remember when we played baseball last spring? When we played together in the park where the ducks are? Remember?"

"Yip."

"Know what that made me think of?"

"Nope."

"I thought of when my dad first played baseball with me." Tears welled up.

"How come?" Jeff said. He squinched up his nose.

"How come what?" The handkerchief.

"Daaa-ud, I mean how come you thought of that?"

"I don't know—I just did. Once Dad and I were playing burn-out—you know?—when you throw back and forth real hard trying to make the other guy say ouch. And I threw this one real hard and it skipped off his glove and gave him a black eye. Playing baseball with you, it made me think of playing with my own dad and it made me happy. Back then, when I was playing with him, I never knew there'd be a you."

"Your dad died, right?"

"That's right, but that's not what I'm talking about. I'm talking about before that. When I was little like you are. Little kids don't realize you were little once too. It just . . ." Martin could feel the point laboring down to nothing, but he kept wanting to say something magic. "It just seems real . . . real interesting to me that my dad played baseball with me and then I played it with you years and years later. And you and him, you never met. You're flesh and blood, but you never met. I'm the bridge between you."

Jeff was looking out toward the playground. "Hey, Dad . . ." Martin waited. "Wanna see the gym? It's time for lunch."

Martin stood up, hurt. "Nah. I gotta go to work." He kissed Jeff on top of his blond head and squeezed him a good one. "I love you, boy," he told him, and Jeff's eyes wandered back toward the north door.

"I love you too, Poppsy," Jeff said, still looking away. "I don't get it. Why did you come to school?"

Martin was heading back toward the car. "I needed to know about vegetables. Grown-ups don't know everything, you know."

"Hey, Dad," Jeff shouted as he pulled open the door to the school, "guess what?"

"What?" Martin spoke over the top of his car and across part of the school yard.

"Daren's got poison oak."

"It'll go away." Martin smiled, getting into the car. When he looked back that way, Jeff had gone into the school.

What an odd state of mind, Martin thought, to wander through the suburbs in broad daylight, drifting with the radio and the flow of traffic. These disc jockeys, they had the city mood perfectly calibrated with their rattling jokes and timed, practiced chaos. At the stoplights, he watched the other drivers. How many of them too were wandering? He came across the northside, all the way to Lake Michigan, and drove a short distance south on Lake Shore Drive until he came to Belmont Harbor.

He parked at the far end of the parking lot and, in the wind and long shadows, sat motionless. There was a woman he knew and he thought of her now, because she always talked to him about being lonely and maybe she was alone now for all he knew, and she had talked to him about keeping a bottle of gin under the bed for nighttime, whether because she was afraid or because she was bored or because she needed love and had no chance of ever having it. It had been a revelation to hear her talk about being alone. She'd been in every kind of therapy known to woman, she'd even been Rolfed in a motel room in Danville, all for the company of it, because other possibilities seemed to have expired. She'd raised her children—they were gone from her except for desperate phone calls they'd make to her in the night, the kind that brought up the heartbeat and made sleep impossible for nights afterward; because she was nearly forty-seven, she felt she was about to slip darkly, alone, into the hole.

Today Martin knew how she felt, as he watched the October waves on the lake. The sun dropped just behind the tall bank of apartment buildings west of Lake Shore Drive, and a chill sat him up. He'd met her, this woman, in a strange town. In a Mexican restaurant they talked with their heads close so even now he could remember the glitter in her makeup, the slightly caked mascara in her eyelashes when she'd cried a couple of times, the warning she gave him about being unfaithful, voice of experience: "I'm not married anymore because of something like this," she said to him. "I found out he was seeing someone else and I left him inside the hour. I took the kids." She was staring right at him. She knew what she was saying to him, the sign she was giving. "If you love a person and the person isn't faithful, there's no hurt like it." She made him think hard about that.

There was a phone booth in the lobby of the Drake Hotel, not far from Belmont Harbor.

"South Ridge Legal Services," a voice said at the other end of the line.

"I'm calling a guy named Skidmore."

"I'm sorry," the voice said, "we're closed. Can I take a message?"

"Closed?"

"Yessir," said the voice, flat, bored, unapologetic.

"I just wanted to tell this guy Skidmore . . . I wanted to tell him what to do with a red hot poker."

"I see. That doesn't sound too nice, sir. May I say who called?" The man on the other end spoke in a monotone.

"Tell him this is your old pal and worst enemy from when you were twelve."

"I see. That's nice. That sounds very nice, I would say." Skidmore would not sound surprised nor break character. "What shall I tell him you are up to these days?"

"Tell him it's none of his business."

"I see," Skidmore said. "That doesn't sound very nice. Where shall I tell him you are calling from?"

"Las Vegas, on the strip."

"Nice. That's nice. Say hello to Wayne Newton for him." They both laughed. "Shall I tell him you were drunk when you called, like you usually are?"

"I don't recognize the accent," Martin told him. "It isn't quite British, is it?"

"Kind of a mix, I'd say," Skidmore said. "Sophisticated, don't you think?"

"Not really."

"You were in a religious thing last time you called, seems like. Drunk and very religious. We talked about baseball and the absence of an afterlife."

"I don't remember," Martin said.

"Drunk." Skidmore mumbled it away from the phone.

"Your letters," Martin said, "are meaner than usual lately."

"Don't start it. I'm not mean."

"I'm not the only one who thinks you are."

"I know. Let's not get into it, wha'dya say?"

"How's legal services for the poor in Nebraska?"

"Terrible. I'm not such a great lawyer, I'm afraid. McFarland says I hate Indians and won't admit it."

"I expect he's right."

"Cut the crap, you don't know. You don't know me anymore. Every cell in my body has turned over once since way back the hell when—the old days."

"Some things don't turn over with the cells," Martin said. He heard a resolute sigh on the other end.

Skidmore changed the subject. "I'm living in this trailer—in my office, you know? And I've got this Indian woman around here somewhere. Fifty years old. I just saw her go by the window here a minute ago, chasing a blue jay with a god-damned tomahawk." The low familiar mean laugh.

"Fifty," Martin said.

"Nothing like it. We like to rassle," Skidmore said in his best boys-will-be-boys central Illinois idiom, but with the subsequent affectations of Australia crowding in.

"Rassle?" Martin said, and he laughed in spite of himself.

The wires buzzed. Maybe this would be the last time they would ever talk. Letters were easier than phone calls. Nowhere in this world could Martin quite find the Skidmore he knew a long time ago, but the handwriting, it had never changed. Always, on the brink of making a call to Skidmore, he noticed his motivation. It was always a wave of feeling alone, wanting to be friends again.

"Ken Boyer died."

"Yup," Skidmore said. Cardinal third baseman, their old common hero. "How's the wife and kid, Rod or whatever his name is?"

"His name is Jeff."

"Right. How's he? Gonna have a bunch more?"

"Everyone's fine. Thanks for asking," Martin said.

Again the phone line buzzed.

"Rough old world," Martin said. Maybe he could convey something by suggestion.

"Plenty rough," Skidmore said. Silence. Then he said, "God. What a laughable jerk."

Quiet again.

"I always think, if I could just put together the right set of words or something," Martin said.

"Well, outgrow it," Skidmore said. "It's pitiful."

Now the full flood of sadness was coming up again on Martin, and he let the phone call die. The buzz in his ear remained, and there was nothing from Skidmore to stop it. Trying to keep his voice flat, Martin said, "There isn't any friendship anymore. Or something."

"I know," Skidmore said. "Go home. Vegas is no place for a man in your frame of mind."

"Shit. It was built by people in my frame of mind. Anyway, I'm in Chicago."

"I gotta go. I'm an attorney. Time is money. Get off the sauce and go home, is my advice. Play catch with Rod." Skidmore hung up.

Martin responded to the operator by feeding in the change, and then opened the door just a little to shut the ceiling light

off. Across the lobby, through the front doors, he watched a
Mercedes being unloaded by two bellmen. The sun was almost down.

Nine o'clock. The hotel lobby's colors seemed faster when
he was coming out of the smoky lounge than they had seemed
when he went in. The phone booth was still in approximately
the same place, give or take. The floor sloped in a way Martin
hadn't noticed earlier. For three hours he'd hung suspended in
a vision of himself in a mirror, through some upside-down
glasses hanging in a rack behind the bar. This time he called
collect.

"Hello," she said.

"Hello."

She paused, recognizing the voice. "Well. Where might you
be?"

"I'm downtown at the Drake Hotel, case someone asks. I'm
okay."

"Sure you are."

"I am."

"This is getting to be a regular thing."

"I wouldn't say that," Martin muttered.

"You what?"

"I took a drive," he said. "Just ended up down here."

"You took a drive? Is that what you want me to believe?"

"You don't know shit about men," he said.

"I see."

He didn't think she quite did see yet. "Do you understand
what I'm saying? You don't know shit about men." His voice
banged against the wall of the phone booth, banged back into
his own ears. "I've been meaning to tell you that."

"I think I've pretty much got it," she said. She didn't say
anything for a moment and neither did Martin. Finally she

said, "What's to understand? I missed a meeting tonight because of this and I'm in a lousy mood. You stay downtown 'til you either get it straight or sleep it off. You got somebody to drive you?"

"I'll be home in an hour or so."

"Who'll drive?" she said.

"Look, I'm resoundingly alone and shall do the driving," Martin said.

"Delightful."

The phone line was quiet for a while. "Do you understand me, about what I was saying?" he finally asked.

"Which was?"

Martin momentarily forgot. This was not a good situation.

She said, "Jeffrey finally mentioned around bedtime that you'd been to school to see him. So I called Charlotte Rudolph and she said you'd terrorized the librarian in the school hall at lunch—threatened to tear the principal's office to pieces or something. Do you ever think about anyone else?"

"Like who?"

"Like your son."

"He was fine. We had a nice chat. Don't use him—he was fine. Don't use him on me because you missed a sales meeting. You miss those all the time. You hate those goddamned sales meetings."

"He was embarrassed. He told me so."

"He did not. He wasn't embarrassed."

"He was," she said. "You embarrassed him."

Martin thought about that. Maybe it was true.

"Look," she said. "I've been worried. I need to know what's going on so I can make some plans for myself. What's going on? Is this the great midlife crisis?"

"That would be the easy conclusion, my dear," he said. "Or

the pre-midlife fore-crisis. I called them about silent retreats.
He asked me what I've done for the Almighty lately."

"Are there any silent retreats anymore?"

"Yes, but they ain't silent and they ain't retreats. I told him
I can have an encounter any time I want one, but I can't get
silence when I need it. He said silence is self-indulgent, something like that."

"What's wrong with self-indulgence, or did he say?"

"We didn't talk very long." He took a deep breath. He was
buzzing, the line was buzzing, the colors in the hotel lobby
were buzzing. "I'll drive with maximum carefulness and caution."

"To the extent you can differentiate," she said.

Martin hung it up. "I'm having a willful adventure here," he
said to the hung-up phone. A lady in a glittering gown and
jewelry buzzed across the lobby. He opened the door of the
booth just enough to let the ceiling light go out, and from the
dark observed her. He could imagine what her aloof, urbane
arms would feel like around him, what look in her self-
absorbed eye there would be if they were together.

It was ten-thirty when he pulled up in front of the rectory at
St. Michael's in Wheaton. The front-right tire of the car
jumped the curb. Martin, accepting chaos as a way of life, left
it that way. He crossed the wide amber-lighted street, walked
into the shadows up the front walk, felt the chill around his
ankles as he carefully climbed the shadowed front porch steps
and knocked on the door. The porch light came on, yellow. A
Franciscan priest cracked the door and looked out, then
flipped the chain lock and opened it wide. "Yes, can I help
you?" he said, his hands deep in his long brown habit, the
white ropes dangling far down.

"Bless me, Father—for I am drunk."

"Funny," the priest said. "But I've heard funnier. You must be Silent Retreats himself. I think I recognize the voice."

"I doubt it. Every cell in my body has turned over since this morning."

The priest gestured for Martin to come in, and Martin bowed past him, walking carefully so as not to fall. The priest indicated a parlorlike room off to the right, and Martin went in there.

"Looks like you've been trying to work out your own redemption."

"Are you going to keep saying things like that all the time I'm here?"

"Sorry. Have a seat."

When Martin sat down, he noticed that the priest was pulling a pistol out of his habit and setting it on the umbrella stand behind the front door.

"Sorry," the priest said. "Not very attractive, a man of the cloth bearing arms. Some joker robbed us last month—got the Bishop's Relief Fund collection. Scared hell out of the Monsignor."

"I'm serious," Martin said. "You gonna blow somebody away with that thing? Blow him out of his socks right on your front porch?"

"Yeah, I know—I probably won't shoot anybody."

"Don't you guys carry insurance for the Bishop's collection or whatever?" Martin rubbed his face. The beard was back. "You know, you might consider a dog. Experience tells me you can keep the poor from crowding in on you if you simply buy a large, well-trained killer dog." Martin's head was buzzing. "I think if I kept a .38 around I'd be afraid I'd use it on myself, and I'm not even celibate on purpose. I would never use a killer dog on myself, no matter how loathsome things got."

"You have a number of interesting points there," the priest said. "How about some coffee?"

"Tell me the truth. Is that thing loaded?"

"Hey—touché on the gun, okay? I'm sorry I met you at the door with a gun."

"No, no, don't apologize to me," Martin said. "Black and no sugar. I'll just sit here a while. Semi-upright. On this couch."

"That would be fine," the priest said. He headed for the kitchen. Martin stared at the picture of Christ on the wall. It was an ordinary picture of a man, only Martin knew it was Christ because of how the guy was holding his hands. When had they stopped painting halos so you knew who was holy?

The priest was back with a huge mug of coffee and two aspirin. "For the hangover," he said. "I don't know your name still. I'm Thomas Simon." He seemed to have a regular chair, and he relaxed in it and let Martin sip at the scalding coffee. The floors of the whole house were bare gleaming hardwood, dark. The warm glow of the low light bent down on them and made the hour seem very late. The priest watched him, and Martin was aware he was watching. Martin had a flash of the woman that morning, leaning over toward him, shouting through the window that she'd help. He tried to think about her. Stopping, that was a nice thing she did. Then she was completely gone. He wanted to run an ad in the paper that might find her. What would the ad say?

"You don't have to tell me your name if you don't want to," the priest said.

"Are we gonna start sharing now?" Martin said. The furniture was spare, the floor dark and clean, the lights dimmer and dimmer, and the house was completely still.

Fiona's Rooms

Skidmore had a woman named Fiona, a strange woman who looked like she hated everything because of how she painted her eyes. There's a picture of Yank and Fiona, before Yank left, taken at a farmhouse south of Long Pine in 1980. Yank is toasting the camera with a silver can of malt liquor, and he's trying to smile but he can't quite pull it off. His beard is shaved crooked, and, to hold back his long hippie hair, he's wearing the elastic waistband from his jockey shorts around his head. Fiona is standing straight, even under the weight of Yank's left arm, which she seems to have shouldered in order to hold him up. There is a blur through Fiona's face, like a question she didn't know she had. The picture was taken on the front porch of the farmhouse, and far off in the distance behind them is the road sign pointing toward the strange little ravine town of Long Pine, located a mile and a half south of the hardroad. The sign is really a painting of a pine tree, tall and narrow and slanting off at an angle—quasi-Indian art. It looks phallic, or like a giant green corndog waiting to be launched.

Yank served in Vietnam, and he had a great stereo to show for it. It was Yank who actually selected the dreary three rooms above a bar in downtown Fort Robinson, this after they'd hurriedly abandoned the Long Pine farm when things suddenly went bad and Yank couldn't swing his end of the rent. They'd lived in Long Pine five months, and had hoped to stay there through the harvest, Yank working at the elevator, Fiona singing in The Gulley and cooking at the hotel. But there'd been a fight of some kind—Fiona would never know all there was to know about Yank—and someone was cut with a razor, and there'd been some bad money exchanged for something, Fiona wasn't sure what. Anyway, it had suddenly come to Yank that it was time to leave. They had wearily slouched into Fort Robinson in the middle of a July night, courtesy of a lonesome trucker hauling used cars to Cheyenne. Yank carried the stereo, and Fiona carried the clothes and her banged-up guitar. It was a new beginning.

Yank painted the apartment a uniform glossy white. He built a great platform bed in the bedroom, which faced west and caught a full blast of summer sun beginning in the middle of each afternoon. And when all this work was done, he settled in for the long haul, went out looking for a job. He had his rich brown hippie hair cut at an actual barbershop for the first time since the army, to show he was serious. Using a little of the money Fiona's ex-husband was then sending along to help her out, he bought a new pair of wheat-colored Levi's and a fancy shirt; and, as always, he made friends with the local cowboys, joining them in the mornings for red beer in the bar down below the apartment. Fiona noticed that he seemed real happy, and for about six days it looked like he was completely stabilized. Then one afternoon the stereo turned up missing and Fiona found out he had traded an Indian even for a Yamaha 750 and hit the road without notice. She ceremoniously hung the Long Pine farmhouse picture on the glossy white wall over the platform bed.

That was in 1980. Yank had been a fine lover, but Fiona seemed to understand his departure, and she liked to think that she could do very well alone. In 1979 she'd hitchhiked penniless out of Valdosta following her divorce. She claimed to be a singer and a writer, and she'd told her ex-husband that when she got out west she was going to write something great. He sent checks to provide a base for her to do just that. From the Long Pine farm, she'd sent a story or two to show him she was "producing," and the boys at The Gulley took a picture of her singing on the barroom stage so she could send that, too. There was never a sign from her husband that he'd received these items, but he kept sending along money and Fiona figured that must mean something. Yank had really liked Fiona's singing, but he didn't give a damn what she was writing, or how she wrote. He was, however, real impressed that she was smart enough to be a writer and still liked him. He raved and raved when she bought an old Olympia portable typewriter and he saw how fast she could go on it.

Yank gave Fiona quite a lot to write about. She set her typewriter on a stocky library table that miraculously was furnished with the place. She moved the table under the tall windows in the bedroom so that sometimes she could look up and stare out over the alley, out over the town, westward out toward the Pine Ridge, and think about Yank, what he must be doing, what he had done, how he used to touch her, and what he had said. Grist for the mill, she thought to herself. Good material, she thought, and she put it all down. Next to her table on the right was the radiator. On the left was her stack of stories and a couple of novels, written before this her "blue cowgirl period," as she called it. Beneath the big bed was her journal, in which each evening she wrote about her life, following intricate directions given to her by her niece, who had once taken a course in creative writing.

Skidmore was a lawyer in Fort Robinson, and before he had Fiona, he was a depressed person because he had just come through a time when he had a woman named Jolinda, a strong Dakota Sioux woman who was forty-eight years old and lived in a concrete-block house out on the reservation. Jolinda loved Skidmore very much, and she was quite a novelty to him, too. Skidmore had loved Chinese women and a black lady from the southside of Chicago, and he'd loved a wicked German fräulein he traveled with on a Eurail pass back in '71, and he'd loved a redheaded professional women's basketball player from Chattanooga, and he had loved a short blond law student from the University of Louisville when he was studying there—a fancy girl whom he still often dreamed of. But most of all, Skidmore loved the girth of his experience, and the time came when the Indian experiment got old, the long drive out to the reservation became bleak, and Jolinda's requirements crowded him. Soon after that, he didn't go out there much anymore. He didn't say anything to Jolinda about his fading sentiments. He simply withdrew. He hoped in time she would be able to fill the void with some glorious offspring of Crazy Horse, some ambitious and brave grandson of Red Cloud, some full-blooded descendant of great warriors, if such had survived.

It was, in fact, on the one hundred and fourth anniversary of the bayoneting of Crazy Horse on the streets of Fort Robinson (the fort, not the nearby town named after the fort) that Jolinda ingested the rough equivalent of her weight in Pine-Sol. That night Skidmore sat by his phone, as though someone would call or he would call someone, while they worked hard over Jolinda in the emergency room. The terror and guilt made his ears ring—the panic caused his blood to rush so hard that small capillaries broke in the whites of his eyes and his mouth dried out. He sat in the dark of his office, which was also his home, which was also a trailer in the Pine Ridge–Fort Robinson trailer court. Through the walls of the trailer, Skidmore could hear his clients—drunken Indian braves squawking their tires at the A&W down on the highway, Chevy loads of high school girls laughing dark and loud at the stoplight nearby. The tension crushed in on him, and sitting there in the dark, Skidmore devised a method for killing himself if word came that Jolinda had died. He decided to shoot himself up on the Pine Ridge, where no one would find him and his remains would simply become prairie powder. Or he would find an anonymous pine, in among thousands of others in a forest, and he would hang himself in the top of it, his body concealed in a plastic Glad bag to foil the buzzards and the magpies and to blunt the shock to any poor backpacker who might come upon the scene. He would go away to the wilderness alone and take his own wretched life, in reparation for what he had done to Jolinda that caused her to drink a toxic substance because of her all-consuming love for him. Anyway, word came in the night that Jolinda had lived and Skidmore let himself off the hook. But he never went to her again, and he always worried that he would encounter her along the dusty Fort Robinson streets. He watched for her so as to duck into a store if she should come by.

Skidmore's office was the South Ridge Legal Services Organization, law for the poor, and he had a secretary named Peg who arrived at the trailer each morning at nine. As Skidmore's law practice faltered onward, Peg said nothing, but did her duty at the typewriter and the filing cabinet. Skidmore often wondered what Peg thought of him as she observed his wasted movement and his confused ways. He was constantly distracted by his aching guilt over Jolinda, and he knew it showed. Three times a week, in jeans and blue jogging shoes, coat and tie, he walked up the hill from the trailer court to the old courthouse where he shouted and groaned and objected client after client directly into jail. The judges hated him because he often resorted to loud talk instead of strong argument, and they were not receptive to his continuous charges of racism. They would hold against him on principle. The district attorney and other prosecutors didn't even know Skidmore was in the courtroom, and easily cut through his half-baked, knee-jerk liberal, laughably ineffectual arguments. Skidmore was losing heart, finally. He was feeling too old to be a social worker, no longer able to tolerate and rationalize the self-destruction poor people seemed to continuously bring on themselves, or so he saw it. There were three shootings and two stabbings a year in his trailer court alone.

And Fiona didn't really hate everything, despite the dark pitiless stare she drew over her eyes. She'd learned that from the rock stars. The fact was, she was wide open to the world. The severe eye makeup was probably a lucky thing, keeping the whole world from gravitating in upon her and delaying the continuous typing of novels and stories that was proceeding in the rooms above the downtown bar. After Yank's departure, Fiona found that she could feed herself and live, although sparsely, on the monthly check from Valdosta, and her productivity soared. On Tuesdays, as a matter of organization, she fixed her plumbing or went to the laundromat, and in the afternoon, by long-established and hard-to-break habit, she might play her guitar and sing—quietly, so that the sound didn't go through the floor and draw a bunch of curious and drunken cowboys. Or she would bake some bread—a week's worth—anything to get away from the typewriter. A day of rest, it was something else her niece had learned in the writing class, and Fiona stuck by it to the letter. She hated filth, and despite its whiteness, because the apartment was old and dusty, she cleaned it obsessively, down on her hands and knees, humming country tunes and thinking about all her stories.

In all this, Fiona rarely said anything to anyone in Fort Robinson, and Fort Robinson, if it ever really knew she had come to town, gradually forgot. Except for the cowboys down-stairs, who sort of knew Fiona through the cowboy talk Yank had engaged in when he was down there mornings trying to make friends. From time to time, as a result of that talk, Fiona would have to endure the curious advances of drunks when she was returning from the park or a trip to the laun-dromat. She was a puzzle to the cowboys because she was obviously a street woman but never seemed to come out and play. Sometimes they would wait for her at the bar's side door, located right on the slanting stairs she had to climb to her rooms. She learned to go by them quickly, and usually one among them would moderate the others and there wouldn't be any violence. But one day when she was returning from the laundromat, Fiona encountered a lone drunk high on the stairs in the shadows, near the door to the apartment. He came at her, knocked her down the stairs, laundry and all, and awkwardly crashed down the stairs after her. He seemed hell-bent on having her right on the downtown sidewalk. But Fiona, ever since her hitchhiking days, had carried a five-inch Buck hunting blade concealed in her boot. She pulled it on this drunk, and she put it against his chest, just below his hairy old throat, and she backed him into the bar. She backed him across the bar, backed him into the men's room, right up against the locked door of the only stall in the place where he couldn't back up any farther. The sheriff was on the pot, un-fortunately. He overheard Fiona, in a low voice, tell her would-be assailant that she would have cut his balls off if they'd been in there alone, but she could see boots under the stall door. She didn't know the boots belonged to the sheriff. When he was finished he flushed the toilet and went upstairs and arrested her. He explained that his brother was her land-lord and also the owner of the bar downstairs, and that neither of them, he nor his brother, would stand by while trash like

Fiona degraded the premises, and this business of pulling knives on the clientele would have to stop also.

Which is how she met Skidmore, public defender. On the merits of Skidmore's professional legal counsel, she was convicted and fined, and, unable to pay the fine, spent a week in the Dawes County jail in Chadron. These events gave Fiona, who was accustomed to the desperate life, material for yet another novel and she didn't even hate Skidmore for his incompetence. In fact, they became friends, and he got her apartment back for her by collecting on an old debt. Skidmore had once helped the sheriff's brother sidestep a paternity suit.

That autumn Skidmore found his way to Fiona's rooms on many afternoons. He would climb the slanting staircase and knock—they developed a little code, two taps, then three taps, so she would know it was him and not the sleaze from downstairs back to settle the score. She did worry about that.

Sometimes when he arrived, Skidmore would be depressed, and sometimes he would be angry or cranky, because of what he was going through over at the courthouse. Because Fiona had no phone, her place was truly shelter, and Skidmore liked to go there because her rooms were so clean and fragrant and she never yelled at him, and her bed was always crisp and white, and her love was a new adventure. In the afternoon, they could lie in the sun that came through the tall windows, and together they could stare off into the far distance at the tan-colored fields of cut wheat, the pine-rimmed bluffs, the whole vast land. Through the open windows, the autumn air would come into the room, hot but at least moving, and spread flat across Fiona's writing table and the big bed Yank built before he went away.

Fiona knew Skidmore, too, was just passing through. Long ago she'd stopped counting on men or expecting much from them. She never said a lot to him about the past or future. She wrote in her journal that the two of them were like two separate small orbiting particles—their coming together was a random thing. But Skidmore wanted to claim her, in some way to get her to love him and him alone and with great devotion. He asked her to move to the trailer—even promised to get rid of Peg—but Fiona made excuses. She said she liked her writing table. She said she hated trailers. She said for all she knew Yank was just on a trip with his new motorcycle and would be back within a couple of years. They both laughed, and Skidmore started paying the rent to the sheriff's brother. He never told Fiona about the Dakota Sioux woman and the Pine-Sol, but sometimes Fiona saw panic and desperation in Skidmore's eyes, aloneness and futility, distraction. Sometimes he was rough, and his humor was hard and grim. He seemed to take more than he gave, and sadly.

She wrote in her journal: "Sometimes I sense that we are only moments from one of those confessions or surrenders that are suddenly blurted out and change people's lives." She would watch him closely, wondering what was on his mind.

Skidmore called Fiona his "blue cowgirl," because she had confided in him that she got the idea to leave Valdosta from the book *Even Cowgirls Get the Blues*, which she was reading the very day her divorce finally came through. In her own mind and probably in reality, the "blue cowgirl" phase had ended with Yank and the move from the Long Pine farmhouse. Having put that period behind her, she no longer appreciated allusions to it. She was now seeking "liberation," and liberation was the subject of her writing, liberation from her own past and from the traditional limitations of traditional womanhood, but liberation even beyond those things—liberation generally, the elusive freedom suggested by the very ring of the word. That was the current phase for Fiona.

She was subscribing to literary magazines and *Harper's* and

Atlantic, and it seemed like every single story had a woman in it who started lifting weights. Fiona couldn't afford weights, but she started toning up, doing exercises every day. She read in *Time* that fitness was what was happening for today's woman—that's what *Time* referred to them as, today's woman—and so Fiona did daily exercises, jumping jacks, push-ups, sit-ups, stretching exercises. She practiced kung-fu moves she found in a *Cosmopolitan* she'd borrowed from the laundromat. She took up nothing that demanded the purchase of special shoes, special support, or special designer sweat clothes.

The afternoon he first learned about all this, Skidmore arrived as usual and shifted his shopping bag full of Stroh's to the other arm so he could hammer out the code on the door with his right hand, when he noticed the door was ajar. He cautiously pushed it open and from there could hear her in the kitchen. In there, he found her on the floor doing sit-ups.

"Why's the door unlocked?"

"Saw you coming up the sidewalk from the window— didn't want you to interrupt, so I opened it between sets. I'll be done in a minute." She was wearing nothing but the sweatbands on her arms and a pair of navy blue panties.

"What's going on?" Skidmore asked, popping open a beer.

"Check it out," she grunted, pointing toward the news magazine on the kitchen table. She was working out on a small black throw rug, a feeble cushion between her and the old linoleum. Her hair was glossy from exertion.

"I thought you wrote in the afternoon."

"What's it to you?" she said, smiling as her face came up. Her hands were behind her head, and her feet were locked down by tucking her toes under the kitchen cabinet. "Hang around," she said. "Push-ups are next."

"Push-ups? Getting ready to enlist?"

"Funny. Trying to make me lose count or what?"

"How about a beer?"

"Never touch it."

"Oh yeah? Since when?"

"Since this morning. Stop it, you're making me lose count."

"Sandwich?"

She stopped. "Will you please get out of here? You're em-barrassing me. I'm toning up. Read the magazine. I'm twenty-nine years old—I've got to get after it while the getting is good."

"I'm thirty-five," Skidmore said, his arms up in the air to indicate that even at that age he was in good condition.

"I didn't ask," she said. She rolled over and started a set of push-ups. Her face turned purple as she worked. Skidmore was looking at her pretty back and the backs of her legs, all imprinted by the ancient kitchen linoleum because the throw rug was too little.

"Look, quit it," he said. "This behavior is extreme."

She sat up. "See these?" she said. She seemed to be indicat-ing her breasts. "These are your pecs," she said.

"Boys only have one," Skidmore said, toasting her with his can of Stroh's.

"Very funny." She rolled over and went back to sit-ups. After a while she paused again. "You get a lot of strength if you do a bunch of push-ups and a bunch of sit-ups every day. Arms like a meatpacker in six months."

"Sounds lovely. You can join the circus."

She laughed. "That's what you know, you ape!" She stood up and pulled the *Time* magazine off the kitchen shelf. "Read it, Jack. Women aren't going to take it anymore." She was smiling at him.

"Take it from who?"

"Men—what do you think?"

"Take what?"

"It," she said. "It."

"Oh." Skidmore drank his beer. "Guess I better read the magazine."

Fiona came to have the opinion that her writing was improved by these exercises. Besides hitchhiking—which was physical exercise, she would hasten to clarify—she had not taken much interest in sports or exertion and had had little appreciation for the psychological benefits such activities accorded the avid and consistent athlete. Now she found that she had double the energy she used to have, and late at night, instead of drifting off into a muddled sleep, she would still be able to read. She took up reading poetry, memorizing poems she really liked and lines from all the novels she was reading, and suddenly many things she read seemed directly relevant to her.

By the end of the warm-weather time, the days had a definite pattern—the heat and bright sunlight building out of breezy, shaded mornings. Each day was scheduled around the mail watch, anticipation of a check from her ex-husband or a rejection notice from some magazine or a letter from her niece. After noon, the sun would come across her writing table, across Fiona, across the floor to her bed, and then up the glossy white wall to the picture of her and Yank at the farmhouse in Long Pine; then the sunlight would wane to a rose color on the white wall, and finally the light would die altogether. At some point in the afternoon, the odd, secretive Skidmore might appear, but not necessarily, and if he did, he would knock in code on the apartment door. Invariably he arrived harassed and pitiful.

"I think it's the way you look," she told him one day.

"What is?" They were eating potato chips and drinking beer—she was back to beer by then. They were sitting on the black exercise rug, in the best approximation of the lotus position either of them could muster. Skidmore was playing his Fleetwood Mac tapes on a portable cassette dictaphone the government had bought him for depositions. The beer was cold.

"You lose because you don't look like the judge used to look before he was a judge. You don't seem to aspire to the same things he aspires to—you don't appear to aspire to his station. So what possible use for you could he have? You, in your Brooks running shoes and jeans. He looks at you and says, 'What in the hell is THIS, anyway?'"

"Because of how I look, the judge runs Indian brave and redneck alike off to the state farm and the county jail—because of how I look?"

"You got it, Rondo," she said, grinning at him.

"How about how you look?"

"Here it comes." Fiona's long, graceful arms waved big in the air. "There will now be five solid minutes of male retaliation." She looked over at him and grinned.

"Okay, let's have it," she said, throwing a potato chip at him. "Let's have some good old male retaliation!" She stood up and stepped back, crouching low, then lobbing more potato chips. "C'mon, tell me, how do I look?"

Laughing, he chucked a potato chip back at her. In the second volley, she took cover behind the closet door in the kitchen area and he under the kitchen table. "Your eyes—that screwy mascara effect. Did you ever think you might have spent time in the Dawes County jail this summer because of the hooker eye makeup?" She made a run for the refrigerator and from that advantage lofted ice cubes across the room.

"I spent time in jail because I was being defended by a distracted, uninspired public defender." One ice cube grazed his shoulder, another slid across the table, then gently dropped off the edge onto his head. "Bingo!" Fiona shouted, ringing up the score.

"That did it!" Skidmore said, and, both of them laughing, he stood up as if to inspire a whole brigade of reinforcements, then stormed the walls, deflecting ice cubes and potato chips. When he caught her, a short wrestling match ensued which bent, veered, curved, swooped, came finally in even turns of its own accord to the sun-filled bed.

When they had made love and were basking on the white sheets, Skidmore finally popped the question: "Why can't we make a deal? I'll let you do push-ups all day and not laugh about it. And you, someday soon, please, take down that goddamned picture of you and whatshisname." Skidmore was staring at it.

"I like that picture," she said to him.

All through the summer it went on, with Skidmore at the trailer in the night most nights, or hurrying at least to be there by the time Peg arrived in the morning, and three times each week he walked up the hill from the trailer court, ten blocks to the courthouse, where he shouted, wailed, and mismotioned poor people straight into the custody of the state. He daydreamed constantly of his regretful involvement on the reservation, and in night dreams he saw Jolinda buried under rocks in the Black Hills, down with the bones of Crazy Horse in a secret place, or he heard her voice coming from the dismal shadows of the concrete-block house out on the Ridge. Sometimes, in peaceful dreams, Jolinda would suddenly intrude, sad or angry, her presence terrible and real. A process had begun in which Skidmore was recasting remembered events with himself as victim.

"I'm a terrible lawyer," he once mumbled to Fiona as they sat on the bed in the sun. "Something else, too. I hate these goddamned drunken Indians."

"If you hate them so much, why are you here?"

"My question precisely." He got up and walked over to her writing table, sat down. "Do you write about the Indians any?"

"Nope."

"I don't seem to be able to defend them. They kill each other, they drive their cars at high speed into poles and cattle. What do they think they're doing?"

"Why are you here, then?"

"They don't seem to be able to organize. They jump each other and each other's wives. They play pool fifteen hours a day."

"Then how come you're here?"

"I'm running from all my friends and acquaintances back in Illinois. They think I'm mean."

"And why do they think that?" Fiona asked, but by then he was paging through a book of poems that was on her desk. Perhaps he hadn't heard the question.

November came, cloudy. Nebraska began to bone up for hard winter and the late afternoons were dim and uncertain. Skidmore tried again to get Fiona to move in, and again she said no. Reagan's budget cuts were a low waving axe over his program and his job, and Skidmore was beginning to feel temporary. He wanted Fiona to go with him. He was haunted by the Indian woman, and wanted to put many miles between himself and her. He kept expecting her to knock on his door. On the street, he would think he saw her and he would wince inside himself and his heart would jump. It wouldn't be her. The wind on many nights would come down from the Black Hills, pick up a howl in the long draws and narrow passes, would roll along the piney bluffs whistling, then flat and quick would whip down the long valley and slam into the trailer court. Skidmore would shiver in his bed. Sometimes he would stand in the dark at his bedroom window and watch the gravel dust sweep up into the yard light and then run downwind like a ghost.

Or sometimes a windless cold would stand on Fort Robinson, and Skidmore would become jumpy from the sounds outside, the yakking of dogs and the howling of kids, the loud shouting of cowboys and Indians getting things straight with their wives. In the rare times when Fiona would let him stay at her place the whole night, he would hurry back to the trailer right at dawn, cold to the core. Most of the time Fiona preferred to have him gone so she could read and exercise before bed. She slept soundly, the bedroom snug from the steamy radiator. The windows would fog up with the steam and her breathing.

One morning she found something odd in her mail. There was a note in scrawly handwriting:

I'm watching.

Fiona said nothing to Skidmore about this message. She assumed the drunk she'd threatened in the summer was back for more. Or that Yank had returned. When she went to the laundry or the grocery, she found herself looking for Yank along the street or standing in the shadows between the buildings. She hoped he was back—she'd missed him and wondered how he was. She assumed he'd seen Skidmore's comings and goings, and was reacting possessively. There was an edge of menace in the method, which Fiona kept trying to ignore. Yet she knew Yank was capable of menace and more.

One morning the veil of condensation dripped down her windows as she was typing and she looked out over the alley behind the bar, out half a block to the next street, and there, in front of the old wood-frame building that was once the trading post, she saw an old blue pickup truck idling in the cold, a weathered camper on the back. Inside, looking her way, Fiona could see a woman, bundled up. In the mailbox that day, a second note arrived:

I remain to be watching.

Many times in the following days, Fiona and the woman would watch each other from their separate places. One afternoon when Skidmore drifted over to Fiona's, she didn't answer the coded knock. He didn't have a key, but the rickety door was easily finessed with his old plastic law school ID card. It was the middle of the afternoon and he assumed Fiona was late getting back from the laundromat. Inside, he looked around the place. He had never been in the rooms when Fiona wasn't there too. This apartment was a great comfort to him—clean, smelling of Fiona and her toil and her blind, senseless, somehow pitiful but lovely optimism. The warmth of the rooms went deep inside Skidmore, giving him a sense of well-being. He decided he would go in and read something she was working on. He was always hesitant to ask if he could do that. He set his beer down on the kitchen table and pulled off his coat. As he did so, Fiona suddenly appeared in the door of the bedroom.

"How did you get in?" She seemed upset. She was wearing a long terry-cloth bathrobe.

"Didn't you hear me knock?" Skidmore asked, defensive.

"You knocked your way in?"

"There wasn't an answer, so I picked the lock."

"Is that what you always do when there's no answer at a person's house?"

"Sorry. There wasn't an answer, so I let myself in—to drop off the beer. What's the matter anyway?"

"There wasn't an answer so you picked the lock?"

"Look, what's the matter?"

She stared at him until he began to wonder if she'd even heard the question.

"The truth comes in blows," she said.

"Huh?" Skidmore was getting ready to fix a sandwich. There was something disturbing in the air. He tried ignoring it.

"The truth comes in blows. *Henderson the Rain King,* 1959."

"That did it. I've got to confiscate your library card." He was smiling, keeping it light. "What's going on?" he asked.

"I've been looking out the window. Someone's out there."

"There's a whole little town out there," he said. Yet already he was starting to know.

"Come and see."

He followed her into the bedroom. Her robe was long and pink. Skidmore had never seen it before. She pointed out the window, toward the wood storefront on the other street. He was stunned. The blood surged into his head, swelling the arteries in his neck. Even at this distance, he recognized her. She looked old, bundled in black and gray wool, a ragged black scarf.

"She's been sending me notes."

"Notes?"

"Handwritten things, saying she's spying on me."

"It's not spying if she tells you."

"Do you know her?"

Skidmore tried to think. What might Jolinda have said in those notes? "How do you think I'd know her?"

"Maybe one of your Indian families, one of your clients, something?"

"I don't know who she is, with her goddamned crazy notes."

"Better tell me," Fiona said. She was getting dressed.

Skidmore watched out across the way, avoiding Fiona's eyes. If he looked at her, he knew what she would look like. She would look just a little afraid, but there would be an edge of determination there also, and that was the part of the look that would mean trouble. She was not going to let this pass. And neither would Jolinda. The radiator pipes rattled and knocked with the rushing of steam. Out on the street, Jolinda gave Skidmore a big, ominous Indian wave.

"Well," Fiona said. She pulled on her jeans, the long familiar legs disappearing behind the light blue. "I'm gonna talk to her and find out what in hell's going on around here." Fast, she pulled on a blue and white flannel shirt, disappearing into clothes. She sat on the bed and strapped her sheathed knife to the outside of her leg, slid on her boots. "Looks like an Indian woman to me," she said, and went out the door.

Skidmore heard her clomp down the slanting stairway. Quickly, he gathered up his beer and his tapes and his tape recorder, and put all the stuff in a shopping bag. Then he too left, latching behind him the door to the apartment, scurrying off down the hill toward his trailer. All the way home, he kept an eye out.

Arcola Girls

On Saturday night, Arcola girls would come north on the two-lane for the dance. The road, Route 45, was flat, and the grass grew right up to the edge, crowding in on them, narrowing the alley of their headlight beam. With their windows open they could smell the warm, damp night air and the cornfields as they came. They could hear everywhere the swarms of crickets. Sometimes grasshoppers would land right on the windshield or thump onto the hood. Crows would sweep from the wires, stay on the road until the last moment, picking at run-over barn cats and field mice. The car tires would thump on the seams of the concrete road. It was a seven-mile drive.

By eight in the evening their white Chevys and green Mustangs and burgundy Corvairs would be cruising through the drive-in and making the Webster Park loop. They would glide through the downtown, past the community building where the dance was just getting started. Sometimes you'd hear their tires screech as they stopped, or they'd peel out at the intersection, showing off. You could hear them laughing.

One of them, named Kelly, had beautiful blond hair, long like that of Mary Travers. There was one named Karen who was famous for singing like Connie Francis, and sometimes at the dance she'd join the band and sing "Where the Boys Are," just for fun. Another, Sandra, was very tall, and her hair was ratted in a bubble after the fashion. She had odd eye-habits, always seeming to observe. Sometimes, playing in the park, she'd be running—her strides were long and confident like a boy's.

They all wore shorts and colorful sweatshirts, white tennis shoes. At the dance they would huddle together in a corner, doing committee work on the latest rumor, the latest dirty joke. Sandra, alert in the corners of her eyes, would look over her shoulder in case anyone was coming.

"I think you love those girls," my girlfriend said to me on the phone one night, "the way you watch them."

There were two bad S curves in the road from Arcola. They were where the highway was rerouted fifty yards west of itself for a certain short stretch because it would always flood in a heavy rain and people would get killed. So, instead, people got killed in the curves. Late one night in that particular summer, early June, Karen, with another Arcola girl named Marie, ran off the road at high speed on their way home. They went over the ditch and deep into the weeds, through a fence, flipped into a field. They weren't found until morning.

The crumpled ghost of their Chevy rusted most of the summer and part of the fall where the wrecker let it down, half a block from the Dairy Queen in the wreck lot of Ford Motor Sales. I don't know what the fascination was, but sometimes I'd go by there. Through the crunched, blue-tinted windows, in the folds of the damp, bent seats, I could see a Beatles album and a soggy package of Kools. There were stains of blood in the driver's seat. One of their shoes was decomposing in the gravel next to the car. I'd find myself staring. This was before Vietnam really got going. Back then, the whole idea of people dying who were about my age was a rare and somehow fascinating thing. The Arcola girls, Karen and Marie, they were the first I remember.

There was one Arcola girl named Rhonda Hart, a wild girl with dark brown hair and strange, blue catlike eyes. Each Saturday night, late, when the dance was almost over and the room was humid and warm like hot breath, a group would gather around Rhonda, who was by then dancing alone, doing, if the chaperones weren't looking, a pantomime of taking her clothes off to a grinding-on-and-on rendition of "Louie, Louie" that the local bands had turned into the theme of the summer.

I remember that her legs were skinny, but she was round and ample under a pure-white sweatshirt, and her menacing cat eyes stared into the group around her, mostly boys, her lips pouting like a bad girl. She'd make-believe unzip her candy-colored red shorts at the back, make-believe slip her panties off her hips and slide them down the skinny legs to the cold cork-looking floor of the West Ridge community building. A little kick at the last and, imaginary pale pink, they sailed through the imaginary air. And on she danced, her arms out to you. She was pretty good.

At Webster Park there was an old bandstand the Arcola girls used to gather at on summer nights. They would park their cars in the deep shadows. The local high school boys would go there, too, and in the black shade of the park maples they would all play, smoke, make out, the Lord knew what else (there were always whisperings, strange rumors going around). These were country girls. Maybe some of them might not have gotten a second look from the boys in Arcola, but in West Ridge they were exotic and different, from a place that, to us, then, seemed far away. They made the air palpable with sex and play.

The first time I ever heard a girl say "fuck," it was an Arcola girl, and she didn't say it mean or loud, but it seemed to echo all through Webster Park, down the length of it into the cluster of pine trees, beyond that to the ball diamonds, the deserted playground and city pool, the walking gardens.

"You'd love to go out with one of those girls," my girlfriend would sometimes say.

We'd be at the drive-in and one of their cars might spin

through. The curb-hops would jump back to avoid it. I might crane my neck to see who it was.

"Cathy says they're all dumb as posts," she'd say. Cathy was my girlfriend's friend.

"Cathy should talk," I told her. I'd turn up the radio, the manic, rabble-rousing prattle of Dick Biondi, WLS.

That summer a couple of classmates of mine, Bob Reid and Buzz Talbott, slipped into a slumber party in Arcola. They climbed through a bedroom window, bringing with them their sleeping bags and beer. Rumors were it had been some great party. The rumor was that somebody's farmer-dad caught them, though, and there had been a shotgun fired and a quick getaway. Bob Reid, and a kid he paid who was taking shop, had spent an afternoon rubbing out and painting a couple of pockmarks on the white tailgate of his dad's pickup.

Sarah, a buxom little Arcola cheerleader, maybe the prettiest in the whole group, got pregnant that summer and disappeared. They said she went to Texas. It seemed like everything you heard about the Arcola girls was an exotic, strange, wild tale—full of skin and possibilities.

So one Friday afternoon I called up Rhonda Hart to ask her out.

"Tonight?" She seemed real indignant. "Out where?" she said. "For chrissake," she added. She was chewing gum. "Give a girl some notice sometime, will ya?" It was her Mae West act. She was laughing.

"Mattoon. A movie. Champaign—I don't know."

"Mattoon a movie Champaign you don't KNOW?"

Shouldn't have called, I thought to myself. Her voice was hard and confident. The Righteous Brothers were playing in the background. I'm different from her, I was thinking. She knows more about the world.

"We could just go talk or something. I don't know," I said. It was all wrong.

"I'm not sure I know who you are even," she said.

"My name's Tom Nichols," I told her. I tried to explain myself to her. Told her I was a friend of Bob Reid and ran cross-country with Talbott. Tried to recall for her times when I was the guy *with* somebody she *did* know when we were all doing something she might remember, such as getting a pizza or buying a Coke at the Sinclair station like a bunch of us did one night and all stood around making wisecracks.

"Well, let's drive around West Ridge—we don't have to go any place special," she said.

"That'd be okay," I said. "I thought a movie maybe."

She was quiet a moment. "So you don't wanna be seen with me or what?"

"Nah. I just want—I don't know—quiet or something, that's all."

"Right." She laughed. She really liked that one.

"Wanna go dancing?" she said. "Up at the Chances R? I heard the Artistics are up there. I love their lead singer—he looks exactly like Elvis. Let's go dancing."

Sometimes I'd see her cruising with Bob Reid in his pickup. I knew she occasionally went out with him, and he was never known to dance. So what did they do when *they* went out? Couldn't we just do that, whatever it was?

"Okay," I said. "We'll find a dance or something."

"You don't sound real enthused."

"I'm enthused."

"You don't sound like it."

"Look," I said, "I must be a little enthused, I'm calling you up."

"Down, boy," she said, laughing, chewing her gum. She thought about it for a while.

"Don't make it a gift from the gods or something," I said finally.

"Right," she said. "Hang on." She put the phone against

something soft to muffle the sound, and was shouting. Then I heard the phone clank down and she was gone, to ask her mom. You'd always forget that Arcola girls had to ask their moms.

"Yeah, I can go," she said when she came back all breathless. "What time?"

"Eight. Suit yourself," I said.

"Dancing, right?" She seemed to be setting it out as a condition.

"Eight o'clock," I said.

"Seven or eight?" she said.

"Whatever."

After I hung up I went out in the backyard and sat in a lawn chair. I was nervous about this. Rhonda seemed different from my girlfriend, rougher and faster. Then my sister yelled from the house that I had a call.

"Hi. This is Rhonda," she said. I didn't say anything. I expected a cancellation. "Remember me?" she said, and laughed. "One more thing. Let's make it around ten-thirty, and you meet me at the bandstand at the park. What do you say?"

"Ten-thirty?"

"Right." She was talking quieter than in the first call.

"No way," I said.

"I got something going I forgot about. I can get loose by ten-thirty."

"No."

"What's wrong?"

"It's too late."

"Look," she said, "I want to introduce you to my friends. I'll ride up with Kelly, and you can bring me home. You know Kelly?" Kelly had the silky, white-blond hair, freckles.

"Yeah, I know her."

"Well, I just talked to her, and she doesn't know you."

"I think I'm losing control of this."

"Ha." She seemed to fade away. Then she was back. "You can handle it. See you at the bandstand. Ten-thirty. Wait if I'm late." She hung up.

At eight I was on the highway to Arcola. I'd decided to try to get to Rhonda before Kelly did. The sun was going down and the Illinois sky was red in the west. The locusts were loud, wheeting in a pulsating rhythm. Much later the moon would rise full and red, blood moon. Jupiter would linger near it all across the sky, stalking. The whole thing was a mistake.

I'd never been to Arcola on my own mission, but I found her house, using the phone book in the booth just outside a place downtown called the Youth Center. I parked down the street on the opposite side and watched the house in my mirror. It was dusk. I got out of the car and walked back toward the place, trying to think what to say. I hadn't thought of anything by the time I knocked and Rhonda's mother came to the door. She was all fixed up, maybe thirty-nine or forty years old. Her perfume wafted through the screen door.

"Hi," I said. "Is Rhonda home?" I told her my name.

"You're Tom? I thought she was with you," she said.

I turned around to see if she was, a little joke. "Nope." Rhonda's mom didn't laugh.

"I'm kind of late," I said. "Are you sure she isn't here?"

"God, I'm almost *sure* she's gone," she said, "but I'll check." Her voice was raspy, had that same worldliness as Rhonda's.

She asked me in and had me sit on the couch. There was what appeared to be a half-gone seven-and-seven on the coffee table. I heard her go up the stairs. There was a cat on the couch with me, staring at me, and there was the tank of fish in the room that I'd been able to see from the car. The whole room had the fragrance of Rhonda's mom's perfume.

"Look," she said when she came back in, "I can't find her. I think she went out already. I thought I heard you come to pick her up half an hour ago. I'm really sorry, but she's gone."

I sat there on the couch, looking at her.

"There are a couple of places you might find her, is all I can tell you," she said, sitting down next to the cat and facing me. I looked out the window into the Arcola night. I noticed that sometimes she herself was looking out, over my shoulder.

I didn't say anything. I didn't move.

"She might have gone to West Ridge, is all I know. Although if she did she's in trouble."

Rhonda's mother was wearing a cotton blouse, a tight dark skirt. Her deeply tanned hand was on the back of the couch near me. Her fingernails were ruby red. The house was quiet, immaculately clean. My quietness was giving her some trouble. On the wall was a picture of Rhonda when she was little. Next to her her father, a truck driver. They were posing in front of his fancy new semi.

"I'm very sorry about this," she said to me. Her teeth were kind of crooked.

"Maybe she took off because I was late or something."

"I don't think so. There must have been some misunderstanding. She was looking forward to this. She really was. She probably told you, I've had her grounded for a couple of weeks because of that drunken slumber party business. She's supposed to be with *you* right now. The condition for this whole thing was that she was going to the movies with you. She's in trouble."

"Well," I said. "It was a misunderstanding maybe."

She was very pretty in a grown-up way, as she shrugged her shoulders and half smiled at me. "Well, she's in trouble." Rhonda's mom was standing up then, my invitation to go. "Good-night, Tom," she said. "I'm sorry about this."

On the way back to the car I looked up at the sky. Moonless, clear as a bell. But a moon was coming—I remembered that from the night before. As I was pulling away, I noticed that a car behind me was passing slowly. I thought it might be Rhonda and Kelly. I drove around the block, and in those few moments Rhonda's mom had turned off the lights and locked up and was darting across the dark yard to the car. It was a white Oldsmobile Starfire with the wide band of stainless steel on the side. I couldn't see the driver before the arching trees and distance intervened.

I imagined that Rhonda had gone north with Kelly and that West Ridge was now aware of my foiled, clandestine date. I decided to drive around the streets of Arcola for a while. West Ridge and Arcola, they were little towns. You could stand in the center of either of them, facing north, and see the bean fields at the city limits to the left and the right; standing there at dawn you could hear the roosters welcome the day out on the farms. In both towns there were the same white clapboard houses with an occasional red brick estate, the same livery stalls down along the Illinois Central railroad where the Amish parked when they came in from the country to shop. There was a grain elevator on the railroad, too, and a lumberyard, and an old hotel downtown. All the themes of West Ridge played out in a variation in Arcola.

I passed the Arcola policeman parked in the shadows up an alley, waiting. I could see the glow from his cigar as I passed. I would turn left at this corner, right at this one, for no reason, but it was a small town and soon I was in front of Rhonda's house again. The lights were all off, except for a lamp near the fish tank in the living room. I decided to park and sit a while.

Before long Kelly's car pulled up next to mine. Rhonda looked over at me. I felt like I'd been caught doing something. Then Kelly pulled ahead of me and parked. I saw the car door open, and Rhonda was coming back my way, walking like a curb-hop in her tennis shoes.

"Is it you?" she said. No recognition whatever.

"I thought we could go south from here and catch a movie in Mattoon," I said.

Now Kelly was coming back, too.

"That's great," Rhonda said, "but it's not the plan. What about my friend?" She introduced me to Kelly, who did not quite look at me. She'd been kind of pretty at a distance, cruising by, but close up she had a hard mouth and a spacey stare. Both girls were chewing gum. I turned up WLS real loud. "What about my friend?" she said, talking over it.

"Does Kelly have a date tonight?" I asked Rhonda.

"No."

"You do, I thought."

· Rhonda looked at Kelly impatiently, like I was missing the point.

"She can come with us if you want," I said.

"Look," she said. "I've got a problem with this. What are you doing at my house?"

I looked up beyond the trees, at the ARCOLA in big block letters on the water tower, lighted from somewhere below. I had once climbed the West Ridge water tower.

"I mean this is *real* creepy," she said. She looked back up the street, chewing her gum mouth-open style. "Did you blow this thing with my mom?"

"Blow what?" I said. "She seemed real nice." Before she could say anything, I said, "Your mom says you're supposed to be with me. Let's just have an ordinary date, wha'd'ya say . . ."

"I've got something I've got to do, that's what I say. Don't you understand that?" She looked at Kelly. "I think he blew it with my mom." Then back at me. "I've got something I've got to do," she said.

"Yeah, yeah. Do that tomorrow night. Go with me now."

"I'm busy tomorrow night."

We both laughed at that one.

"Look," she said. "Kelly and me talked about this. I was thinking maybe you'd come with us."

I stared ahead. No answer.

Finally she said, "Look. Park the car over at the Youth Center and get in with us—we'll swing by and get it later. You know the center?"

I was thinking about it.

"C'mon! I'm in a big hurry." She walked back to the car. Almost there, she turned around and gestured big. "I'm in a *hurry.*"

I parked my car at the Youth Center and climbed in with them. I sat in the back seat. They paid very little attention to me as we drove around. It was clear they were up to something. Maybe they even went a little out of their way to be mysterious.

"She's supposed to be a good one," I heard Kelly say to Rhonda.

"Right. I can imagine." She hummed the tune they play on *Twilight Zone.*

"Seriously, she's got a certificate from some institute or something. What time is it?"

Kelly reached into a grocery bag in the front seat. She pulled out a jar of kosher dills and handed it back to me. "Open this and you get the first one," she said, keeping her eyes on the street. I opened it, took a pickle, and handed the jar up front. They both chomped pickles for a while.

"What time is it?" Kelly asked again. The radio answered the question.

"Slow down, Nutso," Rhonda said as we approached the alley where the cop was. "Hey, Fat Jack!" she shouted and waved as we went by. He remained where he was.

When the evening train whistle sounded from out north of

town, Kelly turned around in an alley and headed back toward the downtown. By the time we got there, the train was through and the Oak Street crossing gates were going back up to let people pass, except nobody was waiting. We drove down a lane along the railroad, a sort of alley. We went alongside the steel quonset-frame warehouses of the local broomcorn factory, passed the railroad depot completely closed down and boarded up, and pulled up in front of an old trailer. Dogs were barking off in the dark.

"Where are we?" I asked them.

"We're at," Kelly said, "a . . . dark . . . old . . . house trailer."

"Wonderful."

She laughed nervously, stared at the place, snapped her gum. Nobody came out. "Looks pretty dark," she said in a loud whisper. The nervous laugh again. "Shall I honk?"

Kelly lightly tapped the horn a couple of times and blinked the lights. The neighborhood dogs intensified their barking. The trailer had burned at some time and had scorch marks above the windows. Several were completely out.

Kelly turned around in her seat and asked me if I would go check in the trailer to see if the woman was in there. She reached down under the dash. "It's worth another pickle to me." She handed me a flashlight.

"What woman?" I asked.

"Jesus! Just go see if anybody's in that trailer. Okay?"

So I went to have a look. The only thing not burned inside the trailer was one overstuffed couch. On it, sure enough, was a woman dressed in black. She was staring straight ahead and the flashlight did not seem to startle her. "Ah. You're here," she said. "Are you Kelly?" she asked.

"No, ma'am. Kelly would be a girl."

"What's that?" she said, coming to the door.

"Kelly would be a girl, ma'am," I said.

"She would, would she? If what?" With my help she stepped down from the trailer to the ground.

"She's in the car, ma'am," I said. She was dressed in a black flowing robe. She smelled like scorched mattresses.

"So. Kelly's a girl is she? Where is she, then?"

"Right, ma'am. She's in the car." I pointed toward the car, and we walked that way. She breathed hard as we went. We had to step over junk.

"Who're you?" she asked.

"I'm a friend of Rhonda's."

"A friend of who?"

"Rhonda." I shined the light ahead so she could see the clear path to the car.

As we were getting there, she asked me, "So how far's this barn?"

"What barn would that be?" I asked.

Kelly heard the question. "Hi," she said. "It's about six miles out."

"Are you Rhonda?"

"Kelly," Kelly and I answered simultaneously.

The woman bent down and looked into the car on Rhonda's side. "Never mind names." Her eyebrows seemed unusually heavy. "I need to be back here in time for the Panama Limited—10:52. Is that going to be a problem, you think?"

"No," said Kelly.

"What's that?"

"No, ma'am," I said, for some reason acting as Kelly's interpreter.

The woman sat in the back seat with me. She was maybe sixty and wore a dark paisley bandana in her graying hair. She was very serious. Kelly started the car, and we headed out.

"Did the train thing work okay?" Kelly asked her.

"It worked very well. I thought it would. It's a whistle-stop, real chancy, and sometimes they don't stop and you end up in Carbondale. But I knew they'd stop for an old woman. I come from the age of trains. We speak the same language." She was smiling as she said this. I tried to picture her, all in black like this, attempting to be a typical passenger on the Illinois Central.

Now that we were heading out of town, the woman said, "Girls, I usually am paid in advance."

Kelly looked over at Rhonda, who rummaged in her purse. She came up with a leather bag of change which Kelly reached over and took and started to hand back. No telling how much. Rhonda stopped her.

"You know Kelly's mother, right?" Rhonda asked.

"Yes," the woman said.

"And we don't want her or anyone else to know about this. You know that?" Kelly said.

"Yes."

Rhonda handed over the bag.

It disappeared into the black flowing clothes. "Onward, ladies," she said, satisfied.

After we left the lights of town, there was very little talk in the car for a while. Occasionally Kelly and Rhonda might confer on the right direction. Out on the country road there was a roar of crickets and frogs. The air was almost hot coming in the back window. I slumped down. We were starting to get far enough north that we were in familiar parking territory for West Ridge. We turned, sure enough, onto the Black River Road, crossed the old iron bridge, and went down into the bottoms. We turned onto the predictable tractor path, went along the river and then across the field toward the barn, *the* barn, the great monument in West Ridge parking lore.

We were about two hundred yards from the barn, on a tractor path serving as border between head-high corn and hip-

high soybeans, when Kelly and I spotted something at exactly
the same moment.

"Oh God, Rhonda, don't look," she said, "don't look," and
she actually groped to cover Rhonda's eyes. We were quietly
passing the tail end of the white Starfire, partly hidden in the
corn. Rhonda stared straight into it as we passed.

"It can't be."

"Don't look," Kelly said.

"What's the deal, ladies?" the old woman said. "You're giving me the heebie-jeebies. What's happening?"

"Nothing," Rhonda said. "We thought we saw somebody,
but we didn't."

"Out here?" the woman asked.

"We thought so," Kelly said. "Wrong again, though." She
tried to almost sing it.

"Wrong again," Rhonda muttered. "Is that dumb, or what?"
she said to Kelly. "Coming here? Is that goddamned stupid, or
what?" She was saying this real quietly, her head down almost
on her knees. "How could this be happening?"

I sat frozen. I realized something amazing. Just as surely as
the summer sky was blue, Rhonda's mom was an Arcola girl,
too.

We went on down the tractor path toward the barn, Rhonda
staying low in her seat and saying nothing. Once she squirmed
up and looked out the back window, but there was nothing to
see.

"You wanna forget this?" Kelly said to her, referring to the
woman in the back seat. "No big deal."

"Oh *come* now, ladies . . ." the woman said.

We parked the car at the side, and all of us went into the
barn. The woman selected a spot on the dirt floor in the middle of the dark, musty space, and Kelly produced six candles
from the same bag she'd gotten the pickles from. The woman

lit them. Kelly and Rhonda sat and the woman sat next to them, a triangle.

Suddenly the woman looked at me. "He will have to join us or get out," she said.

"Sit down here," Rhonda said to me. She was stricken, very tense. I sat down.

"My boy, this is a seance, what we call a 'circle.' We're here to call forth the spirits, and I'm not kidding, the good spirits of departed friends, Karen Ann Kreitzer and Marie Beth McClain. Can you handle it?" She read the names off a small card in her hand, slipped it back into her robe.

I looked at Rhonda.

"They were our friends," she said to me, her voice actually trembling.

I pictured their car in the wreck lot, the blood in the seat, and the shoe in the white gravel. The woman was bowing forward, toward the ground, staring down, changing postures from moment to moment. The candles made the whole barn jump. Gray webs dangled from the crossbeams.

"What happens if somebody drives up in the middle of this?" I whispered to Rhonda.

"We won't be here real long or anything," Kelly said.

The woman's arms were out, embracing us as a group. "Is there someone who can tell us of Karen and Marie?" she asked the night air. The night air was very quiet. "We wish for only good souls to speak to us, friendly souls and no bad souls. Satan lives and we want none of that. Does anyone know of Karen and Marie? And if you do, can you, will you, join our circle?"

The river-bottom sycamores rustled. I realized I could hear the river.

"We join our hands here to form a circle. We invite you to be with us here. We are all concentrating, thinking toward you, remembering you—your eyes, your smile . . ."

Her arms reached out on both sides, and she took the hands of the girls. Then they took mine.

In the candlelight the woman was alternately very soft and friendly looking, then hard and witchlike. It depended on the candlelight, her movements. I realized there was an old red Farmall not far off behind Kelly, an old red hay baler attached to the back.

"Now, ladies, I want to tell you," the woman said, "that these young girls might well not be ready to talk. It may not be easy for them right now."

Rhonda and Kelly said nothing. I was wondering if they had a money-back guarantee. Rhonda's hand was cool and damp, Kelly's hot as fire.

"I suspect that could be the case," the woman said. "That they aren't ready." Again she bowed forward, her arms out, her hands joined to ours. Again she moved side to side, staring off. "We require the help of a friendly soul, a good soul," she said, "in order to speak with Karen Kreitzer."

"Or with Marie," Kelly said very quietly.

"Marie?" the woman said, suddenly tensing up. She held herself very straight, upright, rigid.

Kelly looked at me and rolled her eyes.

"Marie honey, are you sad?" the woman asked. She held herself rigid for several long moments. Amazingly, the woman's eyes teared up.

In a second Rhonda began to cry also.

"I almost had Marie there," the woman said to Kelly. "She was near. Did you feel it? She was with us in this barn. She passed through here. She passed through us." She looked around. "Marie. Please talk to your friends, to Kelly and . . ." She was stumped.

"Rhonda," the girls said in unison.

"Kelly and Rhonda are here to talk to you, Marie."

Silence. A long way off a private plane was swooping in to

land at the West Ridge airfield. I listened to the river, the trees' rustle. I could hear a bird steadily cooing in a tree out there somewhere, peaceful sound, made me feel better. I think I had expected something violent to happen any moment—a barn door to fly open wildly, a ghoul to appear, the old woman's head to do a three-sixty, her eyes to light up like the devil.

"Ladies," the woman said, "this room is full of ghosts—restless souls from this land all around, souls from all ages. There are Indians here and old settlers, pioneers—children and farmers whose bones are buried in this ground. We have made a hole in the firmament and they are crowding to it. Can you sense that they are with us?"

The girls didn't answer.

"Karen? Karen, have you come to speak to us? Will you join our circle? No," she said in just a moment, quietly, "it's Marie who comes near. Marie! Will you speak to your friends? Karen? Are you there, my dear?" The woman's eyes were closed in fierce concentration.

"Karen?" Kelly said quietly into the black.

"What's that?" the woman whispered. "Did you hear that?" She thought Kelly was a spirit talking.

Kelly looked at her. "It was me," she said. Kelly clearly conveyed impatience. This seemed to deflate the woman completely.

"Ladies," she said after a moment, "these are girls who have died very young. Maybe to you your age doesn't seem real young. I believe that they are not yet ready to talk. They are still very sad, I think. There is the sign that they are not happy on the other side. They will be, but they have died young and they aren't happy yet. I'm sorry." She broke hands with Rhonda and Kelly and leaned forward and blew out the candles.

"Or else," she said, "something's distracting you ladies and keeping us from fully communicating."

Abruptly Rhonda went out the door. I suddenly realized where she might be going. Kelly followed me out but ran by me very fast, disappeared on the lane ahead. She wanted to stop Rhonda. I was having a hard time believing Rhonda was really going where it looked like she was. At one point I came around a bend in the path, and could see that Kelly had caught up to her. The two of them were talking, Rhonda waving her arms—she was pretty upset. Kelly had her hands on Rhonda's shoulders—trying to talk sense, it looked like. Then in a moment Rhonda was coming back toward me, and *Kelly* was heading on back toward the car parked in the corn.

"What's going on?" I asked when Rhonda was close enough.

"Kelly's gone bushwhacking," she said. "She's going to get a ride home for her and Ghost-woman." Not knowing I knew what I knew, she lied for my benefit: "I guess Kelly knows those people or something." She looked at me to see if it was going to fly. I let it. "Anyway, I've got Kelly's keys, in case there's a problem," she said. Now she was running back toward the barn with me right behind her. "Give me your keys," she said to me, "so Kelly can get back out here in your car. Then we can go dancing and she can go to West Ridge."

"I don't get this," I said.

"Hang in there," she said.

The windows on Kelly's car had misted up in the night air. The woman was standing next to it. The moon was just up, red and looming low in the east. "The car broke," Rhonda said.

"It what?" the woman said.

"Kelly says it won't start. But you wait here—Kelly's going to get you to the train on time. Him and me . . ." Rhonda indicated me. "We're going to hide from the people in the other car, then stay and guard Kelly's car until Kelly gets back. How's that?"

"You mean she's gone to—er—interrupt those kids parked back yonder?" the woman said.

"Yeah. So you can get to the train. Give these to Kelly," Rhonda said, handing my car keys to the woman.

"Well, what are those kids going to think of me and Kelly out here alone?" she said as the Starfire headlights glanced high off the side of the barn and changed the shadows.

We were retreating into the standing corn. "What are you worried about?" Rhonda shouted. "You've got a whole bag of money."

Later we were near the swimming hole, in a stand of oaks, sycamores, and river willows. Rhonda was munching on a pickle. There were hedge apples on the ground, and I lobbed a few into the river. Maybe she seemed a little shorter than I imagined she was. I'd never stood near her before.

"Pretty strange evening," I said.

She didn't answer. After a while, though, she turned and stood there looking at me. "We paid her seventy bucks." She kept looking at me. I did my best not to react.

The moon was up brighter now, and it gave enough light for me to see the rope I thought I remembered being there, attached high in a sycamore, for swinging out over the water. The night was muggy and hot. Rhonda said nothing.

"Try to tell me what was going on back there."

"You mean Ghost-woman? Just something completely insane," she said. "Kelly gets these great ideas. Kelly's mom knew this nurse up in Champaign who does this stuff—reads palms, all that. I forgot this was the night. That's why I messed you over. Forgot."

"Oh. I thought I was the front man. So you could get out of the house."

She said nothing to that. She was sitting on the riverbank. I sat down next to her.

"My mom's having an affair with the local veterinarian."

She looked downriver into the dark. "Jesus. I'm coming apart," she said. She was quiet for a minute. "I feel so sorry for Dad. I can't think about it," she said. Then she was crying, her head down on her arms, which were resting on her knees.

I sat next to her. I couldn't think of a thing to tell her.

"I thought we might reach Karen," she said after a while. "I really loved her. She was my best friend. My best friend. I'm definitely coming apart."

There was nothing to say. I ate a pickle and regretted it. I rolled a couple of hedge apples down the bank into the water. Finally I stood up and kicked my shoes off, dropped my wallet on the ground next to them. I tested the rope to see if the limb would hold me.

"What if Karen had talked tonight?" I said. "What would she say?"

"Don't tease me. It was a nutty idea. Karen would talk to me if she could. You're going to bust your ass swinging on that thing. I'll tell you what, that woman was a complete fake." After a while she said, "Didn't you think so?" She didn't move. "Kelly says a medium like this one helped her contact her father."

"Kelly wishes," I said. I swung out over the river, a warm wind in my ears. "One thing I know is that Karen and Marie aren't sad. You are, but they aren't." I grabbed a hedge apple, and I swung out over the river, dropping it straight down. It was hard to tell how far above the water I was. I told Rhonda, "There's not anything to say, is why they didn't talk. They died, and that's all."

Her head was down. "I just don't believe your friends can die like that," she said. "Not your friends." By now it seemed to me like she'd been crying off and on for hours.

"It's a real pretty night, you know it? You ought to try to relax."

"Ha. Relax," she said.

I swung out again and again on the rope. I realized it would have been better if she could have been left to herself. "Lucky I'm here to keep you company," I said. At the far point of the arch, I could see all the way to the iron bridge. Out there, the moon broke through the trees, and I could see the movement of the water downstream. Sometimes I could hear a carp break the surface.

"I didn't want to go dancing anyway," I said. When I swung, I could hear the rope grating on the big limb high above. At one point while I was far out on the rope, I heard Rhonda slip into the water. I swung back to the bank, took a run and swung far out again, trying to spot her in the inky black below. I could hear her swimming.

"It's nice and cool," she said.

At the far point this time I let go of the rope and dropped. En route to the water, in a moment when I was anticipating splashing hard into the Black River, in a turning and falling motion in the dark, I happened to glimpse Rhonda's clothes in a little moonlit pile on the riverbank.

Why I Shacked Up
with Martha

Even though she'd been with the company a couple of years, Martha seemed to emerge from nowhere, asking questions, leaning over the desk at work. She was very thin and tall—the bones in her legs long, her arms long and luxurious in how they hung at her side. Visually, she reminded me of an airline stewardess, only less metallic. Her eyes were wide and deep, harbors of secrets, deeper than the deep blue sea. Somewhere down in that well of blue, you knew, was her precious little-girlhood, her past, and her grown-up, secret, pure and rambling sense of womanhood, currently preoccupied by "liberation." Her laugh was quick and strong; she moved forward, or she waited, standing back a little too far— the eye contact always held a shade too long, the laugh a little too appreciative. Had she always behaved this way and I was only just now noticing?

Anyway, I began to get the picture.

"Why don't you join the Chiefs?" my wife had asked about that time, during dinner one evening when one of the silences had lingered longer than usual. "It'll bring you and Scotty closer. Take your mind off work."

"What do I have to do?" I asked her. I felt another increment of my minimal leisure about to evaporate.

"Just be with him. What you do is, you make a vest with

him, a vest for each of you. Sew them yourselves—you two
boys, no help from Mom. That's the rule. And you go camping
a lot. He's growing up. You have to be with him more. He
loves you. He needs your example."

So I joined the Chiefs, to Scott's delight, and received in the
mail days later patterns for father- and son-sized vests. There
were no directions at all on *how* to sew the infernal things,
but there was a notice enclosed that the first Chiefs outing, a
camping trip to the Blue Ridge, would be two weeks from that
very day.

"They don't allow drinking on these trips either," my wife
advised me one afternoon. "It's another rule." She was repot-
ting some coleus and her favorite weeping fig and a lot of
flowers I'd never bothered to learn the names of.

"It's for the boys, after all," she said.

"Where are all these rules written down?" I asked her.

And while all this was going on, I suddenly realized there
were a few things that I'd been meaning to explain to Martha,
this lady at the office, if there were only time. She was just
back from Houston, having served as squad leader or something at the women's convention—International Women's
Year, remember? When she got back she was talking about
having actually shaken the hand of Gloria Steinem.

"A real preternatural experience, right, Martha?" one of the
mail clerks joked.

"Laugh it up, Anthony," she said to him. "It's a hell of a
revolution you're missing." And she toasted him with her coffee cup and all the guys in the office laughed, circling the coffee pot, fingering the donuts, elbowing each other and inter-
jecting last night's scores.

Martha kept going. She said she guessed that in the end it
was the most really fantastic and relevant and meaningful
event she'd ever been part of, something to change a person's

life—all those girls down there caucusing and going out to dinner and drinking in their rooms and storming Houston's string of male strip joints and shouting "Bullshit" at Phyllis Schlafly while she was delivering a dissenting report; and everyone was taking sides on important mainstream issues like lesbianism and so on.

What I wanted to try to explain to her, if I could only get the chance, was that, well, Martha, let's face it, a convention on five million dollars borrowed from the government, held down in some bastion of male domination and capitalistic boyish fun like Houston, with all the accoutrements of conventions, such as soporific speeches by quasi-representatives from endless significant minority elements and "keynotes" from people with "clout"—well, Martha, I hate to tell you but that ain't no way to have a revolution.

I wanted to explain to her that Freud was exactly right when he alleged that anatomy is destiny. (Where would we be without our anatomies, right? Ho, ho.) I wanted to explain to her that the government wouldn't have given the girls money for the convention if it thought for a second that they might be serious about someday making the men secretaries and the women boss. I wanted to explain to her that her big binge on the ERA was a waste of time and breath because, as we learned in the cases of equal opportunity and civil rights legislation, change on paper ain't change, Martha.

But what I really wanted to explain to Martha was that the women's movement was a chic, elitist, fad-laden, bejargoned, prepackaged and predigested media event and not a movement at all, and you could tell that by all the designer T-shirts and cutesy, campy ass-flipping that was going on in the suburbs in the name of equal rights for women. The radicals at the head of it, I wanted to tell her, were probably pretty serious, but let's face it, it was fun in the sun for the others, professionals and wives of professionals who were able to line up a baby-sitter while they went out to "network" or "get involved" or "demonstrate."

And here's a question for you, Martha: what's the women's movement to some lady who drives a school bus and takes in ironing and slumps through the housework and bathing the kids, can't stay home and be a mom because she has to work, so the kids watch television and get fat and flunk school and do dope; she endures hubby's flying tackle at bedtime if hubby still wants to tackle her, but she can't much pay the bills and can't continue to live without digging the credit hole deeper, and she worries all the time and that makes her ugly—what's the women's movement to a woman like that, eh, Martha, with your big ideas? And how many of those women flew down to Houston and got to shake Gloria's hand? Martha and I, we had a lot to discuss.

There was no telling when we'd get the time, because work mercilessly absorbed us both, and of course I was a family man and a Chief, and Martha had a child and husband. In fact, Martha was married to one of the real, all-time ranking assholes, a guy named Bill, who thought for a long time—he was then about thirty-five—that if he just never came home from work, if he went on every trip he could, if he drank every martini ever offered him by any executive in the next echelon up of Buckley-Formitron Digital (BFD), well, someday he'd be president of the whole damn company.

And naturally the people at BFD loved that kind of old-fashioned ambition. They knew Bill was one of the all-time ranking assholes, but, in their case, this was a very big career plus. If he could harness and sustain the energy and determination which made him the asshole he was, and could get some experience in the world of hard knocks, they knew that there was virtually no limit to the asshole Bill could become.

His one real drawback, however, was major by any standard

and caused BFD executives to shake their heads, rub their chins, and pace. BFD was a forward-looking outfit and very much into personnel development (PD, they called it), and there was a lot that the BFD PD consultants and specialists could handle in the way of drawbacks and deficiencies if they had *the right raw material*, so to speak. And ordinarily they would not hesitate to invest in a comer like Bill. But in Bill's particular case, because he was such a broad-based and wide-ranging asshole, the company was frankly hesitant to invest in his executive development. With an asshole of this proportion, they were into an area of numerous unknowns. They knew, for instance, there was an odds-on chance someone would kill Bill and, with that, negate a very significant PD investment. They hadn't become great by taking crazy chances.

There had already been an attempt on this gentleman's young life. As a practical joke, when he was breaking in with the company down in Dallas, he peed in the Listerine bottle of the guy he was on the road with, a redneck salesman from South Texas with flat ears, walleyes, and no discernible sense of humor. For Bill—Martha calls him William—for William, this joke was enormously funny; for the redneck who gargled the pee—well, two days later he caught Bill on the freeway en route to the airport and opened fire on him with a thirty-aught-six. Although he missed Bill himself, he put a three-inch hole in the door of the company car and blew the steering wheel off its mounting, causing a fantastic wreck to occur. Bill was in the hospital ten weeks with broken ribs, broken toes, and a broken face. Of course, the company had to pick up the tab. There was a rumor, unconfirmed, that someone in BFD's personnel development section turned in the redneck for spite, maybe because he missed. Anyway, he's still locked up down at Richmond.

When Martha got back from Houston and hung over my

desk, talking about women's liberation and sexual harassment on the job, her small, pale breasts visible in the shadows
beneath the crisp drapings of her blouse, I determined that I
would have to quite soon make every attempt to explain some
things to that girl.

So one evening (it was my wife's racquetball night and Scott
went with a friend to *Star Wars* for the second time in two
weeks) I slipped over to Martha's apartment to have a chat
(her husband, I knew, was in St. Louis having the last of his
plastic surgery—the face thing had gone on for years). Just my
luck, though, she wasn't there and consequently, with some
misgivings, I left her a note:

Dear Martha:

I came by to explain some things to you, strictly business of
course, and just my luck you aren't home so I have to leave you a
note.

I've been wondering, are you really serious about this women's
liberation thing or are you just trying to make it clear that you
have thin hips, went to Vassar, and are currently underemployed?
I'm wondering because I just read *Newsweek* about the Houston
convention and it sounds like a bunch of bull to me, no offense.
Sounds like a bunch of women going around trying to act like a
bunch of men.

Anyway, I had always thought you were one of the smart ones
and now it just seems like you're going crazy like everybody else,
lured to insanity by Walter Cronkite and Gloria Steinem.

Sincerely,
H. Brodey

For days things were the same. Into my office Martha would
stride, smiling, asking questions, and I remember that, for

me, it was a very strange period. I would watch her eyes for some new recognition, some acknowledgment of my communication. None came. At work and at home I was doing a lot of daydreaming and was probably acting oddly—forgetting things, losing things, not noticing things.

Gradually my wife came to the conclusion that I was unhappy with my work, because, she observed, I *always* seemed distracted when I was unhappy with my work, and in fact there is no doubt about it, I wasn't particularly happy with my work. It wasn't "my" work anyway, and anyway it wasn't particularly "work," but whatever I was doing day in and day out in the plain, sterile box of glass offices on Dupont Circle, I sure wasn't particularly happy with it and my wife was right about that.

But also, confession time, I was gradually becoming quite taken with Martha. In the atmosphere of that office, with its blind, empty toil, if a man weren't distracted by a woman like Martha, he was either a victim of the illusion that he was rising in the company or else he was dazed to a gray blur.

When all is said and done, love is all there is, to coin a phrase. Tell you what. I decided to shack up with Martha at the very first opportunity, blessed soul, because love is all there is; and also to quit my job, just for spite. Wrote a letter to my old friend Wes Hammatt confessing part of my intention (I figured if I wrote it as though it had already happened, it would further incline me to go through with it):

Dear Wesley,

Thought I'd drop you a short note and tell you that things are fine around here and that, just for spite, I quit my job today and am about to embark on a new adventure. You know what I decided? I decided I'm going to be a hell-bent hippie-dad to my boy and a hippie husband to my wife and a middle-aged flake to the rest of the world.

I told the boys down at work that they could take it and fly it straight up Hemingford's chimney for all I cared—laughed in their faces. I walked straight into Maynard L. Hemingford's leopard-skin penthouse office and told him that none of it mattered one way or the other, so I was quitting and that was that. He was pretty startled all right.

Drop me a line and welcome me to the leisure class. And remember this always: love is all there is.

> Your old buddy,
> Harold

In fact, though, in the days right after my note to Martha, when I was beginning to feel disoriented, I was amazed that she offered no sign of ever having received it. I began to think either she hadn't in fact received it, couldn't read my handwriting, or had decided to ignore the fact of my existence outside the controlled and confined dynamics of the office. My worst worry was that somehow my note had been intercepted.

I remember how that concern nagged at me all the way home the Friday before the Chiefs' camping trip. It would have been so comforting if Martha had only given me some sign and not forced me to wonder. When I got home that night, even though I was way too tired and preoccupied to do it, I sewed our vests, out of burlap and corduroy. I thought I had a pretty good design, primitive but vestlike. I had to work most of the night. I kept a bottle of Johnny Walker with me to help me through the hard parts. The project was absorbing, I'll say that, and for a while I forgot Martha existed.

About eleven, I was on the street looking for somewhere to

buy buttons, brown leathery ones that would blend with the style of the vest. I had in mind a sort of Davy Crockett effect, rough and ready, but wash and wear of course. Mine came out a little crooked, especially on the seam under the left arm, and there were a couple of other ragged and uneven places that I went after with scissors to make them look intentional. I learned a few things that kept me from making the same mistakes on Scott's. I was doing all of this in the dead of night, he and my wife sound asleep in another part of the house. For a surprise, I took the liberty of attempting a small monogram on the left side in the front of his. At the time it seemed like the perfect touch.

That morning a van with the words *Tribe 11* painted on the side in Indian writing came by and picked us up for the camping trip to the Blue Ridge. We had our vests in a backpack, to be unveiled whenever everybody else's were, and Scotty was real enthusiastic about the camping part although he was mortified that he'd be the only one with his initials in red script on his Chief vest.

On the ride up, we had a good seat, isolated in back. I had some time to think and sort of relax, doze a little to catch up on the night's sleep. One Chief dad, named Ted, was at the front of our van (seven vans in all were making the trip), taking care of the details and tallying checklists on a clipboard. We were in good hands, so I sat back and allowed my mind to go find Martha. I thought about her lack of communication just when I was needing her to be responsive, and what kind of family obligations such as this she must have been engaged in, exactly the kinds of things that might have prevented her from getting right back to me. I forgave her for a few minutes. I didn't know much about her family, actually, except the stories about her husband. At the office, family realities were usually obscured. I don't know why.

When we got to the campground, high above a bluff Stonewall Jackson once used to reconnoiter the Shenandoah Valley, I was enchanted. This outing was just what I needed. Scott and I pitched our tent on a handsome spot with a fabulous overlook, and at sundown we looked down on the backs of circling hawks far below us yet high above the valley floor. I was still nervous about putting on our underachieved vests (he had already said he'd wear his inside out to hide the monogram). So far no one had vests on, and so I was beginning to assume there would be some kind of ceremony of collective unveiling, some terrible moment when Scott would be embarrassed by his daddy because of the slapdash sewing job I'd done.

Finally the kids drifted off to play and the dads were sitting on some logs around the fire. I seemed to always be standing or sitting near Ted the Organizer. He had built the fire, take-charge guy, with the sticks and logs all standing on end and tipping inwards like a teepee, very precious.

"You're new?" he said to me finally.

"Right," I said.

"Brodey is it?"

"Right." He made a note on his clipboard.

"Pretty up here, don't you think?"

"Fabulous. You always forget a place like this exists so close to D.C."

"It's true."

He seemed pleasant enough to me. His hair was brown and perfectly groomed, and he wore a beard so carefully cropped that it seemed to defeat all rationales for having one. I decided to broach a dreaded subject.

"I've been wanting to ask someone. About the vests, you know?"

"The vests?"

"Right." I was conscious of the other Chief dads around the fire.

"Hey, Ozzie," he said across the fire to one of the dads. "When do we do the vest thing?"

The guy who was apparently Ozzie shrugged that he didn't know, but there was a strange grin also. I sensed a conspiracy. I felt very much on the outside of this group.

"Don't worry about the vests," Ted said. He seemed ready to accept me even if I was not yet a pure Chief dad like the rest.

"I'm not worried. I was just wondering when we put them on. Do we need them on this trip?"

He smiled. Some of the others had heard this exchange and were mumbling among themselves.

"And also I was wondering, does anybody have a copy of the rules and regulations? I wanted to review them. I've never seen them written down."

Ted was shaking his head. "I don't want to sound judgmental," he said, and I braced myself—I was always the guy asking the procedural questions, details, details. "But it's hard to believe, isn't it, that they really expect a bunch of men to sit around sewing vests?"

"I don't think my wife's started ours yet," Ozzie offered from across the fire, and some of the dads laughed. Ted reached into a bag next to the log he was sitting on. He handed me a very cold beer.

"Here's to the rules, Brodey," he said.

It was a great evening. I hadn't felt that relaxed in weeks. That night, peaceful in the tent, Scott asleep next to me, raccoons rummaging in the brush outside, I had a lot of time to think. Martha, a sweet dream, was on my mind. And all her women's lib stuff, what an obsession. I don't mean to suggest that in spirit I was not somewhat in sympathy with some of the things women were saying they stood for in the days of the ERA crusade, to the extent I was able to discern them. It's just that their techniques weren't really very liberated. It's absurd, for instance, to depend so heavily on the government and governmental processes in order to revolt against structures and traditions which have long been culturally dictated, reinforced, perpetuated by government and governmental processes. What fun the boys had watching the girls chain themselves to the statehouse door with their sloganized T-shirts and their falsetto chanting.

But all this had certainly given Martha and me something to talk about, and I was thankful for that. I thought of her, her dark hair, her eyes, imagined those arms around me and mine around her.

Above the tent somewhere in the dark was an owl on the limb of a pine. He hooted the whole night, softly but persistent. At first he was driving me crazy, but I gradually came to terms with the soft cooing. The tone was friendly somehow. I imagined that he was trying to tell me about himself. In the morning there was half a squirrel lying in a heap in front of our tent, a gift. Later I realized it was an omen.

Because. As I said. Martha. Had eyes deeper than the deep blue sea. I had listened raptly to all her high hopes for the ERA and for improving the lot of women, and I'd found myself involved. She'd gone into detail describing the arguments in the feminist literature she read, and all I could do was look at her and love her. When she came across the part in *The Women's Room* where the author says she hates men, one and all, each and every, and that's that, well, Martha talked about that in the office for a week, everyone nodding or making neutral coffee-break-type comments like "Uh-huh," "Yup," or "Sure, Martha, anything you say," and then for them it was back to work as usual, but for me here she came, striding into the office, staring into me with those eyes, leaning way down to point things out, asking whole bunches of questions. I'm damned if I can recall what she was asking. I found myself envying old William. Love is all there is.

In the meantime, time passing, Martha continued on as always, businesslike and business only, never stepping out of role to communicate with me, never confronting me on my letter, left brazenly on her doorstep, never mentioning a thing. I began to wonder what it would take to get a rise out of her.

Then there was the sweet winter morning I'll never forget, when frost had formed on the office windows and the crystal sun had risen to burn it off, and Martha hurried into the office and stood at my desk. She was carrying an envelope and, carefully checking to be certain nobody was close by, said to me, "I thought so."

"You thought what specifically, Martha?" I said. I was trying to work.

"I thought you'd reach out for me sometime."

"How's that?"

"C'mon. You know." She was staring straight at me, her eyes watering. I anticipated the charge of sexual harassment.

"Chrissake, girl," I told her. "Don't talk sign language—I'm a practical man." I was looking past her through my office door and out into the secretarial pool. People were rushing to the Xerox, filing copies, stuffing envelopes, stapling things, making displays, dialing on their phones. "Perhaps you're speaking of my note?"

Quickly checking the door, she leaned forward and kissed me right in front of my left ear, and then whispered, "Yes. You love me."

Then she handed me the envelope and walked out of the office. I sat there, trying to hold myself together. I could hear my heart hammering. I could hear my ears turning red. I felt a solitary drip of sweat slip from under my arm down my side almost to my waist before it was absorbed by a chance fold in my shirt. It was a pretty strange situation. The envelope contained a proposition, no uncertain terms, time and place.

I sat waiting for the sun to rise in the patched asphalt parking lot of the Cedar Hills Motorlodge, a family operation out on the two-lane highway. Not a bird chirped. Not a leaf stirred. The animals in the stand of trees just west of the motel restaurant were motionless. I stared deep into the shadows, followed the vertical lines of the trees from the ground, thousands of lean young hardwoods, up into the tangled confusion of the damp, early spring foliage. Nothing moved.

Then, for a while, I stared at the motel itself, thought about motels in general. The motel office had a curved glass window, 1950's architecture, and, motionless behind the registration desk, in dim light, the night lady sat. I stared at her. She stared back. She seemed not to move. Not even the smoke from her cigarette in an ashtray on the counter seemed to move. It was like she'd been painted there by Edward Hopper. She stared right at me. She kept staring, as I sat there in my car. It was clear to me that she wouldn't suspect a thing.

I was hoping that somewhere out on the highway right then was Martha, speeding along in her Mercedes (imagine this if you can) toward me. Behind the Cedar Hills Motorlodge— Martha had suggested the place because they had waterbeds— behind it was a greenhouse, also a family operation. I found it right at daybreak while I was stretching my legs.

Inside were pots, and tables for pots, and among them all the rocks that kids had thrown, smashing out the windows of the greenhouse, leaving a hulk, faded and broken, causing strange shadows and flashes from the broken crystal in the frosty morning sun. Among the shadows suddenly, among the broken pots on the greenhouse floor, this is no lie, this is how things happen when your conscience is working overtime, I saw the corpse of a dead squirrel and I was stunned with an irrational terror.

I hurried back to the car and disappeared down a country road.

When I skulked into the office about eleven that morning, feeling like my brain had been embalmed, I found this note in a plain envelope on my desk:

Dear Mr. Brodey,

I want to apologize for not making it out west this morning. My little one sliced a toe and had to have stitches last night. William returned from Tucson very late, and I was a little upset. Plus, I backed into Dr. Summer's car over at the emergency room. The timing was all wrong, and I couldn't even contact you to cancel. It must have been an impossible wait, and I'm very sorry. I feel particularly bad because, after all, I asked you.

Martha

Why did I shack up with Martha? Because she asked me— that's one reason. And because, as I have said, I had quite a number of things to explain to her.

Still, this note showed a side of her totally apart from the person of the office game which had begun in light chatter at coffee breaks and which we were trying to consummate at the Cedar Hills Motorlodge. She had a little boy and couldn't even drive right when he was hurt. I could well imagine the battle that was going on inside her, rushing that boy over to the hospital. Maybe her husband had been waiting out at the airport, sitting on his briefcase, needing a ride and wondering what was going on. And then there was this other, this shadowy other person, waiting for her in a motel parking lot out west of town. Suddenly she must have felt like she was bad, like her plan to be unfaithful was making bad things happen to her loved ones. I forgave her for standing me up, even if she really hadn't.

I started wondering about Martha: such a nice person, and she had a whole life out in Arlington in fine circumstances. She had a nice yard and church on Sunday. She had thin hips and the admiration of every male who saw her zip by in her little silver sports car, tasteful golden earrings glinting up in the sun as the wind raised her hair away from her neck. Things had turned out just the way she might have been hoping when she came down the aisle with her pretty little Vassar B.A.

I kept wondering to myself: sure, Bill's a worthless guy, but Lord knows he provides, and, whatever he does for her, it seems to be doing her good, because she's a full blossom of handsome womanhood, and she seems to love her boy, and he's probably a good little kid. Thinking about it all made me wonder. Why me?—why old Harold, in a world full of viable males? Why was Martha wanting to sleep with old systems man Brodey, or Chip, as I was known on the baseball field when I was young? And really, wasn't there nothing but trouble in all this?

After I got Martha's note of apology, I wrote her a note which I passed to her beneath a table at the monthly board meeting:

Dear Martha:

Call me "Chip." It was a long wait and I was disappointed, but I sure do understand what happened and have no hard feelings.

I hope very much that we can rearrange something, unless you've changed your mind. Does your car still work? Is the place out west satisfactory? In all this Martha, I suppose you know there is one thing that puzzles me more than anything else, you being the beautiful woman you are, me seeming perhaps fairly ordinary because of my conscientious and business-like attitude at work. Could you tell I'm a rambling guy, or what? If we are reduced to forever exchanging notes such as this, there is one question I'll need answered more than any other. Martha—why me?

As ever,
Chip

P.S. Please burn all these notes.

She was amazing the way she could deceive. She came into the office and talked the same, laughed the same among the group and made them laugh—she'd be wearing these very pretty white slacks that made her seem tall, and shoes that actually made her tall, and a pretty yellow blouse, and here she'd come, asking questions, "Mr. Brodey, what do you think about this?", "Can you authorize that?", leaning way down, her tummy flat all the way to the cinched-tight waistband. She smelled like flowers to me, and she'd be asking, "Can this be changed?", "Could we call so-and-so for these results?", etc., etc. I'd sit there dreaming of kicking the door shut and kicking off the lights, doing it on the desk. Forget the Cedar Hills Motorlodge and the impossible logistics of comfort.

We were having a lot of trouble setting up our rain-check bout. I would find myself considering calling Martha in the evenings; I thought of driving over to Virginia just to idle by her building a couple of times and watch the amber glow radiate through the curtains and the shadows move. I was acting peculiar at home and at work, and I knew it, but I couldn't get back on track. I was experiencing new emotions, new heat. I was becoming more and more sure of the business of love being all there is.

I felt on the edge of distraction and imagined the whole office knew about us. I almost didn't care. Gradually I was getting to the point where I would have to press the matter, no matter what it meant to my regular life. I sensed my destiny was about to change, that I was about to take a plunge. I tried to calm down, talk myself through it, but I kept thinking about her. The rain check continued to elude us, days passing—time, hours ached by with a dullness absent of mercy.

One day I determined that it was time to do some serious drinking. I called the office and told them I was sick, which was quite true. I headed for this abandoned farmhouse I knew about, out on the Harper's Ferry Road, evidently a favorite setting for the frankest kind of teenage revelry, judging from the mattresses and the shreds of underwear. En route I visited a suburban liquor store to buy a bottle. I selected for this pathological little outing Jack Daniel's. Jack Daniel's stinks worse than any whiskey on the market in North America and is, according to a friend of mine at work, 2 percent cow piss. It goes down very rough, like swallowing sandpaper. But the worst part about Jack Daniel's is the hangover, which is recovered from the way you would recover from the removal of fishhooks in the cortex.

This friend of mine at work almost died drinking Jack Daniel's once, and we know it was the Jack Daniel's that caused it because this friend of mine had ingested nothing but Jack Daniel's for a period of ten days. You would have to agree that in this particular case Jack Daniel's is highly implicated and doesn't come off looking very good. If this friend of mine at work nearly died, I can well imagine that there are cases in which, by ingesting Jack Daniel's, certain men have actually gone to the grave.

And so I selected Jack Daniel's and departed for the Harper's Ferry Road abandoned farmhouse in the early afternoon. I had to think. But that wasn't all. I had to think self-destructively.

There was no glass at all in the windows of the farmhouse, and the ceiling in the kitchen was falling in. All the mattresses and such were on the second floor. I took off my tie and sat on the couch in the living room. There was still flowered wallpaper, and a few other basic amenities had survived, although there was no television. I sat the bottle of Jack on the table before me and stared into it. Then I opened it and took a drink.

An hour later, quite drunk, I was stretching my legs and snooping around, and I accidentally stepped on the business end of a garden rake—its wooden handle flew up and smacked me in the face. There was a lot of blood, and I took off my sportcoat to try to save it—the shirt and pants were hopeless. I recall crashing upstairs and falling out on a mattress which seemed to have been arranged by some darling high school girl so that she could watch the stars while lying on her back. On my back, staring up through the glassless window, I could see clouds in the dusky sky, and I was trying to discern shapes among the clouds when suddenly I saw, whirling among them, a round, black and silver and blue flying saucer.

I have spotty recollections after the initial sighting. I recall seeing something circling to land, and later heard something whirring out in the soybean field, and I could see flashing lights reflected on the ceiling. Presently, a monster was at the top of the stairs, shaped like a five-foot pipe wrench entwined in an ectoplastic tuba and wearing a space helmet. He was staring at me. I figured the tuba part was the digestive tract—tried to make for the car, but my feet just waved in the air ineffectually. Amazingly, that exact movement seemed to be a threat to him. He started yelling in this alien voice, "Mayday! Mayday!" and banged and bumped down the steps and out across the yard. I scared him off waving my legs! He powered up the ship, hit the sky in a cloud of red smoke, turned left over the far fencerow and disappeared straight up. My lawyer believed every word of this until I told him what I'd been drinking.

The fact was, of course, someone had followed me out there and beat me up. I don't think it was William, but it was definitely motivated by William. I found one of my notes to Martha wadded up in my pants pocket while I was checking to see if I'd been robbed, this while the state patrol was bringing me home. My wife later told me the police had thought I was dead when they found me. Figured suicide at first, they said. She told them I was an ordinary systems analyst most of the time but that I'd been real unhappy in my job lately. I told them the rake bit, and the crime lab went out and made plaster casts and verified my story, completely amazing. I told them about the saucer, and they didn't even bother me anymore. Nobody even seemed mystified by the anonymous call the police had received that sent them to the farmhouse in the first place.

I told Wes Hammatt all this stuff. In fact, I wrote him maybe five letters, through the fall, the winter, the spring. I'd been writing to him for years before all this, and I hoped he would find a way to see it all as part of the maturing process of an old friend, that he would understand and maybe, although this was a long shot, commiserate. I really needed understanding. One day he wrote back:

Dear Harold,

Don't go around asking me for approval for your adulterous activities as I am a believer in the sanctity of marriage. A lot of people who know you less well than I do, if they were to read these letters of yours, they'd think you were somewhat of an unstable personality.

Listen here. You tell that Martha person to put on a bra, Harold. That's my advice. I know it isn't helpful to have an old friend tell you "I told you so" but I'm your age, old buddy, and I'm not going through these trials and mental disturbances such as you are from what I'm reading here, going around calling yourself "a rambling guy" like you were some goddamned character in a country music song.

If you still lived in Villa Grove, I'll tell you what, you'd be coaching Little League and girding your loins like everybody else. Why a conservative person like yourself would ever have taken a job in Washington, D.C., and started living the fast life is beyond me. I know a town like that has thousands of good therapists, Harold. Frankly, Joan and I think it might be time.

Keep me posted, and, for the sake of your lovely wife and boy, stay the hell away from the Jack Daniel's. I remain yours in stark and non-supportive candor,

Hammatt

I sat back and tried to think: Is this how the world works? How many ordinary people have secret dilemmas behind their workaday and social facades, all these liberated sexual

choices keeping them awake in their beds at night, the bed-
side clock humming real low like a conscience, their mate
stone-cold asleep at their backs? How many let time pass in
lieu of making big moves and enduring big embarrassments,
turn in earnest to their reports and the payments on the car, to
activities of the Chiefs and the Little League, and, with the
drums of social pressure setting their petty pace, eventually
mature to a gray blur?

I missed a lot of work after the farmhouse ordeal, and I
knew there were rumors I'd had a breakdown. I tried to take
up a fervent interest in flowers, botany.

One afternoon I was at the library studying up on impatiens
(I forget why) when I noticed in my peripheral vision someone
moving among the card files. I sensed it was Martha before I
actually looked up to confirm it.

"Are you okay?" she whispered. She was wearing a tan
skirt, and when she walked down the aisle between the stacks
toward me, each stride of her left leg gave a flash of warm,
tanned skin. She was in tall heels, graceful, her hair parted at
the side and partially covering one eye—she would brush it
back, there would be the flash of her diamond, the flash of her
gold bracelets, earrings.

"I'm okay," I told her.

"We had something going there for a while," she said.

"Almost."

"Those notes. Pretty funny."

"Awful funny," I said. "You burned them, right?"

"Right," she said. "This whole thing—it was a crazy idea,"
she said.

"I know," I said, and I tried to smile. "How's Bill?"

"He's busy," she said. "You know, we—you and I—we almost ruined a beautiful friendship."

"Just about."

"I was willing to risk it," she said, and she laughed shyly.

"Me too." I looked away from her, out a small portal between the stacks which revealed a park across the street. There was a softball game being played by children. It was a Saturday. "I still am," I said.

"We're moving away," she said. "Did you know that?"

"What?" I was conscious of my greasy hair and my broken nose and the way my gut hung over my belt. I never dreamed I'd run into her at the library. "Leaving? Don't tell me that. Why?"

"I've resigned."

"Is it Bill? We need you—the company, that is. Needs you. No kidding. Bill was transferred or something?" This news really unnerved me.

"Something." She smiled.

"Well, let's intervene. People can't just move." She wouldn't say why it was happening. Maybe it was a secret, or maybe people like me, at the edge of another person's life but not in it, don't need answers to such questions.

"Did you break your nose?"

"Does it show?"

"Are you sure you're okay?"

I stared at her for a few moments. My eyes started watering. After a while I said, "Martha, if you're really leaving, there's something I don't understand—never have."

"I know." As she said it, she half laughed.

"Now be serious," I said. "Look at me. I'm a mess here."

"I know what you don't understand," she said.

I stood there, hoping she would just tell me. But she wasn't going to.

"Martha. Why me?"

She stood there smiling. This was a beautiful woman.

"Now, I understand most of it. It's just this one thing that escapes me. It completely escapes me," I said. "This one part of the situation is completely over my head."

"I know," she said, and she leaned forward very quickly and kissed me right in front of my left ear. I could smell her cologne—that sweet "other person" fragrance. I could feel, only inches away, the heat from her luscious white neck. I could hear her breath deep down inside of her, feel it warm on the side of my face. Her arm brushed me as she came near, the silky fabric of her white blouse sliding across my shoulder. Just as quickly then, she was gone, back down the long aisle of stacks. The way she left, I realized she had no business at the library; she'd simply followed me there.

Confession time: I never did shack up with her. Never did. And the ERA never passed, it just laid there. But so what? With the ERA crusade, Martha did, I guess, manage to summon marvelous visions of being liberated and having passion again. For me she was a precious girl, new and vivid in my dreams—at least I had the dreams. But we didn't shack up. And so what if I never quit my job. I have to live, for chrissake.

Infield

I have a flash of Skidmore, playing first base, whose father had played first base before him. He's stretching to take a throw from me at shortstop, and the throw goes over his head, mainly because it's thrown too high but also because he stretched out real fancy before he knew where the ball was going, then couldn't get up to reach the ball, which turned out to be high and not in need of one of his goddamned fancy first-baseman's stretches.

I can still feel the pop in the glove when a grounder is snagged, the jerk in the shoulder from an overhand baseball throw, hard, from deep short and on the run, the rhythm of the footwork, the whip of the arm crossing the body in the follow-through. These were great feelings, yet there was pain in it too, for me anyway. Later I learned there was pain in almost all good feelings.

"What kind of throw was that?" Skidmore's making a scene, yelling at me to get the heat off himself.

The runner rounds first, tears for second. Skidmore's standing next to the bag, his arms out. "Seriously, what kind of throw was that?"

The right fielder sees that Skidmore won't be chasing the ball, gets it himself, and manages to stop the runner from scoring. Skidmore comes to the middle of the field, still looking at me. He's fourteen. This is Pony League, and in those days we played in Levi's with T-shirts colored to differentiate the teams.

"I need an explanation for what kind of goddamned throw that was just now," he says.

I stand out at deep shortstop staring at him.

"Let's have it. What kind of throw was that?"

He's brilliant, and can be very funny. His movements are gawky with a rough adolescence. For some reason I even liked him back then, but he had a terrible mean streak that used to rise up out of him like a second personality—lying, evil, angry, driven.

In adult life, I've accused him of this in letters. I forget when, but it's been just a couple of years ago he wrote me that none of that in the old days was meanness at all. He said it was all irony and I just failed to catch it.

But it was Cliff Webb and Junior Guthrie who got me thinking about baseball, plus the fact that this was opening day for the Cubs up at Wrigley. Like Skidmore, Cliff was an old baseball pal of mine when we were all growing up in this town, and he and I had run into each other in a bar the night before, after all these years.

On this particular morning I had decided to make a tour of our rental properties, to catalogue the repairs that were needed. My wife had been nagging me to get this done for two months—it was tax time. And of course on the day I finally got to it, because of Cliff, I had a headache, so I'd gone to the IGA to get some Extra Strength Anacin, even though it was too late (in order to avoid a hangover, you have to have the presence of mind to take the aspirin at the time you have no presence of mind—one of those little Zen perplexities in the balance of nature as it relates to adulthood).

Incredibly, on the way back to my car on my aspirin run I

encountered Junior Guthrie, another old baseball crony, now with a big beer belly, meandering around out in the IGA parking lot wearing a yellow American Legion bowling shirt and a Chicago Cubs cap.

"Hey, pal, can you jump me?" he was saying. Amazingly, something about the eyes, the old Junior was still down in there somewhere. "Wha'd'ya say? Can you jump me?"

I had the headache and really didn't want to.

"Sure," I said. "You have cables?"

"Pal, you got a car like mine, you carry jumper cables. Over here." He was already heading back to his car, gesturing to me.

The gravelly asphalt lot was depressing in my condition. I spotted his rusted-out tan and brown Cordoba, the vinyl roof fried off by the sun, because it was the only car in the lot with the hood up. I drove around to him and popped my hood, then let him hook us up while I chased the aspirin with coffee from home, then switched on the radio to see if I could catch Paul Harvey.

I think I was staying in the car for fear Junior'd recognize me and I'd get blasted with another round of nostalgia, this while the effects of the first round were still with me. Suddenly I noticed that there was a little raisin of a woman sitting behind the wheel of his car, looking over at me. She had small, brown, nervous eyes, like a squirrel. He'd shout directions to her.

"Okay, crank her." "Okay, shut her off." "Okay, give her a try." "Okay, stop pumpin' her." "Okay, pump her." "Okay, goddamn it, lay off pumpin' her, lay off it."

She huddled behind the wheel following directions. He was shouting through the crack that appears between the motor and the hood when the hood's open.

Watching Junior was difficult for me. I remembered clearly an eleven-year-old second baseman with big white teeth and

floppy hair. I remembered his almost ponylike run and unend-
ing hubbah-hubbah chatter. The optimism of a child. This is
what it had come to?

Finally he looked toward me and said, "Okay, don't rev her.
Let her be. Needs to store it up a minute." He enjoyed my
obedience.

Then, too quickly, he said, "Okay, now rev her," and then he
said to the woman, "PUMP that son of a bitch, Mama—that's
it. Okay, hit it!"

He had the distributor completely loosened and no air filter
over the carb. When she'd hit the starter to turn it over, he'd
go halfway into the dying thing's gaping mouth and wrench
back and forth on the distributor like it was a whale's wisdom
tooth and he was the dentist. His feet were clear off the
ground. He had a stub of a cigar all chewed and sweated on,
which he would light between rounds.

"Ain't gettin' no good contact," he said to me, "—yur bat-
tery's one of them goddamned sidewinders, never can get no
contact from 'em. I'll find somebody else, she'll fire right up."

Translated, this meant his car troubles were my fault.

"Get this goddamned thing goin', I'll take it to the junk-
yard, head back to Kentucky, get me another one. Got this one
down there, cost me one-fifty. Put sixty thousand miles on
her. Guy I play softball with—out at Cabot—he's from Kentucky, told me about it. Lot of stolen cars down there, he says.
Stop pumpin' her so much, Mama, like I goddamned told ya."

"I wasn't pumpin' her!" the woman crackled back at him.

"What?" He hurried around to her window. "Wha'd'ya
say?" She sank down in her seat like he was going to belt her.
"You was pumpin' her, honey. I know that much."

Her face was real wrinkled, resembled the cracked vinyl of
the Cordoba's dashboard. She was dirty, desperate looking,
bent down in that old seat like she was ashamed. For all I

know I might have gone to school with her, too, but she was beyond recognition now.

"Okay, crank her up," he says to her, back in front of the car, and she tries, the motor making a terrible grinding noise. Never jump somebody when you've got a headache. I was not optimistic that the car would ever start again.

"Goddamned starter's the problem. Get this thing started, I'll head over to the parts shop—there's a parts shop around here somewhere—head over there and get me another starter. And some starter fluid. If she's gonna start, she'll start with starter fluid. NOW, MAMA! HIT IT! That's it—PUMP the son of a bitch. Hold it, you're floodin' her. Damn. Flooded."

He comes around to my window, bends down so our noses, or rather my nose and the end of his cigar, are eight inches apart. "That there's my girlfriend," he says so she can't hear. "She loves me—hard to figure, I know. You'd think my brother could buy me a car. I gave him a kidney and he ain't rejected it yet. Doc says most of 'em are rejected by now, but not mine. Never paid me nothin', some brother."

I got out of my running car and went with him up beside the front end. I watched him climb in and out of the motor.

"Now wait," I said. "You gave your brother a kidney?"

"Damn straight," he says. He pulls up his dirty bowling shirt and there's the scar. It starts just above the tip of his pelvis on the right, and heads northeast most of the way to the opposite shoulder. Half of an X, right up his body, pink and angry looking like my hernia scar, only two feet longer, I swear, and heading across tender territory, the white and light-blue flabby sticking-out human frog abdomen. "Yeah, worked all his life and he never knew he had a bad heart, eighteen hours a day without givin' it a thought."

I was trying to remember Junior Guthrie's brother. Couldn't.

"Then they tell him his heart's givin' out and he gets all

these bypasses, and then his kidney gives out 'cause of his heart gave out, and he gets a kidney from me, two hundred bucks a week on drugs to keep him from rejecting it, you know that new stuff they got now? Well, my brother's fadin' fast after all this help he's gettin' from doctors, but the kidney's cooking along like nothin' ever happened, shit."

Again he dives down into the motor, his feet kicking in the air. Over his shoulder, he yells above the grinding of the car, "Doc says if he dies they'll get it back for me."

His whole body is pivoting on his beer belly, which is pressed down over the fender into the area where the containers for windshield-wiper fluid and coolant used to be.

"Hit it, honey, that's it," he says to the woman, and wrenches the distributor for all it's worth. And, incredibly, the car starts. "Yup, my brother's in the garbage business and the trucks is always breakin' down. We got a couple of 'em on their ass in the garage all the time, all spread out all over everywhere gettin' rebuilt. Don't tell me about distributors, I tell 'em, it's just the timing's off and the chain has to come around, and you gotta hit it just right. Good work, Mama," he says, as I climb back in my car.

He unhooks the cables and thanks me, latches down my hood with appreciated reverence for my car, and comes around to my window again.

"This is a fine automobile."

He is bending down, squinting at me, smiling. He turns his head and spits a piece of his cigar.

"I know you, right?"

"I don't think so," I said. "You a Cub fan?"

"What?"

"I see your cap—you gonna watch the Cubs this afternoon? First day of the season."

"Nah. This here's my brother's hat. You're Carl Landen, am

I right? Took me a second because of the beard. Makes you look like a salesman. Good to see you. I'm Junior Guthrie."

"Junior," I said. "Good to see you."

"Hey, honey, this is Carl Landen, guy I played baseball with when I was a kid. His dad was the doctor that died, remember I told ya? Long time ago?" He looked back at me, smiling, but neither of us could think of a thing to say.

"Well," I said finally, "you take care."

"You knew it, didn't you?" He was asking hopefully, as if trying in a friendly way to find out if he'd not changed so much after all.

As I backed out, I saw he had a ball glove in the back window of the car.

"I wasn't sure, Junior. You know how that goes. You take care."

The rest of the morning I toured the rentals, head hurting and kind of cranky except I was by myself so maybe also a little lonesome—I think I was lonesome for my boy. I wanted to talk baseball with him. He was over at school sitting in a desk, bored stiff, age eleven. I mooched three fingers' worth of whiskey from the cleaning ladies at one of our places around noon. Under the sink I found a glass left by the last tenants and washed it with some of the cleaning ladies' Spic and Span. They must have thought they had a pretty cool boss, to tip one with them out there on the job.

I planned this to be the house I hit around noon, because it was partially furnished from inventory. It had TV and cable so I could pick up WGN (if the cable hadn't been disconnected yet—tenants had moved out the day before). There was a cot in the house, and a lamp, again, left behind by a former tenant—it was shiny black and shaped like the head of a horse, red shade.

The headache hadn't given out with the first hit of aspirin, and I'd taken more around ten-thirty, but still no give. So about noon, after I belted down the cleaning ladies' whiskey and they were gone, I stretched out on the cot, the TV droning with a soap opera. I think I still had the headache, but I couldn't feel it.

Lying out on that cot in our rental, I started thinking about my dad and baseball and Skidmore and all those kids I knew like Junior and Cliff who grew up, and all the things I learned. It was the same stuff my boy was going through now.

From the upstairs windows, the back bedroom, at my childhood home across town (my mom still lives there), I remember looking down into the yard one night. There wasn't a moon; the light from the stars lit the yard only a little. Near the doghouse, on a long chain, was my springer spaniel, Tad. He was lying down, but his head was up, on guard. He was watching the undergrowth. He would look deep into the black shade of the lilacs. His chain would clink in the dark. He was guarding his very best friend, my father, who was stretched out on the picnic table nearby, watching the stars.

From my lighted room, through the window screen and down into the dark, I could barely see him. He didn't move. I was listening to the Cardinal game on the radio—Harry Caray, Jack Buck, Joe Garagiola. Vinegar Bend Mizell was on the mound, high-kicking lefty. Infield of Stan Musial, Don Blasingame, Alvin Dark, Eddie Kasko. Outfield, Wally Moon in left, maybe Curt Flood, but I forget center field really, Joe Cunningham in right for sure. Behind the plate, Hal Smith. They were playing the Pirates. 1957. This was when *I* was eleven.

"Who's winning?" Dad asked me. He could see me clearly.

"Cards. Cunningham stole home again."

"Great." His voice was barely audible.

"What're you doing?" I asked him. His father had died that winter. He'd missed a last chance to see his father alive in the previous fall. Dad had gone out west on a quick trip to hunt pheasants and had neglected swinging through the old Nebraska hometown to see his folks. He was having a hard time getting over it.

"Looking at the stars. You start to get a sense of the dimension after a while. Come here," he said.

I went out and sat next to him on the table. He pointed out a dim formation overhead that, if you looked away from it just a bit, you could see was really a kite-shaped cluster of seven stars.

"Pleiades," he said. "Look real close and you can tell some of them are farther away than the others. You can catch the depth of it. Go get the binoculars." I got them but we didn't use them long. I knew, I thought I knew, what was on my dad's mind.

"What was it Grandpa said, in the hospital?" I asked him.

He sighed. "He said, 'Jesus, Mary, and Joseph.' Then he took a deep breath, and he died."

He was quiet a minute or so. "The Bishop out in Lincoln, he says they're going to name Grandpa a Knight of St. Benedict. It's a great honor, recognizing him as a holy man. The Pope has to do it."

"You think Grandpa's looking down on us right now?"

He didn't answer for a while, looking up, breathing quietly. It wasn't a question to answer, really, but just to think about. In those days the rural Illinois sky sparkled deep and black.

"I wouldn't know," Dad said finally.

That summer I saw my first professional ballgame, in the old Busch Stadium on Grand Avenue in St. Louis. My father, his good friend and partner in medical practice Bob Swift, and I stayed in a nearby hotel called the Fairgrounds, and drove across town to the zoo that Sunday morning.

On the way, we went to mass in the St. Louis Cathedral, unfinished in a hundred years of work, scaffolding high in the vaulted ceiling where the man who made the mosaics labored day after day, the altar candles far below. As we drove around the city, I remember that I would sit in the back seat of the car, and up in front Dad and Bob would be talking about patients, or investments, or other things that often seemed too convoluted to keep paying attention to. So mostly I absorbed the warm, sunny streets of St. Louis.

We ate lunch near the stadium, in a bar, sitting toward the back. Right now I can summon the smell of beer and that primitive air conditioning, see the reflection of the front windows and the gleam of traffic off the dark linoleum, taste the ham sandwich eaten too fast, the anticipation of the ball park in less than an hour.

But when we came through the gates of the old Busch Stadium—formerly called Sportsman's Park and still called that by most of the fans—when we came up the walkway to find our seats, we popped into a strange, finished, green world like I'd never seen before. Every angle, every hue was planned, coordinated—the game was urbane and civilized, not like the pasture-type game, dry and weedy, we played at home. The afternoon air was heating up. People who behaved randomly and at odds outside acted in concert at the ball park, standing together and cheering or laughing when Cards manager Freddie Hutchinson kicked the dirt or someone stumbled rounding first. The crowd had a rousing, a great comforting, somehow knowing, collective voice.

Bob Swift had interned at Barnes Hospital in St. Louis, and knew all there was to know about the ball park. Hand on my shoulder, he pointed out, against the back screen, Harry Caray, in slicked-back hair and black-and-white checked pants, conducting the dugout show for radio, interviewing Larry Jackson, last night's winning pitcher. The big batting cage loomed over the plate, and the venerable old catcher Walker Cooper, wad of tobacco in his jowl, was cracking line drives.

At home, I pictured the ballplayers as kids. At the ball park, I was amazed by the dark shadow of beard on the face of Blasingame, "the Blazer," as he was called. He was littler than I thought. Moon's eyebrows were astonishing, Kasko wore glasses, Cunningham was bald. Those were men out there.

The first time I saw Musial at the plate, his unusual stance (often described on the radio) amazed me. Perhaps I had pictured Babe Ruth or the drawing I had of Casey at the Bat, or the action photo I had of Ted Williams hitting the long ball with a big arching swing, a vicious, Y-chromosome rip. In reality, Musial's stance seemed soft, relaxed, almost like dance. The front foot was pointed forward, toward the pitcher, the rear foot back toward the catcher. The front knee bent inward, graceful; the bat was held too high and way too far back. The head was out over the plate and tilted a little. His stance communicated artistry, individuality, himself. By then he was getting to be a grand old man of baseball, his late thirties. During the game, when he blasted a home run, the crack of the bat communicated immediately that the park would never hold it. The enormous swelling roar of the crowd conveyed not only happiness but respect. The ball bounced on the roof of the upper deck in right field, up where the light tower was. The scoreboard Budweiser eagle flapped its wings and a little red Cardinal made of neon darted around the stadium. The stroke itself had been a level, easy, sweeping movement, not a wild-ass swing like you'd get from Kaline, Clemente, Frank Robinson. Not the tight, big-armed body turn of Yogi Berra.

Somewhere along the way Musial broke the cadence of a sprint and settled into the relaxed stride of the home-run hitter in his parade lap, the crowd standing, amazed and happy.

Baseball was different without interpretation, without Harry Caray or Dizzy Dean communicating it to you. You had to really watch. It was happening at some distance away. We were far down the left-field line, almost to the outfield wall, nearly a block away from home plate. The crack of the bat arrived a moment after the swing, the ball already lofting high toward right field, camouflaged by the shirts of patrons in the upper deck. Or on grounders the third baseman might already be reacting to his right, reflexively, as the sound of the hit just arrived.

Vernon Law was on the mound for the Pirates that day. A tall straight man, kind of thin. Sitting almost out to the left-field wall you could still hear the pop of his fastball in the catcher's glove.

On a ball hit to left I remember watching Wally Moon, the handsome young Texan, rookie of the year three years before, who replaced the retired and venerable Enos Slaughter, reach back and lay the ball on the flat plane of green air. All I could compare the geometry and motion to was pool, the great green carpet of perfectly groomed grass like a pool table, flat, the smooth flight of the ball as though it were coasting not across the hot afternoon air but green felt, flat marble. The motion of his throwing was thrilling, how he reached back, stepped forward in a long low stride, the arm coming straight over the top, fast like the hammer on a pistol. The flight of the ball was low and fast—it skipped like a bullet on the infield dirt, the Blazer taking it on the short hop right at the bag. Big league, I thought to myself.

My dad got up from the seat next to me in the third inning, asking if Bob or I wanted something, saying he'd be right back.

Bob Swift stayed with me, one empty seat away. He'd lean over and fill me in on things, the enormous black man selling beer, sweating, his voice full and shouting, for fifteen years an institution at the ball park.

I was enthralled. I stared through the binoculars at the players and the crowd. My dad's absence bothered me a little, but not terribly—sometimes I'd say something to him, forgetting he was gone. I stared until the heavy steel on my nose and against my eyes began to hurt, but I kept staring. The binoculars were very powerful, and because I'd used them on planets I could focus them as sharply as they could be focused. The creamy white and scarlet and blue and yellow of those old cotton uniforms was dazzling against the deep green of the grass field under the brilliant afternoon sun.

As long as I live I'll remember one strange thing that happened that day. Using the binoculars, I followed a foul ball up and back into the crowd, watched the fans scramble and laugh and spill their Coke and popcorn. I watched one lady laugh at her friends, and the guy who got the ball turned and waved at Harry Caray in the radio booth, knowing Harry would observe on the air, "Nice catch by a fan down long the first-base line!"

But suddenly, as I panned the crowd, there in my vision was my own dad—far away from me, he was standing along the concourse, leaning against a steel pillar, a beer in hand, watching the game alone from shadows.

I remember my father very well in those times, at my ballgames. He stood out by the railroad maple down beyond third base at the very field where my son plays now. The Illinois Central had put out a plaque, inlaid in a sort of gravestone, commemorating the planting of the tree on Arbor Day 1905, and my father would invariably be sitting on it during the games, if he could be there at all. A few times he had the old

8-mm Brownie with him and would level it at me. I've seen the films in recent days. I remember how I felt then, but when I see the pictures only one impression hits now: I was pretty little.

As I've said, I was playing shortstop in those days. Later, in college, I played third. They don't now, and really never did, expect a shortstop to be a hitter. I console my own son with this to no avail. There was only one thing a shortstop need be able to do, and that was cover the ground. His area in the big leagues is seventy feet of real estate from behind second to twenty feet on the second-base side of third, and in addition he must be able to range into foul territory behind third, about where the IC maple is at the Pony League diamond, to rein in foul balls the third baseman ordinarily has no angle on.

The third baseman fielding foul balls down the line has his back to the infield, must stop, turn, understand where to throw, and throw. The shortstop makes this play somewhat facing the infield, somewhat set to throw. When the shortstop fields grounders to his right, he must be able to throw overhand to first, putting a vertical spin on the ball, or else the ball will float. When he fields to his left, back behind second, he must throw sidearm, quick and snappy like a second baseman, or with the long whipping action if he is throwing from farther out. In turning the double play, he must choose which side of the bag to work as he pivots, according to how the runner coming into second decides to try to take him out, and also according to how the ball arrives from the second baseman or the first baseman, whoever initiates the play.

In those Pony League days, just as in the days of American Legion, Skidmore played first because his father played first, and his father, Leonard Skidmore, was our coach. My father was a local doctor, and he'd played shortstop as a boy. He and Leonard Skidmore were good friends. Now my boy plays shortstop. So there you are. The infield has continuity through the ages.

Another memory: I'm standing across the street from the Catholic church, on the vast green lawn of the Douglas County courthouse. Father O'Daniel is pacing his front sidewalk, reading his breviary. I sit against the old silver maple under which an earlier generation of kids in the neighborhood had fashioned a makeshift home plate. Unlike the IC maple, this tree is tall and old and many times broken by lightning meant for the steeple it sheltered. It's a workhorse, a government tree. Its limbs are white with the shit of starlings and pigeons, not songbirds. A bored ballplayer years before had chiseled "Honus Wagner was here" into the trunk. It was a lie and he chiseled on the north side, opposite the church, out of sight.

"How's sixth grade?" Father O'Daniel shouts over to me after a while. "It's going okay?"

"Yes, Father."

He's the one I confess self-abuse to every Saturday afternoon. No telling what all those other people are confessing to him, who stand silently with me in the confession line along the back wall of the church. There was a show on *Ford Theatre* one night of a priest who had had a murder confessed to him, then couldn't help the police because of the confidentiality code of the confessional.

Father O'Daniel had been in a car accident several months before, hurrying back to town to do a wedding after playing golf too long, and for what seemed like an endless number of spring Sundays he said mass on crutches, the altar boys, mostly eighth graders, helping him to the podium where he stormed after the parishioners to get them to contribute more, more for the new Catholic school he dreamed of.

I served mass on weekdays that summer. I would go to his house on summer mornings. Together we'd walk across to the church, not saying much, and in the sacristy dress for the celebration. He muttered to himself in Latin, kissed the stole before putting it on. The wood floor creaked. I rinsed and filled the cruets with water and wine. Then he rang a little bell, and we walked onto the altar. Two little ladies and a farmer, the morning's congregation, rose to their feet. And the tone-deaf lady who provided the music let her rip from the balcony.

Now, on the front sidewalk, he paced too quickly, trying to heal the leg and say his office at the same time. Two birds, one stone. Like Jackie Gleason, a little traveling music. Sometimes he took a turn and went down the narrow white sidewalk between the church and the rectory. He'd been the local parish priest for thirty years.

"Want me to pop you a few?" he said just when I was afraid he wasn't in the mood.

"Yes, Father. If you have time."

He came across Van Allen Street, book in hand. "Did you bring the 33?"

"Yes, Father. The 30's cracked anyway." Father O'Daniel liked my "Larry Doby" 30, but he liked my "Duke Snider" 33 even more.

He put his breviary on the courthouse pedestal, above a bronze frieze of a scene from the Civil War, Columbia leading the wounded Union soldiers to safety. He was raised in Ireland and didn't play baseball as a boy. But he was a talented golfer and therefore could hit flies virtually straight up so high they made the well-groomed expanse of the courthouse lawn seem small. I remember very well the tininess of the ball against the blue sky, the thrilling speed it would gather in its fall from that great height, the occasional tricks of the wind, warm and humid. Major league infield pop-ups.

Father O'Daniel raved and raved at how I could range under those fly balls and haul them in. The courthouse lawn was dotted with trees, particularly one very tall cottonwood and of course the silver maple. I learned to catch a fly ball even when it nicked a few leaves, or thocked off a solid limb and went a strange direction. I would chase it, dive for it. The ground was soft loam, sweet-smelling. The satisfaction of catching the ball before it hit the ground has stayed with me my whole life. Sometimes my boy will let one drop right in front of him. He only does it to drive me crazy but still I don't see how he can stand it.

Actually, though I never told Father O'Daniel, the 33 was too big for me. I bought it at Western Auto one afternoon for him to use.

"How's your mom?"

"Great," I said.

"How's your dad?" he asked me. He was my dad and mom's friend. He probably knew Dad better than I did. I often wonder . . .

"I don't know how he is," I said. "I don't see him much."

The pain I had in my arm in my baseball years was a dull ache, not the slack disconnected feeling when the rotator cuff goes in the shoulder, a pain baseball men will tell you is the beginning of the end. This pain of mine was above the elbow, inside the arm and toward the back of it, and it came I'm sure from the whipping action of throwing, which God did not design an arm, and particularly the elbow, to do. It especially hurt on those cold blue evenings of spring when the team was out there getting ready for the season but the season hadn't begun because it was too cold to play baseball. Many nights I couldn't sleep because of my arm, and I worried that it was the beginning-of-the-end pain. I couldn't have stood to be told that. Baseball was everything for me then.

I was playing with other pains, too. Pony League was the first league in which spikes were worn, and at shortstop you get spiked in the various activities around second base, covering second on throws from the catcher when a runner steals, covering second on double-play balls hit to the right side of the diamond. I had been stitched in one knee for what seemed like the better part of the whole summer, strange as that may sound. I had chased a fly ball down the third-base line, beyond the IC maple in foul territory, a towering fly ball, chased it beyond foul territory out onto the access road—there was no fence then—I could not let this ball fall to the ground—and ran full speed head-on into two girls who were riding by on their bikes. We all went down in a heap and the ball landed among us.

Every move I made that summer, it seemed, tore the stitches. And I had the usual strawberries on my butt and legs from sliding on the hard sandy base paths. The worst place to slide in back-country (that is, not professional) baseball is home, because invariably the dirt has eroded from around the plate, which has dried out and gotten brittle and extracts its pound of flesh as you slice yourself over it. And invariably the dirt of the back-country baseball infield is either gritty and sandy or like concrete.

Another common wound is a swollen mouth, from bad bounces. If the infielder is getting swollen ears instead, bench him. He's not watching the ball. I tell my son, watch the ball.

It was in that summer that I came to understand my father was an alcoholic, and so in those baseball summers there was also an oppressive pain of the spirit that seemed to invade everything. The films he took of me playing tended to hop a little sometimes, and the focus was dubious. Many young men, I know now, will recall the same experience—terrifying and humiliating. Your father would stand beneath the IC maple down by third, and he would embarrass you with distracting, weak, complaining taunts, some of which would bring a laugh from the other parents in the crowd. The time came when I dreaded that he would even show up.

In my sophomore year in high school, after six years of handling all this the best I could, probably the culminating thing of my childhood happened. He had come to one of my games, as usual not falling-down drunk but too loud. That night I got home before he did after the game. I waited for him in the garage. I sat around, on the lawnmower, on a pile of drying logs, in a swing in the backyard, eventually on the back bumper of Mom's car. Waiting. He was taking too long to get from the same place I'd come from. I'd gotten a ride with someone else. I didn't know what I was going to say, but I'd decided I wasn't going to take any more of this shit from him.

Finally the lights swept up the driveway. Instinctively, I retreated. I jumped and grabbed a crossbeam in the garage, and swung up into the dark upper reaches where we stored scrap lumber and extra shingles.

He pulled in right under me. I noticed, watching him from above, how alone, and how tired, he seemed when he climbed out of the car. Like me, as it has turned out, my father was often alone. He pulled a box from the back seat and hid it carefully under logs at the back of the garage. Then he straightened himself, straightened his shirt, and shuffled out and across the gravel in his leather soles, into the house.

It was a cache of Old Fitzgerald. I got my .22 and I set the box on the hood of the car and I reduced it to sweet-smelling glassy rubble, and put a couple of rounds through the windshield for good measure. I'd say six shots altogether.

On the stairs in the house later that night, he caught me, me going down, him coming up. He'd slipped out there for a nightcap and made the discovery. "Watch yourself, Junior," he said to me. He had a hold of my shirt. "I'm not perfect. I never said I was." He didn't seem like my father as he said this. I looked right in his eyes and got a terrible feeling. He was giving me a warning from the underworld, one bad boy to another.

Memory: The sun is going down. Irv, an older man, holds an old 34-inch Nelly Fox thick-handled bat, the handle wrapped with friction tape. Irv is wearing bib overalls, black workboots he scuttles through the dust in. I'm sitting on the bleachers, ball glove next to me. Home from college, 1966. Irv shouts at his boy, who is out in left waiting for the ball. "Keep it low," he says. "Just 'cause the guy hits you a high one doesn't mean you throw a damned pop-fly back in." He spits. "Low, son. Low." Irv gestures low. "Think of it," he says. "Shortest distance between two things. Keep it low."

Now he lifts the bat to his shoulder. It has gotten four shades of dark darker since the lecture began. He smacks a hard line drive, left center. The boy comes across, takes it on the bounce, and fires it to the plate—you hear him grunt. He's six or seven years younger than me, maybe a freshman in high school. The ball hisses as it flies, skips once and slams against the green boards of the backstop behind the plate.

"Hell of a throw, son." He smiles, the bat down again at his side, staring out toward the outfield. "That was a great throw."

I applaud. I want into the action. Like all people in this town, when Irv looks at me it's with the searching-through-

time look—can he find a face in my face that's a face he
knows?

"Wanna shag a few?" he says.

"I'll take the cut-off," I tell him, and his son backs up to the
fence as I trot out to shortstop. Left fielders need to hit the
cut-off man.

Now I'm standing on the field I played Pony League on,
about eighty yards from the little field I learned on. A thousand evenings like this come to mind. I remember this diamond when it had no grass, was solid dirt, and the wind
would always kick it up into your eyes. And I remember, with
a lot of pain, the railroad maple where Dad would stand to
watch my ballgames, and the commemorative stone beneath
its now embracing shade.

From there he'd point the old Brownie movie camera at me.
In our home movies, blanching out with age, the leaves of this
old tree when it was years younger wave in the foreground.
"Gives it depth," the photographer would tell us from the
dark on projection night.

There were old white outhouses on that end of the park,
and I remember sitting in there on a one-holer looking at the
splayed obstetrical graffiti and not knowing what I was looking at or if the drawing was for some reason upside down. The
word *fuck* was frequently carved with pocketknives in the
pine of the outhouses. Successive paint-jobs had miserably
failed to cover over generations and tides of *fuck* going back
who knew how far. I looked around from my position to see if
the outhouses were still out there. They weren't.

"You're Landen's boy," Irv says to me, points at me with the
bat. He found my face. "Aren't ya?"

"Yes."

"We were real sorry," he says. He cracks a line drive to his
son, down the left-field line.

I fade over to the line and out, until I'm between third and Irv's son and have both hands in the air for the cut-off. The boy sends the ball to the plate. Before it gets there, his dad is yelling. "What are you *doing*? Everybody's *running*! You can't throw people out from there! Hit the shortstop! Hit him! His dad brought you into this world!"

That kid, Irv's son, later married a girl named Missy Dodd.

In college, 1966, about two years after my father was killed in a car wreck, Skidmore and I had a major falling-out. It was simple why. At a party which I did not attend, he'd quietly passed along to those who were attending that my father, dead two years, had had, in earlier days, an affair with some woman in town. I never knew the source of this rumor, but always suspected Skidmore's dad was somehow at the root of it.

The next morning I was in bed when my mom yelled up that I had a phone call.

"Hi, it's me." It was a girl named Kitty whom I sometimes dated.

"Last night," she said, "your pal Skidmore said something I think you ought to know about. He said your dad had an affair a few years ago, with that lady Mrs. Dodd, at the hospital."

I sat there. Something like that had never occurred to me. In fact, it took me a laughable ten seconds to imagine what my girlfriend meant by the word "affair." Then my initial reaction was that this was another vicious thing Skidmore dreamed up to say, being mean in a lot of ways. But then I realized something about him—that his meanness was rarely in outright lies, more often in the brutal administering of the truth.

"He said there might even have been a child," Kitty said.

I knew Mrs. Dodd's youngest daughter, who was then about nine. By subtraction, we came to the summer of 1957. I recalled seeing him through the binoculars, standing alone in the shadows at the ball park.

I could tell you a great story about Leonard Skidmore, my old coach. He was a first baseman way back when, but when the war came and he was drafted he went to Europe and you might think he forgot baseball. It happened that he was in the Battle of the Bulge, and so was Warren Spahn. In the evenings Leonard would scout out a catcher's mitt and let Spahnnie throw a few. Spahn was already well known, famous even. His return from his duty fighting the war was anxiously awaited by Johnny Sain and the Boston Braves. To hear him tell it, Leonard had to get a slab of ham from the mess officer to put inside the catcher's mitt, to take out a little of the big-league sting. Anyway, there they were, my friend Skidmore's dad and Warren Spahn, playing catch at the Battle of the Bulge.

Cliff Webb, who had provided me with my Opening Day hangover, was three years older than me, and it turned out that he had mostly played catcher later on. He had always seemed easygoing, but now, in middle age, he had very oily skin and nervous, worried eyes. He'd sat down next to me at the bar (I'd been there a while), recognized me past the beard in just a few seconds, and, even though we hadn't seen each other in twenty years, a minute didn't pass before he embarked on a long joke about tits and the Pope.

I had heard that he had a reputation for being tough on wives—in fact, had been in jail for beating up one of them. Which was a lot like his father, who'd been in jail for something right during the time Cliff and I'd been playing ball together. I assumed the scars on his face were where his women raked him as they were going down for the count.

"I remember your dad," he said. "Yelling at you to hit behind the runner. Hell, at the time I didn't even know what he meant. He'd yell, 'Okay, touch any base, touch any base!' "

Cliff was laughing. "There we were, twelve or whatever. Your dad, he must have known a lot about baseball."

"He did," I told him. "He was an old infielder and the game got inside him when he was little. Like us." I recalled one night after going to a game between the Cardinals and the Giants we went to the coffee shop at the hotel and Dad ended up sitting at the counter talking baseball with Harvey Kuenn. "Remember him?"

"Managed the Brewers in '82, right? Against St. Louis in fact, right?"

"This was around '63 or so. Kuenn waś a third baseman then, and outfield of course."

"Well, he was something, your dad. I'll bet everyone on our old team remembers how he yelled for you."

"*At* me, was more like it." I laughed, but I didn't think it was so funny.

"Whatever happened to that asshole Skidmore?"

I always wonder how people weather time in other people's memories.

"Lives in Nebraska. He's an attorney."

"Oh boy, that's about what I'd expect. He go to Vietnam, do you know?"

"Nope."

"You?"

"Nope."

Cliff needed to talk about Vietnam, so we did, getting plowed on beer which he was buying for us by the pitcher. I was turned on my stool and had a good view of the whole bar. I in fact was deep in eye games with a woman sitting at a corner table way off behind him. She was my age, maybe younger, but hard—maybe older, who could tell in the dark?

He was talking about Vietnam, but now he was selling for State Farm and a lot of that kind of language invaded his speech and bored me. After he told me about the war, he briefly skirted his marriages, then hit upon the topic of an old fishing rod he loved. Once in a while I'd glance over his right shoulder at the girl in the corner. She seemed shy in a way, looking down. But then she'd be looking my way the next time I looked hers. A couple of times we held the gaze until one or the other of us looked away.

He was repeating himself—I'd missed something in the conversation. "Hey, you ever play softball? I said—looks like you're in pretty good shape."

"No. Wish I did, though."

The girl in the corner, her hair was dark brown, held back with a small ribbon and a flower.

"Wish I did," I said.

Vietnam kept sneaking back into his conversation. He'd been a marine, and had a very rough time. Fifteen years had passed, and it still wasn't settled inside of him. He said he'd like to go back. He said it was where he knew himself best.

The girl in the corner half smiled at me once. She seemed to be alone, although in a little town like this it was in terribly bad taste for a girl to show up at a bar alone. It made me wonder about her.

Cliff was talking about Hill 881 and how he'd watched from a hilltop as North Vietnamese tanks ran over some little villages on the way to the siege of Khe San. Once the girl seemed almost to toast me with her beer—she raised it, nodded my way. Suddenly Cliff said, "You gonna listen to me or watch her?" I looked back at him, startled. He was looking right at me, his eyes watering. He turned and looked at her, then back. "Really. I'm supposed to meet some people anyway." He polished off the last of his beer.

"Sorry, Cliff. I really am."

"Well, damn. It's irritating." He'd gotten my apology but he was angry and seemed to want more. "I hate talkin' to somebody, their eyes climbing the wall."

"I don't blame you," I said.

"You gonna talk to me, or you gonna watch her?" he said, his face just a little red in the creases.

"Well, since you ask, Cliff—I'm gonna do both," I told him, putting my hand on his shoulder. "I'm not perfect either."

The girl in the bar, she wasn't Missy Dodd, who is probably my half sister. The town isn't *that* small.

I know this town too well, and the people in it. I really ought to move away. When I go to my boy's ballgames, I frankly can't stand to watch the game from the bleachers, among Dad's old patients who will take the time to tell me about an ailment or ask me something I don't know the answer to about how things have turned out since his death. And I don't know what his last words were—car wrecks can kill you without last words. I don't know if he's up there looking down. I dodge those people the way Dad did. Sometimes I actually even take the video camera and find that great shade down beyond third base under the IC maple, where the angle on shortstop is good for picture-taking at sundown and a fellow can have a drink if he needs one.

The Valence of
Common Ions

I'm at Chamberlain's Funeral Home standing in a crowd of mourners, separated momentarily from my date. Actually she's a mourner and I'm simply accompanying her. It's her friend who has died—a twenty-eight-year-old woman killed in a collision at an intersection. She was thrown out of the car, so the casket's closed.

The visitation seems to have brought together a blend of people who don't know each other, but it's a large crowd. Then again, Chamberlain's is a large funeral home, and there are four visitations going on simultaneously. A sign at the door directs you. In the Cambridge Room are the Arnold mourners; in the Coventry Room there are the friends and family of Miles Overman; the Kensington Room has Miss Milly Key's loved ones; and we're in the Devonshire Room.

This is a shocking death. A man has read some scripture, standing near the head of the casket, and the dead woman's sister has read a poem the woman wrote when she was little. High school kids, dressed up, are crying. I imagine they're her cousins, or friends of younger brothers or sisters. There are old people, perhaps grandparents or friends of parents or grandparents. The woman was a nurse, and there are ten or so nurses in attendance in their white uniforms. The people are talking quietly in this large room, which has flowers banked up against the wall all around.

Two children are near the casket, and I watch them. For a while they whisper. But when I look back, the game seems to have become tag of some kind, low-key but with the potential to escalate. The taller boy, maybe five years old, hides in the flowers. The littler guy, about four, goes in and gets him. At that point an older woman politely asks them to settle down, but she's cautious. For all she knows, these are children of the deceased.

There's a man who happens to be standing near me, and he quietly observes that the tall one belongs, he thinks, to the dead woman's sister, who is distraught and, after her reading, has been taken to a small chapel located in the center of the building which services—he uses that word, *services*—all four areas of the funeral home. The chapel has a mauve-colored skylight. He describes it to me from a time when he'd been in there on some other sad occasion. And the littler kid, he confesses, he had thought belonged to me, because I'm the only one in the room he can't match to other people. I tell him I have no children here and am not even currently married. The words sound odd coming out of my mouth. It's a new thing.

Our conversation isn't very good. I can't think of much to say, and don't really want him to say much either. We talk very quietly. I note with a little impatience that he's one of those people who have the practiced ability to sneak in what they evidently consider to be compelling autobiographical details. For instance, he says, while we're discussing the time he was at this funeral home before, "The man who died was a guy I used to know when I was playing Triple A in the Detroit organization—he'd been dating this woman who hated me who looked like a lady I used to live with back in '76."

I have a friend named Dubie—he and I go way back—and if

Dubie had said something like this I'd razz hell out of him. But he wouldn't. This guy then works it into the conversation that he's a psychologist, has his own practice, is newly married. His hair is thinning, and he parts it just above his ear, combing the whole works over. I don't ask how he rationalizes this psychologically. His eyes drift while I'm talking, surveying the crowd until his turn rolls around again. I'm feeling low and critical, and he's the handy victim of it. I didn't know this woman. I feel that I shouldn't be here.

At last Roberta, my date, comes up, and she knows him. Her mascara is dampening down onto her lower eyelids. "Hi, Albert—you've met Daniel?"

Albert says he has, but shakes my hand anyway. She's dabbing at her eyes with pink Kleenex. Her eyes are green and sharp. She's been in a cluster of women toward the back of the room, all of them about her age, all of them friends of the dead woman, many of them the nurses who came in a group.

"How you been, Bobbie?" Albert asks, briefly embracing her, using the telltale nickname from the old days. She says she's been great, and some flowers by the casket go over sideways. One boy jumps reflexively and actually bumps the casket. Roses slide to the floor. The boys head for the hallway, trying to walk like gentlemen, but it turns into a race. In the quiet, distracted mourning of the room, few people really notice this activity.

A man in a dark suit wearing a Chamberlain's name tag steps from the crowd like the Secret Service and firmly asks the boys to go outside, and the low drone of conversation resumes. He escorts them to the door and as they go by me I hear him ask, in his practiced funeral-home whisper, who their parents are. It turns out they're in the Arnold party, the Cambridge Room.

"This is something, huh," Albert says. He's speaking of the

tragedy. He shakes his head. He's really trying to get into the mourning thing, but he's so self-absorbed he can't quite pull it off.

"How's Howard, do you know?" Roberta asks. Howard is the husband of the dead woman. He was in the wreck, too. To me, Roberta's voice betrays that she doesn't think much of Albert. Can Albert feel this? I wonder.

"He's okay," Albert says. "Fair condition. He was going to make it today if he could, but I don't know."

"Albert's real close to Howard—they go fishing," Roberta tells me. "Who's got the baby?" she asks.

"I don't know," Albert says. The tone shows he doesn't have children of his own. "Howard busted his collarbone and bumped his head real good. But he may come. His friends are here, that's for sure."

"Right," Roberta says.

"Well, like I say . . ." he says. He moves himself so that his upcoming remark won't be heard by anyone but us, but with us has the proper gravity. "Howard likes to drive these little Jap cars. This was a fancy little Toyota he was in. Spun him around, man . . ."

Roberta doesn't want to hear much more of that. I feel the tugs at my arm.

"Lucky the baby wasn't in the car," Albert says. "The back end's wadded up like . . ." He stops short of the metaphor. "Little cars are fine," he goes on, "if you can get some assurance the one that hits you will be little. That's what I always think about."

"Say hi to Jackie, will you?" Roberta says, retreating.

"Sure," he says. "She's just over there." He points, almost as though he expects us to hurry over but then he notices we aren't. "Take care, Bobbie," he says, and half turns away.

"Would you not leave me standing again?" I say to Roberta

when we're just a little bit alone, and even as I say it I regret the selfishness of it.

"Sorry," she says. "This has to be strange for you. I *am* sorry. It's just that . . . everyone's so shocked." She's crying.

"I know," I say. "I'm sorry. For some reason that guy back there, he really got on my nerves."

She's wiping her eyes by tracing over and under her mascara with a corner of the Kleenex, talking quietly. "Albert's hall-of-fame psychological utterance," she says, "was his observation that when he married Jackie she had a low *profile* of herself."

"Jesus. Was he serious?"

"I think so. He said it at a party in front of a bunch of professional people who didn't know he was joking if he was."

I look back at him, still alone, still half-turned.

She's crying again. "Boy, this is very hard—a lot of these people were very close to Michelle. Nobody knows what to say."

Roberta sees another friend, and we go over to her. Roberta has her arm through mine. I'm proud to be with her.

"Hi, Angel—this is Daniel."

"How do you do, Daniel." Angel and Roberta embrace for a moment.

"Angel is really Dr. Gehret, my chemistry prof," Roberta tells me. Roberta is close to completing nurse's training over at UC–Davis. Angel's is a name Roberta has mentioned many times. She is a gracious, classy woman. She shakes my hand, elegant in all her movements. Her hand is bones. She's dressed in black, and whatever her perfume is transfers to me. She's perhaps five years older than I am, her early forties. Roberta is thirty.

"I can't stand this," Angel says. Her eyes too are damp. "She just had a baby."

Roberta now has one arm through mine and one through

Angel's. "That's Michelle's mom and dad over there," she says, indicating with an unobtrusive nod of the head. It's hard to see them, with the group of friends around them. "Howard'll come through this, don't you think? Maybe somehow he'll make it." Roberta is just saying these things. She doesn't really know what she's saying. She's just trying to say something. "He always says he's a survivor—Howard does. He always says that."

Angel's looking toward the box. She says, "You know, Michelle wanted this baby so badly."

Roberta wears her hair frizzy, bookish, or like she's just been rained on. I notice that her nose, pink now along with her eyes, is fine, very delicate, much like my ex-wife's. This resemblance is a new revelation to me. We stand there together for some time, no one saying anything.

"Have you seen the note on that one bouquet?" Angel asks after a while. We haven't. "It's there on the end. The card says, 'Best Wishes for a Quick Recovery.' Is that ghastly?"

I look in that direction. Now no one is within twenty feet of the casket. The roses that had fallen are back in their place. Staring at the box, I try to picture this woman named Michelle in there. On a tripod next to the casket is a small studio portrait of her in her nursing uniform. But to take that picture and extract reality from it, and place that reality in the dark gray metallic casket. Hard to do for a stranger, let alone loved ones. Michelle. Embalmed. Ready for the grave. Good-bye.

We stand quietly for a while, looking at the thinning group. People are leaving the visitation in clusters, friends, families. I hear someone say they have to go to the grocery store now.

Roberta's head is down, and Angel tries to comfort her. "There's nothing any of us can do," she says. Then the three of us are in the parking lot—a damp spring evening. On the street at the end of the driveway cars are sliding by under the amber streetlights. Everything seems to have a sparkle, a shine. Off somewhere I hear a cat fight.

"People always say that," my girlfriend says. "That there's nothing we can do. I'm going to figure out something. I'm going to do *something*." I don't know Roberta well enough to know what this means.

"Roberta, call me sometime, please?" Angel says. A gracious smile. "I'm over in Calistoga now. Won't you? Maybe you could come and play the piano for me. Have you heard her play, Daniel?"

"It's hard to think about now. But I'll call you," Roberta says. "I keep thinking of it, looking for an academic excuse."

"Come by and we'll discuss valences of some common ions," Angel says, and she winks.

"Good idea," Roberta says, with a grudging little laugh. "A little bad-grade humor," she says to me.

"Don't you have the periodic table?" Angel asks, her hand on Roberta's arm.

"You mean that chart thing?" Roberta is kidding. They both laugh quietly. "I have it, but I need to find and understand it."

"It's a date, then," Angel says.

The following evenings are difficult for Roberta. On a couple of them, she's at my place. She cries, and spends hours on the phone. She's back to smoking, which she'd quit a couple of years before I met her. I listen while she talks to friends, sitting at my kitchen table with the lights out and the long white cord of the phone stretched from the far wall. She occupies herself this way while I'm working in the darkroom just a few feet away.

The night after the funeral she calls Howard. "Hey, Howard," she says. "It's Roberta. You okay?"

"I know," she says.

The pictures I'm working with were taken from about two-thousand feet. This particular work is for a developer who wants to tuck a mall into a hillside.

"Well, is the family gone?—not yet?" Roberta is asking Howard.

"Look, I didn't call to ask what I can do. Are you relieved and refreshed by that?" She laughs, all indications being that this struck a chord with Howard. "I'm gonna *tell* you what I'm going to do—little change of pace, right."

"Right," she says, levity subsiding. "I know, Howard.

The pictures I'm developing show highways and neighborhoods, the roofs of used-car places, an occasional line of traffic at a light. Even at so low an altitude, over a dense population, I don't see anything readily identifiable as a person—except for maybe those small specks dotting the edge of a backyard pool. Staring down through the camera sometimes I imagine that I'm looking instead through a microscope, into a petri dish. There's a rough eruption of green mold in the corner, microscopic cauliflower—wait, it's a forest. At 2,500 feet, a cemetery is easy to identify, the stones in rank and file, an occasional canopy, an occasional burst of color from flowers. But you don't see many people. People from above are about the size of their hats.

"Look here," she says to Howard, taking a deep breath. "I'm carting in food tomorrow. Might last you a couple of days if you ration it."

I peer through the curtain, reminding her of the other offer.

"Oh yeah, and my friend Daniel—you've not met him yet. He's a professional photographer. If you find a picture, Howard—of Michelle, you know?—get it to me and we'll make it big and pretty, for posterity. That little girl of yours, someday she'll . . ." There's no way Roberta will make it through this sentence.

I look back out at her.

"I gotta go, Howard—right—I love you, too. Hang in there. Have your mom be sure to throw the door open wide around noon tomorrow. I'll be on the run."

"Okay," she says then, after a moment, and clicks off. She puts her head down on her arms on the table.

A few years ago I was doing a job for a surveyor. This was back in Illinois, and actually, completely without knowing it at the time, I recorded a stop-action sequence of an auto accident. It was all silently unfolding down there, inside the view of my camera, and I didn't notice. I was looking at something else, trying to fly at the same time as usual.

I noticed it in the darkroom while I was bringing the pictures up a few days later. I went through my pile of the week's newspapers trying to find out if anyone was hurt. Didn't find anything. I guess I could have asked the police.

A week after the funeral we're driving up Angel's long driveway in Calistoga. Being out in the car with Roberta makes me feel wonderful and guilty, like stolen moments. I have to keep reminding myself that my divorce is final. The change in my life is dizzying.

Angel, dressed in sandals with a little lift to them, a dazzling white, frilly blouse, and Levi's, is all the way at the back and waving us to drive around. The driveway comes around the house and blends into a large patio and garden. Angel's still holding the hose—she's been watering a terrace of flowers. Twisting the nozzle, she stops the water, drops the hose in the grass.

"You came!" she says when we stop, and her arms engulf

Roberta as she gets out of the car. "I didn't think you'd come even when you called and said you were on the way."

"Why's that?" Roberta asks.

"Hello, Daniel," Angel says over Roberta's shoulder, over the top of the car. "Good to see you again."

She orients us, points in the direction of the Palisades to the east, then toward the Mayacamas, the direction of Santa Rosa, Bodega Bay. She takes us back to an area around the pool. She pours us a glass of wine. Roberta and I sit on wrought-iron patio chairs in the shade of a white canvas umbrella, and Angel is partly in the sun in an ancient, weathered rocking chair. Her black hair has silver in it. She has it gathered up in back.

"Do you know Napa wines, Daniel?" she asks. "This is a Chardonnay—you won't find better in California."

She must think I'm from North Dakota or something. I listen and smile. I like her is why.

"It's aged in oak casks. Like the reds. Tastes grassy, don't you think?"

"Dan's been up and down the valley in his time," Roberta says protectively. "He lives in San Jose."

"Ah, San Jose," Angel says.

"He used to live way farther north. When he was married. And Chicago."

"Are you divorced, then?" she asks me, the usual measured caution in her voice showing she's allowing for the chance that, like Howard, I might be a widower.

"Freshly."

"Well. Welcome to the world. Don't become too discouraged for a while. It's an adjustment."

"Okay," I say to her.

"Then later let the discouragement get down inside of you and eat you in half like it does the rest of us," she says, laughing bitterly. She clears herself of whatever she means by that and says, "Well, then, how did you two meet?"

"Daniel likes photography," Roberta says.

"I'm an aerial photographer," I tell her.

"I have this vision of a man snapping photos from a high wire." Angel laughs.

"Not high enough," I say.

"No, but I'm getting there," Angel says, laughing even bigger, her eyes bright.

"I mean, I have an airplane," I say, but I feel the comment go flat in the afternoon air.

She's already toasting us, her tough-woman laugh easing back into a warm smile. "To my friends . . ." Her bracelets slip to her elbow. "I'm glad you came. I hated that terrible visitation, didn't you?" She catches my eyes as well as Roberta's over the rim of her glass as she sips. Her mascara is very heavy on top, making her eyelashes essentially one thing. I can't get over the evenness of her beauty.

We're quiet for a moment. "You know, I've heard Howard is taking leave from work and trying to do the baby thing himself." She shakes her head, looks off toward the garden. Suddenly she's battling a wave of emotion. "You just don't imagine people like Michelle . . . this kind of thing happening to . . . not Michelle."

"I know. Not Michelle," Roberta says.

"Did you have children?" Angel asks me. "But of course it's different with men," she says before I can answer.

"I thought we were talking about a man—Howard," I say. "Yes, I have a daughter." But even as I say it I know she won't appreciate my daughter—my daughter won't be real to Angel today. I have a flash, then, of the comfort I used to feel just before falling asleep, knowing my little girl was happy and warm in deep sleep just a few steps away in another room. "My daughter's in Chicago with her mom," I say, to round out the detail, but Angel has moved on.

I watch her lips move, but I don't follow her drift. Since I left home the year before, this is the kind of people I've met continually. Well-groomed singles, making conversation, living in nice houses, surrounded by nice things they got the ideas for from each other or in magazines. Roberta is one, although she doesn't have a house but instead lives in a townhouse among many single nurses a block from the Davis Community Hospital.

Angel says to Roberta, "Donna came by, and Jackie, last week. She really likes you—Jackie does. Really. I mentioned you might visit me soon. She says you're pretty and bright. No argument there. Right, Daniel?"

"Right," I say automatically, and lift the glass as a small toast to Roberta.

"Jackie thinks Albert . . . do you know these people, Daniel?"

I nod and offer that I sort of know Albert.

Angel continues right over that. "She thinks Albert is still yours, Roberta. Yours for the taking."

"Did she say that?"

"Maybe she was just being charming."

"Well. Albert's *anybody's* for the taking," Roberta says.

"Albert and Roberta dated there for a while, Daniel—hardly a matched set, would you say?"

"Hardly."

Roberta has reached over and put her hand on mine on the table.

Then they talk about this person named Donna I've never heard of before, well into the second glass of wine. Donna has taken charge of her life, Angel says. She's not seeing men, and she's completely off pills. She is going to a female counselor in Davis and they seem really to have hit it off. Roberta and Angel talk about the celibacy article in *Cosmopolitan.*

I watch Angel. She's engrossed in Roberta. She brings us both along with her laugh, and once in a while there is a polite glance to me—to keep me included, but this visit is about Roberta. I'm very comfortable with that.

When we go in, I take the Chardonnay and Angel takes Roberta's arm. Together they walk ahead of me. They talk so quietly I can't hear. I flatter myself that they may be talking about me, or at least about men. I think I know better, however. In the house, made mostly of stone and glass, Angel shows us around. She lives alone.

In the kitchen, on the counter, is a textbook. From the front flap Angel pulls out a poster-sized periodic table. "For you," she says to Roberta, and Roberta laughs. "The text is old, so you're missing the eight or nine new elements. Maybe it's a collector's item by now, like a flag with twenty-one stars or something. Post it over the bathroom sink," she says. "You'll have it in no time."

Roberta plays the piano for Angel, who sits next to her reading the music. The room, the whole afternoon, fills with the sound of the piano. Roberta has some boiler-plate sections of classics memorized, including some of Rachmaninoff's second concerto, which I love, and Debussy's "Arabesque," and Angel has a lot of music. I find myself wanting to hear things all the way through, but each piece seems to go a while and then play out. They talk quietly, and sometimes rousing laughter comes across to me. For the most part, I can't hear them. Angel plays then, and she is very good, too. They land in a clump of show tunes, and Roberta sings in that hefty Karen Carpenter style of hers.

I've been in this situation before in my life, it occurs to me.

Sometime. My wife and I had gone somewhere, perhaps to the home of a friend of hers from college. The kids would play outside, and I would find a good chair with a view. Maybe if they had a good bookshelf I'd pull some book down and page through it. And there would be music.

Through the glass wall from where I'm sitting I can see into the far reaches of the yard, well groomed and empty. And I can see the trees and flowers in a rock garden area next to a pond, moving in the warm, gentle wind. I possess the bottle of wine, and in time give myself over to it.

"What is it about Angel?"

Roberta is in bed, stretched out under white sheets. It's several nights later. "I don't know," she says. "Like what?"

I'm in the bathroom staring in the mirror. It's my apartment. Roberta makes me feel old. I try to imagine why she wants to be with me. She didn't know me when I was younger and had more hair and didn't have the beginnings of a paunch.

"She's been single a long time," Roberta offers. "I think she's had it with men, is why she may have seemed a little tough."

"Not at all."

"I asked her if she was going out. She said she'd been dating a Ph.D. named Brad off and on for about a year but it ended. Said he was fine, a real high-energy guy, as they say, and they had fun and all that—he was making big dollars somewhere and they traveled a little. Then suddenly he seemed to sort of lose it, got all soft in the neck, and shortly after that asked her to marry him."

In the mirror I examine my neck.

"Plus, you know. She's teaching, and college is a hard nut to crack when you're . . . whatever they call it."

"A woman?"

"No!" She laughs. "Adjunct."

"Ah. Adjunct."

I hear nothing from Roberta for a few seconds. Then she says, "What are you *doing* in there?"

"Do you have any pictures of Michelle yet?" I say. Inside, I'm thinking of death, my own, alone out here in an apartment with a shopping center across the street. I think of Michelle rocking in the carpeted dark of her casket when it's bumped. I'm wondering if a woman exists whom I might lose control of myself with and fall in love again. I'm wondering if maybe I haven't drifted too far from church. I'm thinking I should call home.

"She was a pretty girl. What are you *doing* in there?" Roberta sounds half irritated, half bored. Muttering, she gets up. It's almost dawn. She dances into a robe of mine, steps into my mirror. "What're you doing?" she asks me.

"Thinking."

"About what?"

I try to give it words. "I just try to imagine how Michelle's husband must feel, knowing she's buried in the ground."

"What does he care about that? His wife is dead. That's the sad thing."

I stare at the mirror. What a composition, the two of us there before me. Who is this girl? Is she an actress portraying my dream girl, portraying my wife? It's like I'm waking up in a strange place after amnesia.

"Did you know I played baseball in college?" I ask her. Her eyes go down. "Did you know I used to work for the paper in New Haven, Connecticut?"

"C'mon," she says. "What's the deal?"

"Did you know I walked Wisconsin for Eugene McCarthy?"

She shakes her head, smiling. "Gosh. You're pretty old." She tickles me in the side, trying to bring me along.

"It's gone if you don't know about it."

"Are you going to start pumping me full of the sixties stuff again? I tell you, it isn't healthy to think your era—or whatever—is the center of the world. Plus, to people like me, it's boring."

"I know."

"You miss your family?" she asks me. That's something that has always amazed me about her. Roberta listens very well. "I understand that," she says. Her arm is around me, hand resting in the small of my back, so comfortable.

"Tell me something," I say. "Did Michelle go to church or anything?"

"Unitarian or . . . one of those. Why?"

"I just . . . I wonder what she thought would become of herself when she died." Hearing myself say this drives me into retreat. "I don't know. I can't get it out of my mind how those little kids actually bumped the box."

"Daniel, the casket didn't move. It wasn't going to fall. Haven't you ever been a pallbearer? Those things are heavy. And anyway, don't make Michelle's tragedy yours. Let *her* have it. Feel sorry for *her*."

"I do. But I didn't know Michelle," I say. "For me, she's death *generally*, the physical aspect. She's pushing up general daisies. It's the general effect."

"Poor Dan." She tries to bring her arm up to my neck, but I'm heading for the other room.

"Poor Daniel what?" I say, sitting down on the bed to pull on my pants. "I'm going to call Dubie—remember him?" Roberta is right there, pushes me back—I'm tangled up in my jeans.

"Those people that dropped in for breakfast when I first knew you?"

"Right. Dubie and I go way back," I say.

"Why don't you just call home? I've got a great idea. Fly

your little girl in and we'll take her for a glider ride in the Valley."

My boots are on the floor under my feet. I'm looking up, the frizzy cascade of Roberta's hair in my face. She's smiling down. "You're a good boy, Dan," she says to me. "I want you to be happy. In the meantime," she says, a smile at once shy and mischievous, "here's the physical aspect," she says, flirting with the movement of her hips against me. "Here's your general effect," she says. She kisses me next to the eyes, holds me still.

"Hello." It's a couple of nights later. I'm in the apartment alone. I decide to call.

"Hi, Dubie. It's Dan."

"Daniel! You okay?"

"I'm doing great."

"It's the middle of the night."

"You notice everything."

"Are you sure you're okay?"

"Yeah." I hear him struggling to sit up in bed. Dubie's a pilot for United Airlines, still lives in Chicago.

"Hey," I say. "Let's catch the Giants one of these days."

"Okay." This sounds uncertain, like he at least suspects this is not the reason for a call in the middle of the night.

"I miss your brand of BS. It's been too long. Plus, the Giants are having a good year."

"Seriously, I'm up for it. I've been wondering about you. Haven't been to the ball park since the last time we went, you and me. I stopped watching them after they traded Clark to St. Louis."

For a few moments I can't think of anything to say.

"I've been wondering how you're doing," he says.

"So how's work?" I ask him.

"Great. I'm in deep shit with some old friends because I crossed the picket line this spring."

"You did?"

"When push came to shove, thirty years with the company just outweighed the union dispute. It wasn't even a hard decision, Dan."

"Sounds okay by me," I say. "But, speaking of deep shit, you're in a little with me."

"I know—don't say it."

"You're a shitty correspondent."

"Ah, I know it. I sure am sorry, Dan . . . I swear, I . . ." He stops himself. He knows there's no excuse. Dubie flies to the coast a lot, and calls while he's here, and used to, after the divorce, at least drop me a card from time to time. He says, "Not everybody can hammer out four-page letters triweekly. Takes me longer to read your letters than it takes you to write 'em. I couldn't keep up."

I hear something in the background, a woman's voice. "You got somebody with you?"

"My wife, you madman."

"Of course. Sorry."

"Everybody gets divorced, thinks everybody else is." He tells her it's me on the phone. "You dating, Dan? Elaine wants to know."

"Same, same."

"Roberta? Was that her name?"

"You remember her?"

"Do I remember? Eggs benedict? She's a doll, kiddo." I hear Dubie take an elbow to the ribs. He laughs.

"Right," I say. "That's her. Breakfast is her forte."

"He says breakfast is her forte," Dubie says to his wife, and she says something back I can't hear. "So what do you hear from Sharon?" he asks me. Sharon's my ex-wife. "Sharon," he says. "What do you hear from her?"

"I hear nothing."

"What about Adrienne? Don't you see her on weekends anymore?" Adrienne's my daughter.

"Nothing. Everything's broken down."

"Jesus, Dan, I don't know how you handle that . . ."

"One day at a time," I tell him.

"We saw 'em a few months ago. They had a hard time there for a while. Sharon was working for three-sixty at Olan Mills or some damn place and losing the house. Adrienne's the cutest little thing on earth. Which one would fully expect from you and Sharon. I don't know, pal."

"I'm up on my payments," I say. "I'm sending them everything I get. Virtually."

"Oh, I know. I don't mean that. It's hard anyway, you know. It's hard for them. And I know it's hard for you, too. It's hard. I'm not saying this to get you down," he says after a moment.

"I know."

I hear Elaine talking again in the background. "Roberta makes you happy?" he asks, evidently relaying a question.

"Yeah," I say. "I don't really think true happiness is in the cards. She's a very good girl. She's one of these thirty-year-old English majors, back to school to become a nurse and make a living. Bright, like an English major; down to earth, like nurses. I think she likes me okay. I'd do anything for her. You know," I say, realizing maybe I'm being too effusive, but I can't stop, I feel the release of pressure, "you know, she's twenty-nine, almost thirty—that's a different generation from us. Really. That crowd doesn't imagine anything that isn't there."

At the end of this, the point lost, I hear him talking in a low voice away from the phone. Then he comes back. "Elaine wants to know if you went through with your post-divorce daydream of buying something phallic like a Corvette or a big motorcycle."

"Doesn't she like phalluses?" I say.

Laughing, Dubie relays the question. "She says she likes phalluses okay, but not on the highway."

I hear Elaine say something else, then Dubie passes it along. "Elaine says she still thinks you and Sharon could have survived if you had just sought counseling. She says she thinks Sharon misses you."

The second he says this, I think of lonely Albert, staring off, nobody to tell his story to. I try to imagine going to him for marriage counseling, fifty bucks a pop.

"Tell Elaine survival wasn't the question."

"Well, what was it?" Dubie asks point-blank. "We're your friends. We've always wondered."

"She wasn't happy, and I wasn't happy. How's that for starters?"

Elaine's talking in the background. "How old's Adrienne?" Dubie's asking me. "When was she born? Elaine wants to know."

"1975," I tell him.

"Lord, I remember that!" He laughs. "You rented that house next to a K Mart dumpster and had that old orange Vega."

"That's pretty much how I'm living now," I say, a joke sort of.

I hear Elaine recalling something, and Dubie listens, then relays it: "Elaine remembers how she and Sharon took off, when we were all up in Vancouver, and we couldn't find them. And then we finally caught up to them in this French-type place, remember? Where they were playing Leonard Cohen."

I remember that very well. We were young then, and I recall courting guiltily the possibility that some night on that trip

Dubie and I might swap, one of those quiet sexual fantasies that pass by, mercifully not acted upon. Now I'm not sure I can even picture Elaine.

"Hey, Dubie," I say. "Tell her to stop with the flashbacks, for Christ's sake. I . . ."

I stop. Both of them are quiet.

"I see," Dubie says after a while.

I feel a sudden swell of emotion in my chest, not immediately recognizable to me. It's anger or sadness, one. "Sharon cared less about me or men in general, Dubie. Tell Elaine that. She spent endless hours over coffee with the witches—no offense to Elaine—in the neighborhood. It took five hours of foreplay every two-and-a-half months just to roll her over. I don't really think I turned her on anymore. It was like, she had her baby so thank you very much. She misses the routine and the income and the security, and she probably will have to get out of that house—the mortgage is a killer. She didn't love me anymore."

In the background Elaine is buzzing, her voice sounding disgusted. "Tell him he ought to check the statistics on how many households there are where it's the woman who's starved sexually."

Just at the end of this, Dubie covers the receiver and says something to her. It seems to be an attempt to get her to back off, because it's very quiet on the other end for a moment after that. Then I think I hear her mumble that I wasn't such a great catch myself. Dubie doesn't relay it, whispers something to her.

"And don't say 'Poor Daniel,'" I say to him.

"How'd you know I was thinking that?" Dubie says quietly, an audible smile. "No, really. I understand."

The word "understand" feels very good coming into my head. I think he does. I think a little communication might have taken place despite Elaine. I tell him how, living alone, suddenly I feel close to death, and far from the time when I was young. I tell him it's strange making love to a woman who didn't know me when I was twenty-six. I don't know why but suddenly I'm telling him about Michelle's visitation. I tell him I didn't even know the girl, or her child or her husband. I tell him about the creepy get-well card, and how it seemed like Michelle's casket actually rocked when it was bumped, even though Roberta didn't think so, and how the flowers fell.

Long Pine

There was a low, flat flow to the road, sundown. Skidmore, who'd been hiking fast since his last ride dropped him in the middle of the sandhills, was sitting now on his old suitcase, the kind with the pouches on the sides, deep in scrufty grass on the road's shoulder, dreaming of law school. Whole minutes passed, he didn't move. Cars flew by, station wagons, sixteen-wheelers blew by and honked loud as they passed and Skidmore didn't move, thinking about a blond he'd known in law school, back in Louisville, back before Fiona and he met—Fiona the wild-eyed impressionable Valdosta girl who carried a Buck hunting knife in her boot and thought she was a writer. Skidmore was thinking of the blond way back before her.

He took a swig off his Jack Daniel's. He'd told that poor fabulous blond girl so many lies and crossed his lying-ass trail so many times with her that the pupils in her eyes actually came to be shaped like question marks. Her mouth held a perpetual pout, and that only made her more beautiful to him. She didn't look half as tough as she turned out to be. Skidmore left her after they had a spat and she fired two shots from her .357 into her own refrigerator as he was walking past it. She finally did become a lawyer, he heard. Skidmore—thinking of it he chuckled almost proudly out there on the road—Skidmore was a razzle-dazzle guy. He could unanswer more questions in a week than most men in a lifetime. It had become a pattern in his life. Give him a relationship and a couple of months on his own resources, and Skidmore could bring ruination on everything—he could bring more ruination than whole defoliation programs, whole societal collapses, whole holy wars. He actually heard one of those bullets whiz past his belt buckle.

Out on the road, though, thinking about that blond, he could only really think of the good things: that he had loved her so much, that there wouldn't ever be another like her, so playful and evil in bed, that he was better for having known her. He didn't want any part of most of his wretched past anymore, but he wouldn't have minded plucking that blond girl out of his memory and standing her up there on the road and telling her he'd be hers forever if she just promised to love him the way she did back in Louisville in law school and not lie like a lot of women. He tried hard to resurrect the texture of her right out there on a highway in Nebraska at nightfall twelve years later.

He was headed for Long Pine, never to be seen again. Fiona, it happens, had lived in Long Pine. She waited tables and sang in some dive there—it was where she met Yank, in fact. She'd talked about it being a hide-out town, full of rogues and crazy women drinking all day and all night. She said it was a town Jimmy Hoffa might be buried in, if he was buried in Nebraska at all, or where the guys who got him were hiding, because it was so weird, disgusting and far from everything else. Nobody from most places had ever heard of Long Pine. The way Fiona talked, Long Pine was the most dreaded, worthless place you ever saw, so Skidmore was headed there to be disgusting like he deserved if he couldn't even get a simple vagabond woman to take a simple picture off her goddamned wall.

Skidmore raised the bottle of Jack Daniel's again. He looked back down the road to see if Indian braves were trailing him. He

squinted, looking way, way down. In Long Pine he wouldn't
have to worry about any of his Fort Robinson past, including all
the Indians and white boys who'd threatened to get him if they
ever got out of the slammer, including that damned exasperat-
ing Fiona, poor, confused ratty little girl holed up above a
sleazy downtown Fort Robinson cowboy bar all knotted up
over her novel, which she already knew could never be as good
as *Even Cowgirls Get the Blues.* Poor Fiona, cornered by art.

It was bad enough that she absolutely refused to remove the
picture of her and Yank from the wall above her bed. (The
picture showed Yank with his arm around her, his left arm,
the hand down lightly on her breast, a menacing look in his
eye. They were drunk, toasting the camera with cans of malt
liquor. Yank was wearing the elastic band from his jockey
shorts around his head.)

"You gotta take that picture down," Skidmore had said to
her. "I don't mean to complain, but you have to cut that picture off the wall."

"Get tough," she told him, laughing. "He's a friend of mine.
It was a time in my life—I like to remember it. I like to remember the farm."

"He left you without notice."

"That's just the way he was," she said.

"I'm asking for some consideration here. Couldn't you
hang it in the hall, or the bathroom, if it has to hang on the
wall around here, and not over the bed?"

"Put it out of your mind, Mister. I'm my own boss and interior decorator. I hang what I want hung. The picture stays."

The look in Yank's eye in the picture would sometimes intrude into Skidmore's daydreams—a rough, wild-ass look,
like the sky was the limit. Skidmore had argued a lot of Indians and white boys into jail who had a look like that in their
eye, and he always knew it wasn't the argument that got

them—it was the look. And in the picture there was a look in Fiona's eye, too. She loved Yank. She was completely accustomed to his desperate style of life. It gave her material to write about. Skidmore could tell she was intrigued by old soldiers like Yank, the romance of having lived on the edge, as opposed to lawyer types like Skidmore who wrangled CO status and wimped out the sixties in the Caribbean. How could Skidmore compete with Yank? That damned picture, it was a real problem.

Then came the day when the straw broke the thing's back. They were going to have a real date, and he would come over and they would walk to a movie or something, stroll in the old cavalry fort just outside of town, and he trudged up the hill from his trailer to her apartment, and what happened? She wasn't there. They had a date! Well, if she felt so free as to run roughshod over an actual date, well then, screw her. Skidmore hit the road. No one was ever better to her, for sure not Yank. Skidmore couldn't live that way anymore. He hit the road. Now *he* was going to live the risky life. He knew her standing him up was the sign she didn't love him with the all-encompassing devotion he required of his women. He knew very well that women will lie to you if you aren't careful. Just by looking at her, you never think a woman will lie (especially if she's one of the types that curl their eyelashes, one of the types that look at you with that one kind of look certain girls look at you with), but she will, she'll lie and keep lying even after that if she wants to, because women, Skidmore was thinking to himself out on the road, are a bunch of liars if you aren't careful. He swallowed four square ounces of Jack Daniel's and another hit for good measure. Then he thought someone was right behind him with a tomahawk and he stood up and whirled around fast, letting out a loud war whoop and at the same time letting fly a karate kick, but he was wrong—

no one was there. In the last light of day, he sat on his suitcase watching a magpie eat a smashed jackrabbit a hundred yards down the road. The white in the magpie's wings flashed pinkish in the setting sun.

Skidmore didn't feel bad at all, leaving Fort Robinson forever. It had been a terrible town, and it held bad memories. He was a terrible lawyer and he knew it, but he knew he could be better if he could just leave his past behind him, these women and all his problems. From where he was standing now, Fort Robinson was eighty miles off to the west and Long Pine was ninety miles off to the east and he couldn't get a ride, and, the sun gone down, the highway finally disappeared in the dark and he was sitting there on his suitcase and all there was, all there was at all, was sky. So that's what he thought about, staring up. He didn't know the name of any of the stars, or which was which. He tried to spot a constellation but couldn't see a one. Somehow, in this mood, he knew if the stars could shit they'd shit on him. His soul was sad, he thought to himself. The road, the land, the deep, black, living void above, they were all silent, and looking up Skidmore began to feel as though he might be pulled right off the earth. What would that feel like? He would disappear straight up, into the sparkling black sky. For a moment it seemed like that would be okay, but then it was terrifying to him. The black well rumbled above him like Judgment Day. He looked down at the ground instead.

It must be guilt, he thought to himself, that keeps me from properly communing with nature. He ran his fingers through his hair and scratched at his scalp. There was a time when he was a little boy and did a lot of camping that he had struggled to become nonchalant in the presence of nature—pushed hard to become nonchalant, in fact, and almost achieved it. Now nature was strange to him.

It must be guilt, he thought to himself. He knew well that

women weren't the only ones who lied. He took a drink. Deep in his heart it occurred to him that maybe he was mean, like all his old friends used to accuse him of before he took off. McFarland still told him he was mean when from time to time they would chance to meet. Sometime, he thought, I'm going to have to stop being dishonest and lying to a bunch of people all the time. He knew the ambivalence toward truth hammered into him in law school was not the problem. He had been particularly acclimated to that way of thinking long before law school. Truth to tell, when he went by to pick up Fiona and she wasn't there, he kind of smiled. He thought it was pretty spunky of her. A little revenge for all the times Skidmore said he'd be there and didn't make it. But you expect that sort of thing from a man—freedom is part of his soul. For Fiona to turn around and do it back—she really got him, he thought to himself, and laughed grudgingly.

Well, whatever. He determined that when he got settled in Long Pine he would examine his poor hurting soul and by an act of will become a better person. He decided to have a glass of red beer when he got to Long Pine, and he'd tell them that he was there to start a law office, and he'd never let them talk him into playing on their goddamned redneck softball teams and chasing women the way all the guys in their thirties did out in Nebraska, usually at Godfather's Pizza or a certain bar, usually after the softball games but sometimes after church or on nights when nothing was scheduled. Television had ruined the whole culture out there, he thought to himself. Everybody tried to act like they were in a Lite Beer commercial.

Skidmore was feeling drunk and lonely. What do they want from me? he thought, pretending that he was a tragic character caught in the complexity of the human dilemma. He tried shouting it, "What do they want from me?", out across the sandhills. Then he thought he heard something in the bushes and sat perfectly still. Maybe it was Jesus answering his painful cry—Jesus appearing to him at last and asking him to become an apostle. "Where have you been, Lord?" Skidmore said aloud. He waited. But nothing supernatural happened.

He loved that blond, he loved her more than anybody else in the world, more than anybody before her and certainly since. Maybe she had fired a couple of shots at him, acts of pure womanly passion—but never, never had she willfully stood him up. He tried to recall her name. He tried hard. She had a strange name, it was Mary, no, it was Helen, no, rhymed with Helen, no, it was Alice, no, what was that name? he thought to himself and the whiskey went down his throat, rolled down, tasting like gasahol.

He looked back and forth, up and down the road. He was completely alone. Yank would come after him. Cut him up for leaving Fiona without notice. Skidmore shook his head. The dark was making him paranoid. He mumbled the Lord's Prayer to himself, a low vocal drone, over and over, and he relaxed. A couple of hours passed in which he was a complete blank. Finally a semi came along.

"Hey, boy, you're gonna die out here if I don't give you a ride," the driver said when Skidmore opened the door on the passenger side. "And I'm gonna die if you don't give me a hit off that bottle in your shirt."

"Kill it, it's yours," Skidmore said, handing it over, then climbing up into the cab and pulling his suitcase up behind him. "We're both gonna die sometime."

"You're right about that, hoss," the driver said. He put the bottle between his legs while he pulled the rig back out onto the highway and shifted up through the gears.

"I've been out there since three this afternoon, I swear.

Goddamn! Nobody wanted to give me a ride." They had to talk pretty loud.

"You oughtta stick your goddamned thumb up in the air sometime, you jerk! It's the sign you wanna hitch a ride with somebody. I was watchin' you when I was comin' up—thought you was a commemorative statue. This Jack Daniel's shit"— he waved the bottle—"it does that to your brain." He rolled his eyes like it already did it to his brain.

"You're drinkin' it all right." Skidmore situated the suitcase against the door so he could lean on it. He considered strapping himself in but didn't. "What're you haulin'?" Skidmore asked him. "Pipe, looks like."

The driver held up the bottle. "Yeah, I used to drink this stuff back in Jackson, everybody did in fact. You'll throw your guts up 'fore the night's over. Me, too, probably."

"So what're you haulin', pipe or what?"

"What's it look like?" the driver said, and laughed way bigger than Skidmore could figure out why. "Steel pipe, to Omaha—where're you headin' for?" the driver asked him.

"Long Pine," Skidmore shouted.

"Long Pine?" He had truckers' head-buzz, too much road, popping too many reds, spaced out on daydreams of the bra-straps through the white dresses of truckstop waitresses bringing him meatloaf and mashed potatoes.

"You been there?"

"Long Pine? Nope—and I ain't goin'," the driver said. "You joinin' 'em for the festivities?"

"Which ones would those be?"

"C'mon. The hooker rodeo."

"Don't know of it," Skidmore said. He planted his feet for a truck-driver joke.

"C'mon Jack, don't bullshit the bullshitter. The hooker rodeo."

"I ain't lyin' . . ." Skidmore noticed he was adopting the dialect of his host. "C'mon," he said, looking over at the driver with a big sixteen-wheel smile, "what is it? Some kind of big-time rodeo?"

"Five hundred hookers ropin' calves in one little half-assed town—I GUESS it's big time. You got more disease in Long Pine this week than exists in all South Dakota during the warm months of the year, except on the reservation. Established fact. The hooker rodeo. Never heard of it?"

"Place is crawlin' with whores?" Skidmore said.

"You're gettin' the picture," the trucker said, giving Skidmore a chance for a hit off his own whiskey. "I'm surprised you haven't heard, goin' there and all." Skidmore took a huge swig, bottoms up, then handed it over to the trucker, who waved it as he talked. "Why, hell, there's posters up in every truckstop from here to Boise." The trucker was getting such delight out of conveying this information that Skidmore suspected the hooker rodeo did not exist outside the cab of this truck.

"Call up somebody on the radio and ask 'em," Skidmore said, pressing the guy with a challenging smile. "Catch some trucker and let's see if he's ever heard of it."

"Sorry, you're just goin' to have to believe me because there ain't nobody out here to call up and I wouldn't be here myself if I didn't have to be." The trucker looked solemn then. "I'll giveya a ride to Omaha, forget Long Pine. Bad place, bad. Don't go to that old hooker rodeo. You don't need a woman that bad."

"Well," Skidmore said, staring out into the small zone the headlights cut for them on the prairie. He was touched by the driver's sincere concern about his welfare. "Well, I don't know. I feel like I wanna go to Long Pine—I been hearin' about the place for a long time. I'm feelin' hopeless and footloose, you know what I mean? Ever get your mind set on something?"

The trucker looked at him. "How come?"

"How come what?" Skidmore said.

"How come you're feelin' footloose? I wanna know. I'm kind of a philosophical guy myself."

"Women, for chrissake," Skidmore blurted out.

"Okay. I know what you mean now," the driver said. He rubbed his hand across his face, checked his mirrors. "If you don't mind, I'd just as leave talk about something else. I'm serious, I don't want to talk about women, I can't stand it, I swear I can't."

"Had to leave my girl, back in Cheyenne." Skidmore was going to talk about it anyway. "Been on the road three days. Heard about Long Pine. It sounds about right for how I'm feelin'."

"How come you're feelin' sad and footloose aside from women? Let's talk about that aspect of it." The trucker drank the last of the whiskey.

Skidmore noticed the truck had sped up. They were hurtling through the dark at seventy with a full load. When the cab bounced, he could feel the trailer's weight pull them back.

"She stood me up," Skidmore said. "lied to me. Kept a picture of her old boyfriend up above the bed to see if she could make me whacko. I took off."

"I'm about to throw your ass off my rig," the trucker said. "I'm goddamned serious here. For all you know, maybe I got a broken heart and this reminds me of something, you know?" He winced up his eyes and bit his lip. "I hate this topic, you get me?"

"She was a hell of a lover, though," Skidmore said, "when she wasn't playin' games. She'd get those long damn legs around me and, those crazy eyes, she'd be lookin' up there at me. Christ." At this speed the road was very bumpy and at times the trailer seemed to whip around back there.

"Watch this," the trucker said. He grabbed the bottle by the neck. He held it with his left hand. Skidmore expected to catch it on the bridge of his nose. "Sling 'em a mile—real accurate." He leaned half out the window of the truck, steering with the other hand. His head and half his body disappeared out the driver's side window, into the dark. Suddenly he fired the bottle over the top of the truck, over the two mounted chrome horns and between the various aerials, and it smashed against a sign that was whipping by which said to slow down to thirty-five for a very sharp curve. Laughing loud, the trucker dropped back behind the wheel real quick, first downshifting and then braking hard. Skidmore came up out of his seat and almost against the windshield, but he got his hands up. The truck whistled through the curve. Skidmore fell back into the seat as the driver accelerated back up to seventy-five.

"I just can't take bad treatment from a woman," Skidmore said. "Lyin' and no devotion, you know? You know what I'm talkin' about?"

The trucker didn't respond, but kept his eyes on the road. He was getting into a bad mood. He was wearing a baseball cap, plastic, one size fits all. He pushed up the bill.

"Should have smacked her, I know it," Skidmore said. "Can't handle a woman treatin' me like that—been crazy since Nam."

He looked over to see if that one landed. Sure enough. "You were in Vietnam? Where at?" The road was old and cracking up. They were both bouncing in their seats.

Skidmore didn't say anything.

"Marines? Regular army, I'll bet." The bill on his cap popped down and he popped it back up. "Regular army, I can tell. Intuition. I was in Two Corps myself, up and down in there—Hundred-and-first. D'you see action?"

Skidmore didn't answer. He stared straight ahead pensively, like a lot of men who've been to hell and lived to tell about it.

Finally the trucker said, "Look here. I know what you mean, okay? We're not the same, none of us are, after the war. Shoulda slapped the shit out of her, no doubt about it. What's she know about gettin' right down to the line, right?"

"Nah, can't hit a woman even if she lies to me, which is usually," Skidmore said, and they both laughed.

"Well, you shoulda slapped her around—that's what I'da done. You gotta right to. How much can a man take? I do it plenty. You got to sometimes. They understand. Sometimes they understand a man better'n you do."

Skidmore decided not to talk to the guy anymore, since he felt so free to finish off his whiskey after bitching about it, and to talk about Fiona like she was a goddamned coonhound. So, leaning over against his suitcase, he slumped down and acted like he fell asleep and after a while he did exactly that.

"You can just fall asleep there if you want to," he heard the trucker say at one point. "No problem for me." All the time he was asleep Skidmore was completely aware of the driver and the pounding of the road. Once he heard the guy say, "You in the reserves? Never mind." After a long time he felt the trucker downshifting and heard the airbrakes set, heard the engine whining down. The trucker reached over to wake Skidmore up. "This here's your place," he said. "Tell ya, I'm good for Omaha and you'd be better off takin' me up on it."

"Listen," Skidmore told him. "I'm a dangerous man—got people after me. You don't know half of it. You want me outta here and don't know it."

"Well, we're half a mile north of town, maybe a little better. Just walk down that old road there. See them lights? That's Long Pine herself, God help ya."

Grabbing the suitcase, Skidmore opened the door and

jumped down into the dark. He thought it might be a trick. He didn't see any town anywhere, but he'd had it with this guy anyway so he thanked him, yelling up into the cab, and the truck wound up and rolled away. Skidmore walked south for ten minutes before he could see anything except stars. When he saw the lights and got closer to them, they were a little blinding themselves, and at one point he lost the road and fell headlong into a narrow sandy ravine, rolling down against an old fence. When he found his bag and climbed up out of there, he was at the Long Pine Cooperative Grain Company. A colossal cattle truck went by fast, heading into town, downshifting as it passed in anticipation of the city limits. Skidmore watched as the truck tore down the main street, throwing grit and dust up into the streetlights, ultimately disappearing under a train trestle at the other end of the street, into the dark beyond. It was 4 A.M. Except for the time-and-temperature sign on the savings and loan, the business district, two blocks long, looked like the set from *Gunsmoke*. Skidmore brushed himself off, noted that his ear was bleeding from the fall, and headed down the street looking for the hotel.

When he found it, he was amazed. It was a four-story, wood-frame structure with outdoor catwalks around all four floors so that, with the gingerbread architecture and trim, it looked like the main part of a huge old riverboat, the prow buried in the sand. Skidmore didn't see one rodeo participant, though he looked. In fact, Long Pine looked pretty dead.

The desk clerk was at least one hundred years old and was capable of assigning rooms and checking people in and out while fully asleep. He put Skidmore in room 556.

"Room 556? There are only four floors."

"This here's the penthouse. It's on the roof. Nice view of the airport. How long you stayin'?"

"Fifteen, twenty years," Skidmore said. "I'm setting up a law practice. You got anything not on the roof?"

"Maybe you ought to practice somewhere else, then come here when you get good at it," the old man said, and he laughed hard at his joke. "Look here, this here's the penthouse, sir—it's our best room, no extra charge 'cause I assigned it to you arbitrarily. Holy shit, what'd you do to your ear?"

"Fell down, nothing serious."

"Look, sir. No offense, but I can see you're completely a drunk man, so I want to tell you something. This here hotel has rules. No visitors we don't know about. They call you from this phone, they don't go just trailin' off up into the place. We got a bouncer, too, case you think I'm kidding. So I advise you to go on up there to 556 and sleep it down. If you don't like the place, we'll change you tomorrow."

"This place full 'cause of the rodeo?" Skidmore asked. He dabbed at his ear with his shirt-sleeve.

"Rodeo?"

"The rodeo, you know." Skidmore winked.

"Ain't no rodeo here I know about," the old guy said. "Used to have one at Winner, but the Indians took it over. Got a helluva go-cart track."

"I'm talking about the rodeo that the . . . the girls take part in. You know."

"Ah, jeez, you mean the HOOKER rodeo!" The old man laughed. Skidmore conveyed his relief that at last he'd communicated.

"You a trucker, or what?" the old guy asked him.

"I told you, I'm an attorney at law."

"Well then," the old guy said, "you're the victim of false advertisement conducted by our city council about a year ago. They put posters up in all the damned truckstops from here to hell and high water. Guess some of 'em are still around. Never was no rodeo of that sort. Just a idea to get a little tourism, and to get the truckers to come in off the main highway just out half a mile. Pretty funny at the time." The old man chuckled and set the key on the counter. "Don't forget the rules, you hear?"

"I hear," Skidmore said. Hesitantly he picked up the ancient, tarnished key to 556.

"One more thing," the old guy said, pulling out a mimeographed sheet from a cubbyhole beneath the counter. "You mentioned you might be hangin' around—play softball?"

"Nope," Skidmore said.

"Nope," the old man said subvocally as he wrote on the sheet. "The lawyers mostly play for the Lutheran church. Ever go to no Lutheran church?"

"Nope," Skidmore said.

"Nope," the old man said, writing again. "If you was to play softball, what position would you be interested in playin'?"

Skidmore stared straight at him, and finally the old man, waiting for a response, looked up from the paper. Skidmore kept staring at him until the old man went back down through his bifocals to the mimeographed sheet. "No softball," he muttered as he wrote.

The room was actually a cupola on the roof of the hotel. It was an ordinary room, just stuck on top. You could step out onto the tarpaper-and-gravel roof and there, right behind the hotel, was the airport runway, blue lights forming a tall upside-down V fading away up the horizonless dark. Skidmore went into the bathroom and threw up for several minutes. Just his luck, the toilet stopped up and overflowed. He had kicked off his boots and now his white socks were soaked in upchucked whiskey. Exasperated, he fell backwards onto the bed and didn't wake up until three the following afternoon.

He woke up because the phone was ringing. He would have answered it immediately but his head fell off. His head fell off and rolled across the floor so that the hanging-out tongue involuntarily licked the hotel room linoleum each time the head went face down. Or at least it felt like his head fell off. After a while he realized his head was still on and he couldn't think what he'd just seen go across the floor. Groggily he answered the phone.

"Hello."

"Front desk, sir," the caller said. "We have a gentleman down here who would like to see you. He's wearing a Nazi helmet with Viking antlers on the side. He says he would like to discuss Federal Express."

Skidmore was staring down at the linoleum pattern. "I see. Did you get his name?" he asked.

"No. He's right here, if you want to speak to him."

"Just get his name, if you wouldn't mind."

Skidmore heard scuffling on the other end of the line, and then someone else had the phone.

"Hello?" the person said.

"Yes?"

"Sir? I wonder if you couldn't come down here a moment, before they start happy hour and everybody in this whole town gets drunk and freaked out." The voice seemed rather polite.

"What is it that I can do for you?"

"Well, are you the lawyer or is this the wrong room?"

There was a good idea, Skidmore thought to himself. "This is the wrong room, I'm sorry. This is room 317. No lawyer here," he laughed. "Haulin' cattle, Cheyenne to Omaha. Need a ride?"

"Listen, sir, I'm real sorry about this. Excuse me one moment."

Then Skidmore heard him speaking to the desk clerk. "You scrawny son of a bitch, you hooked me up to the wrong room—what room was it?" he said. Sounded like a scuffle.

"Room 556," the clerk answered. Sounded like something was around his neck.

"Sir, I'm real sorry. We've got the wrong number here. I didn't mean to bother you. We're recruitin' lawyers for the Federal Express, the softball team, you know? I apologize, and my friends apologize."

"That's just fine, young man," Skidmore said. "No trouble at all. Good afternoon to you." He hung up.

Fast, Skidmore got his suitcase and his boots and quickly tied the bedsheets together. As he left the room, the phone began ringing again. Hanging the sheets around a drainpipe at the back of the hotel, he tossed down his suitcase and lowered himself to the fourth-floor catwalk, strolled to the fire escape, went down it and found his suitcase, then walked over to the Airport Bar and Grill for a late breakfast.

Eating, he sat in a booth close to the front window, so he could watch activities on the roof of the hotel and, by looking up an alleyway, could also see if it was all-clear out front. Several members of what was evidently a motorcycle gang stirred around out front. They had Federal Express written on the backs of their T-shirts, above a skull and crossed softball bats. After a while, the mad dog who had called him came storming out the front door of the hotel, climbed on his motorcycle, and sped away doing a wheely and causing dirt to fly straight up behind him like a rooster tail. The rest of the gang followed, raising a storm of dust and noise in the downtown area. After downing five scrambled eggs and a glass of red beer, Skidmore went back over to the hotel. The desk clerk on this shift was a young man, and Skidmore sat his bag down and asked for a room.

"How long will you be staying?" the clerk asked.

"One night," Skidmore said. He filled out the register, using the name of his friend McFarland, who was completely fictitious. Early in his adult life Skidmore had created McFarland to have someone to talk to, a very best friend—and McFarland, luckily, over the years, had consented to allow the friendship to continue. While not positive, Skidmore was fairly sure the friendship would not be harmed by his taking the liberty of using McFarland's name in this special instance.

"I think we should settle the bill for one night right now, Mr. McFarland. Would that be okay? It comes to fourteen-fifty."

"I understand," Skidmore said, and paid the man. He noticed that he was involuntarily talking like McFarland, lending credence to a notion he was developing about the power and creativity of the human mind.

"I couldn't help but notice the helmeted gentleman who left here a few minutes ago."

The clerk laughed, shaking his head. "We get some crazies. That's why we have to have rules. Visitors call from down here. No women on the fire escape—we'll throw both of ya out. And so on. Used to have a printed sheet with the rules—can't find 'em." He handed Skidmore a room key. "Mr. McFarland, you'll be in room 209. It's on the second floor. Take the elevator, go to your left on two and follow the numbers. It's after 207, I forget which side of the hall."

Skidmore went to his new room.

"Dear Blondy," he wrote, nervously idling away the evening with a letter after finding his room and cleaning up. While cleaning up, he discovered he'd ripped his pants and underwear sliding down the drainpipe. Carefully, he tore the elastic band off, knotted it to size seven-and-a-quarter, and put it on

his head to keep his hair back while he bent into the letter.
Once in a while, when he'd look up from writing, he'd see
himself in the mirror above the desk.

Dear Blondy,

I really do remember your name, but I like to call you Blondy
because of your hair, which, you recall, was blond, etc. Well, I
believe you are probably wondering what I have done with my
life since law school. Well, I have been to Norway twice and
have, other than that, whiled away my middle years on Indian
reservations and in small towns near Indian reservations, doing
legal work for and against Indians and white boys, etc. I was
going to be a litigator at one time, you will recall, but this is
more like social work. How have you been? Yesterday, I was out
hitchhiking, just for fun. I had been in Ft. Robinson, Nebraska,
and, on the spur of the moment, divined that I might only
change towns, a matter of 90 miles here or there, and reach
ultimate happiness. I arrived here last night. On the way in from
the highway, I accidently fell in a ditch and almost broke my ear.
But I think it'll be a nice town to raise a family in.

I know you're wondering how about the women, aren't there any
women in your life, etc., and the answer is really no. I used to
chase a lot of girls, and I admit that even when I was chasing you
I was chasing a girl. That last sentence was a joke. I don't write
many letters. Anyway, I have this friend, McFarland, and I did
ask him some of this stuff, about girls, and he said the one way
to find ultimate happiness was to stop thinking so much about
it. Have you met McFarland? I keep forgetting. He's great with
the advice but he's the best friend I have. So, how have you been
or have I already asked?

One thing I've learned in middle age is not to trust any woman
who is not yet a memory. Such as Fiona, whom I only just left.
She was not very dependable when it came to taking down pho-

tographs of old lovers, small things like that, plus she stood me up when we were having an actual date. I know this is boring. I think I mention it to let you know if I was ever a shit to you that I am now getting my just deserves, or whatever, etc.

I'll tell you something. I remember you. Do you remember me, if you know what I mean? It would be a valuable thing to me to know that you remember me. I remember you. You're the best I ever had. I like how you laughed, and I like how you really did want me sometimes if I hadn't been completely obnoxious recently. When I had you I didn't know what I had. And I didn't know then how lonely I'd be later. Etc. I don't know what to do now.

> With love,
> Skidmore.

In the drawer of the desk there was stationery, and he took out an envelope and addressed it: *Blondy, Box 2439, University of Louisville School of Law, Belnap Campus, Louisville, KY Please forward if necessary.* Carefully, Skidmore folded the paper and put it in the envelope. For a while he shadowboxed and made fast wisecracks into the mirror. His hangover had completely subsided, he noticed, but the letter had made him feel blue. He thought maybe he would just go up on the roof of the hotel and contemplate leaping for a while, get some fresh air. About then the telephone rang. For a moment he stared at it. He didn't even own a ball glove.

"Hello."

"Hello, this is the front desk." Skidmore recognized the voice of the old man again. "Is this Mr. McFarland?"

"Yes," Skidmore said. He prepared himself. "What is it?"

"Well, sir, could you come down here, please?"

"I don't believe so, no. What is it? Why are you calling me?"

"Sir, this lady is down here and she's crying."

Skidmore's head swam. "What's her name? Why are you calling me?"

"She wants to talk to you. I'll put her on."

"No, hell no, you just ask her—what's her name?"

Skidmore heard the desk clerk ask the person her name. It sounded like a scuffle broke out, and then she was on the phone.

"There's a goddamned law about signing into a hotel under the wrong name," Fiona said. She was crying. "What did I do wrong, for chrissake? Why did you leave? I just went to the drugstore to get you some after-shave. It was going to be a gift since we were going on a goddamned real date. I wait for you all the damned time, you can't wait for me five minutes while I buy you some after-shave?"

Skidmore was staring down at his letter to Blondy. "How did you find me?" he said.

"How did I find you?" she said. "How did I find you?" Skidmore could imagine the tears streaming out through her wild-woman eye makeup, her wild-woman hair across her face, caught in the muck.

"I knew you'd come to Long Pine. You were so fascinated when I told you about the place. Jesus." He could hear her wiping her nose. Skidmore couldn't believe she was down in the lobby. "I'm a wreck because of this, damn you. I knew you'd come here, plain as day," she said, "you all do." She wiped her nose again. "Maybe you could just tell me what the hell is going on. Do you love me or what?" she said.

Poor Skidmore, cornered by Fiona. He eyed the sheets on the hotel room bed and tried to think what floor he was on.

Marguerite Howe

I think back on all the waitresses I've watched—roadhouses, coffee shops, airport restaurants. I watch them because it occupies me while eating lunch, and admittedly maybe because I'm lonely in a way women never understand, and probably because I'm tired of watching soap operas in these canned-decor motel rooms with their high traffic bedspreads, tired of stripping down and taking futile, half-sleep, beer-induced naps, lulled by the sound of cars out on the highway where I should be.

And I watch because waitresses are fascinating, the way they cope with routine, their eyes down, their thank-you's flat and self-protective. Sometimes I might say something to them or write a note to them on a napkin as I leave, or I might leave saying nothing but taking a little of them with me in what I've seen and wondered. Sometimes coming out of the restaurant is disorienting, like coming out of a movie. I scan the terrain for clues as to where I am, what year it is. Waitresses deal with you as a customer, and in that way are a lot like the rest of the world. But by observing and wondering, I do at least manage to keep myself from thinking about all the other things I think about when I'm on the road.

Like all the times I bashed my head. Like the dizzy hour in the washroom back at South Ward, sixth grade, sitting on an old porcelain sink, staring down at the gray, matrix-marble floor, smelling the powdered soap and wadded paper towels, the whole room gray from the gray of frosted-glass windows serving as shelter from a gray day. Then a cloud like a gray whale, in from the corner of vision, and slam. When I wake up there's blood, a wide lake on the marble floor. I think to myself that there's been a disaster, and in a way there has, one of those little private ones that come back much later on. The teacher who found me shrieked and woke me up—she thought I'd killed myself. Mild kidney infection, the doctor says. That's what makes you blind. You broke your nose.

Then another time, the great family car wreck. Passing a truck on an old two-lane, we fly off the road going sixty, hit a culvert. Here's a 1958 Oldsmobile doing cartwheels down a fencerow, barbed wire, wooded underbrush, knee-high corn, flying suitcases and disintegrating windows. It lands upside down. Again I wake up bleeding. Elsewhere, someone squealing like pigs. Concussion, the nurse says—you'll be okay. Still have dreams about that one. Miss my brother Ben.

I do know about getting the old head bashed. In college I had a fight with a guy from town. The Fonz I call him in my memory. I'd gone out with his girl once. A long time after that I was going for a Coke at the bowling alley, and as I was crossing the parking lot he tore out from behind the building in an old Ford and tried to run me down. I shot him the bird; then I saw the brake lights and heard the wheels lock. He backed up. I bent down to look across the front seat at him, just as he was climbing out on the other side.

As he came around the rear of his car, I noticed that the Fonz was a little guy and I recall thinking I would win. Next thing I knew I had a bicycle chain around my head. I recall trying to go with it instead of pulling my face off, and somewhere in there my head hit the curb and the car and Lord

knows what else. I finally got a hold of the little shit and decided to kill him, but some bowler pulled me off. Nasty, the
doctor says—between the two of you I'll be here all night.

Anyway. The weightroom at the old memorial gym, University of Virginia, was a white cell, shaped like a perfect cube,
with ancient brick walls and tall windows like the interior of
an old church. This weightroom, it was not the weightroom
of the athletes. It was for ordinary students. We had the pre-
Nautilus machines, universals with fraying cables, free
weights with old bars that were rusty and sweat-pitted. The
weightlifters here were not lifting in order to make the team.
At the end of it, there was not a standing ovation from the
crowd and a kiss from the cheerleaders. There weren't mirrors, there weren't radios like in the beach-blanket weight-
rooms of the stars. There were no immediate gratifications
whatever. Except for this certain girl who would pass the door
of the weightroom on the way to the pool and, in passing,
glance in. Half an hour later she'd pass again returning to her
locker.

It was a visual thing. She had dark oval eyes, olive-colored
skin, straight silky black hair. I never knew her name—in my
mind, I called her simply Ann. Day after day she passed the
weightroom, always that moment of looking our way. I know
we all watched for her, all of us who lifted at that particular
time of the afternoon, although nothing was said. I'd see her
other places, on Emmett Street at the crossover for instance,
or in the periodical section at the library, or drinking beer at
Poe's with her sorority sisters laughing around her. Once we
bumped back to back coming through the turnstiles at the
bookstore. She never particularly saw me, or at least there
was never a moment of recognition or acknowledgment. I was
not the recurring theme for Ann that she was for me.

Anyway, I met her years later, or so I thought. And this is

when I got smacked in the head in New Haven. I imagined that I recognized her at a party. In fact, this person I thought was her was the hostess of the party. It was a reception at her house in connection with a symposium we and several other Texas oil companies were attending at Yale. She was living with the artist Jerome Slater, had lived with him for a while when he was at Oxford and all during the first African tour, and his friends were at this party too, half of them gay, I surmised, and the other half, I swear to Christ, speaking French. And then there were menopausal matrons and all the usual execs and functionaries, full of mutual and fleeting admiration for one another, oil and art, art and oil, money and money, it was a great party. I was with Sarah Beecher, from our Chicago office. But don't tell my wife.

Sometimes I think back on the people who are dead. Brother Ben, seven, upside down in a cornfield. My friend Carl T. Palmer, who died in the crash of a 727 on its approach to Dulles International. I wonder what Carl thought when he heard the pine trees tickling the belly of the plane. They found his ring finger, with ring. But if there is one death among the people who are dead that makes me know I can die, I can really, really, die, it is the death of Sarah Beecher in deep, cold water, Lake Michigan. I'm told Sarah was swept off the deck of a prominent industrialist's sailboat while trying, during a squall, to explain what we meant in the sixties when we said something was irrelevant. I guess that's how it happens.

But anyway, she was alive and well in New Haven the night I thought I had finally found that long-lost UVa girl, lo after fifteen years of watching for her to step out of the crowd and be like she was back in the days at memorial gym, the image of perfection, the sweet inspiration, distant and silent and coy.

Imagine my surprise when Sarah and I arrived at this quaint

little Trumbull Street apartment building, climbed the narrow stairs to the right flat, and tapped on the door—and there
she was, taking me away in the breeze of her dress and perfume with the startling olive skin, the oval eyes lined with
dark lashes, the piercing greenish brown eyes smiling at us
both. At Sarah the way beautiful women look at one another
in the company of men, at me without an ounce of recognition.

"Good evening," she said. "Come in—they're just getting
started in the living room. I'm Marguerite Howe." Long arms,
the lovely carriage of a swimmer even then.

I watched and waited. I was going to have to ask and make
an idiot of myself. I was patient, watching close, trying to
make sure. From certain angles, yes. From others—maybe. A
guy (Foster Petty, I called him in my mind) struck up a conversation with us that was mostly for Sarah, and I disengaged,
found the perimeter of the room and took to looking at the
paintings on the wall, mostly Slater's.

They were evidently from his "bridge period," bridges and
bridges only, those of the old stone and old steel, and he
seemed most taken by the arching formation just over the
river, and by the equal but opposite reflection of the arching
formation in the surface of the water passing below, which
would also give you ripples of sky and river-bank trees. He
would depict the birch and the sycamore, and there would be
stones flat and water-swept right at the water's surface, right
at the water's edge. There was one picture of a bridge over an
ice-packed river, and one of a bridge vaulting a dry riverbed.
But for the most part, Marguerite's boyfriend had water in his
rivers, flowing steady, one must suppose, all the way down to
the sea.

Presently, I went straight to Marguerite, who was standing
ornamentally next to the tall, thin artist. "I hate to say this,

but haven't we . . . I mean, at some time in the past, a long time ago, I think, haven't we . . ."

"Met before?" Marguerite said.

"I was wondering the same thing, exactly," I said.

"I don't believe so." She looked away. Marguerite and Jerome were so urbane and worldly that they almost collapsed from boredom. Slater came from a world where this kind of approach is not used even for the sake of humor, and he wheeled abruptly and disappeared into the kitchen.

"No, I think we have. Really."

"I've never been to Texas."

I looked down at my own name tag, *Bob Price, Market Dev., Dallas*. "Oh, that! I'm not from Texas. I'm from Illinois."

"I love Chicago. Don't I, Jerome?" Then she noticed he was gone. "I was there in 1974. I was there with Jerome in 1979— Jerome is who just left." She grinned. "He tried acting, at the Goodman. Do you know the Goodman? That was fun. I love Chicago."

"Chicago isn't it, my dear, if you'd shut up a minute."

She laughed abruptly, stonily. "Oh, this is real cute— where's Jerome." She looked back toward the kitchen.

"I'm serious," I said. "We accidentally bumped asses once in the college bookstore, University of Virginia." Her jaw may have dropped as I said this. I was losing her fast now.

"Think now. Charlottesville, '68. Jeffersonian democracy? The blessing of the hounds, the old engineering building, Mincer's, the pool at Mem Gym." I waited for her to soften. Nothing. "I can't be wrong. I'm never wrong about a face. I spotted my first-grade teacher on the ferry from Patras to Brindizi."

"I've never been from Patras to Brindizi, and I've never been to Charlotte. Don't you think I remember what school I went to? I do the Northeast mostly."

"Charlottes-ville. You *what* the Northeast?"

"Never been there. Never have."

"How can you say this to me?"

"Please," she said. "It's a mistake."

"Oh, bull."

She looked straight at me. I had decided on an impolite course of action, hoping maybe a fight would break out and I could skulk away unnoticed.

"Really," I said straight into her face. "Be serious. You used to like to swim, maybe still do. You wore your hair long. Striped swimsuit." If this was the right girl, she was going to be amazed by my attention to detail.

I looked across the room and saw that Sarah was totally absorbed in conversation. Foster was very smooth, his hair razor-cut, his tie carefully loosened, his eyebrows combed. I checked several times and Sarah never looked up.

I was beginning, it is true, to allow that this woman was not my UVa fantasy girl, only a reasonable facsimile. She was sipping an old-fashioned. We were all sipping old-fashioneds by then. Her mouth was harder than the mouth of the girl I remembered, or maybe it was her mood, or maybe the rigors of passing time. Maybe we were all harder and softer than we used to be.

"Look," I said, and I took her arm, walked along beside her. "Try to see it my way. I never make this kind of total error about a face. I have to go with my instincts."

"Would you not," she said laughing. She looked at me and I let go of her arm. Luckily she didn't dart away.

At this time, I noticed a quick, attentive glimpse from Sarah, just in the act of turning as Marguerite whispered to me, "The coffee's in the kitchen."

How do you know in the afternoon when you are drinking too much beer that you are going to need all your faculties in order to be articulate that evening? I was in a bind, being in a strange town, in the company of Sarah Beecher who, at that time, had progressed beyond relevance to feminism and didn't take shit from anybody.

Marguerite must have had a lot of parties. She knew to roll up the rug and let us spill and wet on the heavily waxed hardwood if it came to that. She was using these very hefty glasses, with a thick glass base and her initials, MMH, etched on the side.

"I can't help but notice that your name begins with MMH, and I think I even might exactly recall that the girl I'm thinking of, back in Virginia, pretty pretty girl—this whole thing is quite complimentary if you think of it—I'm sure her name was MMH, something like that almost exactly." I was laughing sheepishly. "At worst, we have a *major* coincidence on our hands."

"Look, Bob, go talk to your companion. She's lonesome for you."

"She would appreciate that—I'm serious." I turned the both of us so that my lips could not be read from across the room. "But it's you I want."

Here I achieved Marguerite's full attention. I set my sights on living through the next three minutes. The chances were fair provided she didn't shout for Jerome. The stage was set for a soap opera. Sarah's glass was already in the air, ice sailing away from it in slow motion, the drink splashing on people and causing them to contort their faces and fall away in stopaction, hurky-jerky style like when the film comes off the sprocket.

Bob, Maggie, Sarah—you think about all the soap-opera triangles you've seen. Maggie doesn't agree it's a triangle, says it's a square. Sarah's a nurse at the hospital, has many emergencies. Bob is a doctor, lawyer, and successful archi-

tect, runs a women's magazine on the side. The two women are wonderful, but different; Bob is different, but wonderful. Everyone is attracted to everyone. Suddenly Sarah inexplicably murders Sylvia, Bob's second wife's first husband's fiancée; Sylvia comes back in dreams, gives Sarah a case of the nerves. Sarah confesses, goes to jail, is found insane in a court of soap-opera law. She studies anthropology while in jail, and Maggie assists Bob at the magazine, starts her own talk show for women.

When Sarah gets out of jail, she and Maggie often meet for coffee, discuss Bob. Oblivious to this, Bob goes on business trips where he has many adventures and close calls with girls on the demographic bubble who look alike and want to be stars in the soap operas. Finally, Bob learns that he's adopted, which makes him sad. Sarah reveals she once knew someone who was adopted. Maggie has a baby, puts it up for adoption. Sarah gets a job at the courthouse.

Amazingly, one day the adopted child comes back and wants to talk to Maggie. The child is now seventeen although everyone else on the soap opera has only aged two weeks. Naturally, Bob, Sarah, and Maggie are astonished. They meet for coffee. Someone steps up and asks Bob to sing, so he does, to the astonishment of the regulars in the nightclub, bar, and/or lunch counter. It turns out Bob is not really Bob—he is David. The bad news is he isn't really a doctor; the good news is he isn't really adopted. David goes to jail for not being Bob. Sarah asks, "But where is Bob?"

"He's getting carried away," Maggie Howe says. The ambulance was very well lighted, large gray whales swimming. I have no clear recollection of the following week.

Later Marguerite tried to cheer me up by telling me how this event had really been the turning point of the whole evening. The group loved it evidently, having a body among them. Late arrivals, she said, assumed it was a gangland hit which missed and some poor bastard from Texas got nailed by accident. She did satires on the artists—the artists wanted to believe, man, that there had been an affair, man, and this babe had kept a secret from this dude too long, man, you know, and he had doggedly sought to learn the truth. She had resisted, and he took her arm, man, sex you know, and he started using this big-guy weight on her, man, and she says enough of this shit and she pulls this little silver piece out of her purse and pop, Jack, she blows him away. Went down like a goddamned tree. Dumb oil company guy anyway. Forget it.

According to Marguerite, it took forty minutes for the ambulance to arrive. On Tuesday, when I woke up, the doctors were on the golf course and a nurse—Bunny, I called her—with a small but crucial chip out of her nose and pointy glasses bent over me and said, "Well hello." Through her white dress I could read the designer's name on the elastic band of her bikini panties.

"What happened to me?" I asked her. No answer.

"Sarah's gone back to Chicago," Marguerite told me when she came to visit.

"What happened?" I asked her.

"Sarah said she was real sorry," Marguerite told me. "She said she didn't know why she did it. She said when she threw it she never thought she'd actually hit you. She said she saw red when she realized you were doing your thing again. She said you really bled and you never seemed like the kind of person to bleed."

I sat up, realizing I was in a hospital. My bed was surrounded by airy yellow curtains. "What happened to me?" I asked her again.

"We covered for you at home—bad fall at a party, nothing serious, you were lucky, home by Friday. Your wife bought it, we think."

"Am I okay?" I asked her. I couldn't see straight. I wasn't

sure I could move my toes. She started to talk past my question again. I took hold of her arm. "I need to know what happened to me."

Pretty eyes, she looked down at me. "You got your head bashed, Bob."

You think about women. You know women aren't everything, but once in a while you think they might be. The Sarahs and the Maggie Howes, their pretty smiles and their knitted brows of concern, their hair flying in your eyes. Most of the action is mental, make no mistake. While you may bump into them at the bookstore, they may never know you exist and that you love them. Perhaps no one knows how happy it makes you just to see them walk by. You stare at waitresses. You crane your neck in heavy traffic. You become what they call a womanizer.

While I was in the hospital, Marguerite and I had several nice chats, and later she helped me get my things at the hotel and took me to the plane in her little green Rabbit. By that time I knew the whole thing had been a drunken mistake and that she wasn't my UVa fantasy girl, but she was nice, no doubt about it. She lectured me about my chauvinism.

"What's a woman to you?" she asked. She smiled at me, mercifully. "For you a woman is someone to make you feel like a boy. It isn't good for you, Bob, all these lies and deceptions. Think how it makes the women feel, your wife and everybody. Settle down. Get some character."

This is how intimate we got. Marguerite Howe has my blood in the cracks of her hardwood floor. And she told me to get some character.

I went home and cultivated a lull in my life. I imagined my brain was healing. I operated at a basic level. I decided to stop loathing my job and wanting to rush through the office vomiting into the typewriters. I tried to be faithful and truthful. My wife and I went out to eat a lot. I made it a point to eat basic foods, drink to a basic excess, stay away from the girls at the office and on the road, stop watching the waitresses, concentrate on business, and, also, I took up running. I was a little depressed, and I think now that running was a last-ditch attempt to die a heroic and dynamic premature death rather than the shameful, guilty, regressive, gluttonous, wearisome, promiscuous, and despicable premature death I was headed for. I was feeling guilty about my life, and I was thinking a lot about dying.

A shrink once told me at a party that I should give up drinking and align myself with the stars. I guess that's how those guys work. They say something like that to you and it stays in your head because they're a shrink, and later it occurs to you that you might know what they mean. I decided the reasons I was fading so fast were work, drinking, lying, late nights and pretty girls on the road, and, finally, bad organization.

I decided to address head-on, with a high heart and an eye to the future, the problem of bad organization.

I sorted everything. It was a long-range project. Sorting and labeling. I didn't just label things; I labeled the shelves I put them on. I bought staplers and note cards and a couple of two-drawer filing cabinets for the home. I had a different stack of note cards for each category of my life. Every paper clip had its place. This went on for several months. There was no doubt about it. It was a large glass, and Sarah had hit me right on the button.

In the meantime, back at work, I was doing even more driving than I used to. After Carl Palmer died on the Blue Ridge in that 727, I wasn't interested in airliners. I leased a Buick and spent my thirty-second year on "cruise."

One day in the spring of the year following the Marguerite

Howe disaster, somewhere between Junction City, Kansas, and Denver, I looked into the rearview mirror and there, driving a dark blue BMW, was a beautiful woman, her hair flying in the wind, chic sunglasses, peering coyly around me. When she passed, I watched for her to look my way and I think she might have, just for a second.

I tried to imagine what she must be like, and where she must be going. I tried to imagine the silk threads in her voice, the warm breath. We were on a big four-lane, and I commenced to play a game. For no reason I would signal to change lanes, and move over into the left lane. I was about a quarter of a mile behind her. When we would come to a little rise in the road, in which for only a moment we would be obscured from one another, I'd take that moment and switch real quick into the other lane again. For half an hour I did this, supposing that she was watching my every move in her mirror.

Finally, as I was cruising along in the right-hand lane, I repeated the process again, signaling so she could see, shifting lanes, then waiting for the rise. When it came, I shifted real quick into the right lane again. When I topped the rise so I could see her, I saw to my absolute glee that she had switched to the left lane. And all the way to Denver we were never in the same lane again. I would switch, she would switch to the other. It was a coded conversation of some kind, a dance. Sometimes I would pass her and speed up ahead, and at the first rise I'd switch lanes. In the flat again I'd look back and see that she had switched, too.

Once, and this was the real surprise, I had to get off the four-lane to get gas. I knew the game was over, but I had no more gas. When I came down the entrance ramp back onto the highway—I couldn't believe my eyes—she was parked on the shoulder waiting and rushed off again ahead of me to play some more.

On the outskirts of Denver we came to a moment that, I

guess, had been inevitable all along. The moment designed to resist loss. We were on a city street by this time, and finally she signaled to pull into a big, empty parking lot. Which she did. After seven hours of this strange game, there was the desire to meet, to say hello. As I went by, I saw her watching me in the mirror. I saw the realization hit her that I was not turning in, that we wouldn't meet. She looked down. I drove on, washed away in traffic. Five minutes later I changed my mind and went back, but she was gone, of course.

Anyway, I'm in a restaurant alone, on the road. I'm watching waitresses. When I leave they are completely behind me, like Sarah, like Maggie Howe. Several of them are clustered in a back booth (all the booths are vinyl, cracked at the wear points). And here comes another one, evidently off-duty. Mary Proletary, I call her in my mind. Bless her—see how she scans the place when she comes through the door. Either she knows herself in some solid, truckstop way, or she doesn't but doesn't know she doesn't.

Anyway, you can tell she pulls no punches. Her cheeks are rosy; she's still young. She isn't a quasi-professional like me, carrying flip charts and slide-tape programs around in her trunk—a labor guy, trying to live the executive illusion. Mary doesn't have to consult, tell people what they already know so they'll pay her. She never has to use the term "application-oriented" in anything she does. She never says "bottom line."

She comes into the place in her off-hours—I wonder why. I watch her. She's showing the other waitresses pictures of her baby. They peer down through cigarette smoke and black eyeliner. They smile and laugh together, rubbing shoulders as they huddle over the picture. It's interesting to watch them look at her. I'll bet they wonder about Mary, and Mary's boyfriend, whom I estimate to be a trucker from Memphis.

Mary is wearing a sundress, and I can see the straps from

her bathing suit Xeroxed into her skin. Her hair is frizzed and peroxide reddish blond. Her walk is steady and solid, straight ahead. Her lower legs are full of the genes of work, her back narrow so the bones show. She's been granted seven years to flower and bear young before she plunges into the dim middle world I'm peering at her from, anonymous, scarred, guilty— futile life, totally unrelated to anything a person ever dreamed of or wanted. Lonely, burning, storms. I dread returning to the car and the four-lane highway, using the credit card to call the office and tell them the Dallas estimates drawn from Boston data.

I watch those waitresses. They wonder about old Mary, and Mary's boyfriend whom they've never seen except in the shadow of a baby's snapshot. They wonder, watching her, about how happy she seems, and how she manages to hang on the way the customer in this place tips.

Rosie

Here I was, or part of me, trying to explain to someone, Rosie T., why there's no God, and I was drinking. Almost always on the road I'm drinking—usually Johnny Walker black from a silver hip-flask McClure gave me before he died of the good life—all of this on top of black beans and beer.

"I think about the blood," I was saying. Over the years, I'd become accustomed to the mean anger I could now feel getting loose from me. "Here's God's son, sent to the world to save us. He's going to do this by, what they say, 'dying for our sins'—but first he says 'Do this in remembrance of me' and he starts eating his own body and drinking his own blood. This I'm supposed to explain to my children. Rosie—are you with me? I swear, what in hell was that guy doing? We're talking about the New Testament here."

There sat Rosie, drinking imported beer, gold earrings glinting in the partial light when a breeze lifted her hair. Her eyes were focused down, and her feet were bare.

"I don't know," I said. "When I was in college, I'd get in these arguments with the priests. They drove me whacko with their opposition to abortion, a belief they held up right next to their patriotic tolerance for napalming the citizenry of small . . . never mind, you remember all that. Abortion was bad, but arming ourselves so that we were second to none in our ability to fry the whole planet—*that* was okay. I said, 'Guys, try to look at it like this: maybe you don't care so

much for the already born but instead are genuinely con-
cerned about the unborn. But look here,' I said, 'if we fry the
whole planet, think how many unborn babies we might kill.'
Of course, this was a wise-ass oversimplification if there ever
was one."

Rosie was peeling the label off her bottle. Sometimes her
expression would change. I'd see an edge of a smile, an edge of
a nod. Faint as these responses were, I chose to accept them as
rapt appreciation for the wit of my argument. We were out by
the tennis courts, under stars visible through the city haze.
Off some distance behind her, the vaguely lit and looming old-
style hotel waited like a mother ship anchored offshore.

"I'm telling you," I told her, "there's nothing more un-
satisfying than trying to nail a bunch of priests for inconsis-
tency."

It's lucky I was drinking, because God is a big topic—bigger
than sex, bigger than fossil fuels, I tried to tell myself, bigger
than ennui, consternation, thwartment, and other charac-
teristics of my professional life. To address the nonexistence
of God, or to presume to address it, required drinking, which
in turn provided me with a good excuse for the quality of my
argument.

"Now, the idea was that he was going to save us by letting
us hang him on the cross and bleed to death, or, I guess, God
was going to save us by letting us do that to his son. We hang
him up there between a couple of thugs and the whole business comes to pass just like the prophets had predicted. Naturally, since they had predicted it, we had to go ahead and do
it."

Rosie's crisp gray skirt and white blouse glowed, her gold
necklace, long and graceful, glittered in the light and shadow.

"Then—let me know when I'm being offensive—he rises
again on the third day, opening the question of 'Is it really

such a sacrifice to send your only begotten son to die on the cross if you have the power to bring him back in glory three days later at the drop of a hat?' You with me?"

Rosie was in the company, out of Boston. I was from Dallas. She took a sip from her green bottle and smiled. On other trips, before this evening, I'd seen her at meetings. She had one of those faces I'd keep seeing, and sometimes we'd even exchange glances. I'd been surprised this evening when, after the last afternoon panel discussion had ended, suddenly it was just the two of us drifting down Connecticut toward a Mexican restaurant she knew about, beyond the embassies, the arches, the long bridge.

"Don't misunderstand me," I said. "I oppose abortion too."

I watched her peel the label, and took another hit from the flask.

"God," I said. "Is that me? Is that my breath I smell?"

Rosie laughed abruptly, her eyes flashing up to mine, bright, clear, very pretty. "You could have said you don't like Mexican food," she muttered, razzing me. Finally, a verbal response.

"I love Mexican food. I was just checking to see if you're listening. I love Mexican food." I relaxed a moment. I could smell her perfume when the cool breeze came around just right. "Jesus," I said, "I'm starting to depress myself."

Rosie brushed at her dark hair. She was a beautiful girl. When in the past I had seen her, she would be sitting in corners of hotel bars, in intense conversations with someone, or striding down hallways among her friends, laughing and gesturing big. There was something captivating about her movement—bold, confident, but still very soft.

"I don't drink like this at home," I told her. Her eyes were down again now. "The blitherings of a drunk. By the way, I don't mean to run roughshod over whatever it is you believe—I'm not doing that, am I? You have to look at these as the blitherings of a corporate drunk or whatever—quick, change the subject. Extricate me."

She was looking down, no signals. Her hands folded now, motionless in her lap. Her beer on the table almost gone.

"I told those priests, I said, 'Look guys, if there's a God, why isn't war a sin? What do you want?' I said. 'War contains rape and lying, insanity—sometimes people even get killed. There's inebriation and profanity, stealing, promiscuity—what do you want?'"

I heard myself resort to old letters-to-the-editor, old complaining missives to the draft board, old 1960's runnings-off-of-the-mouth.

"'So where's the mainstream American church which follows the footsteps of the Prince of Peace and says absolutely no to war?' I said to them, 'Some churches say no to dancing. A lot of them take very brave stands on gambling and birth control. On the topic of frying the planet, however, there's some question. Right? You get high-level debate on that one. You get damned near to the Amish before you find religions extreme enough to oppose war.'" Rosie just sat there. I was wearing out.

Now she looked up and muttered, "So you say there's no God because of what churches do?"

"Hell," I said, "I don't know. There probably *is* a God. He probably planned all this as a test."

I was now beginning to feel like I'd been drinking the scotch through my eyes. Rosie remained at rest, her legs up on the wrought-iron table (skirt perfectly tucked and folded for modesty), her face rosy-cheeked from imported beer and the night air.

"Oh well." I was trying to back myself down. "Talk, talk—how did I get on this godforsaken subject?" I put the bottom

of the flask against the sky. Out came the last of the Johnny
Walker, down my throat sore from raving.

"My goodness, but you sure told those priests, didn't you,
at your college, back in the good old sixties." Rosie was looking down, as always, at the bottle, at her hands.

"Okay, sorry—I'm wound up." I smiled, trying to slide off
the hook with a flanking maneuver. "If I offended you, I'm
sorry."

"Not at all," she said. "Actually, I don't know what in hell
you've been talking about."

My face froze in a waxy half-grin. I tried to push a chuckle
out through the wax, but it wouldn't go. I was leaning forward, a posture left over from my last glorious moments as a
religion bullshitter. I had the need to swallow, but I was afraid
I would gulp audibly so I resisted, but this made me almost
choke. She was right, of course. When I'd started the conversation, it had been ordinary and banal subliminal seduction
fare, getting to know one another and so on. But I'd caught an
old ideological thermal, and the thermal and the scotch conspired to ruin me. Now Rosie's face wore a polite, perhaps
even a shy, smile. She knew she got me.

What a strange test. Two people otherwise married, out by
the courts in the middle of the night. Was it my imagination,
or had the growth in the number of business meetings held in
hotels exactly paralleled the growth in the number of professional women in business?

What a life. Waiting or hurrying in the airports, waving big
at the taxi stands, hopping in and out of friends' cars at the
various bars after meetings, that's the way things were, and in
the hotels thousands of faces passed by me, thousands, motivated at cross-purposes, full of plans and secrets and wondering. Their briefcases and careful choice of clothes, the un-

spoken whole life behind their eyes—home, where the reality was, where the real, not plastic, loves were—home, behind them somewhere, or half thought of in the half-finished letter in the breast pocket or worthless little toy picked up in the airport gift shop.

I leaned back in my chair and sweated out my penance. The air was getting damp, and there was a chill. The morning fog, it appeared, would not be confined inside my head but would spread to the streets, bridges, alleys between tall buildings, would hover on the Potomac.

After a while she said, "You seem so angry at something." She looked at me. "Are you like that? Seriously. Your whole face changes."

"Doesn't sound like me to me," I said, trying to laugh it off.

"I don't know," she said.

It seemed like that was about it. Time to pack it in. Count it as a miss—attribute it to anger in the eye of the beholder.

After a while Rosie took a long sigh, and her chin came up, her eyes, and she was saying something, almost too quietly. "My mother died three months ago."

She quickly waved off a gesture of mine that I was so sorry, and she was going on.

"She was fifty-five and no great friend of my father. I have memories of loud fights. But, anyway, she had cancer, which had been in whatever they call it—remission—for a couple of years, then came back.

"She knew she was dying, but the doctors tell you not to think that way, so every time she did she had to do it with guilt, as if the *fact* wasn't bad enough. We sort of thought she'd come to terms with dying—I guess people can. But right at the end she was real disturbed, wild in her eyes—she was grabbing out at things next to her bed, shouting, crying. God, that's with me forever.

"The doctor said she was really unconscious, couldn't feel a thing, bullshit, bullshit—she was supremely lucid.

"My father was in and out—he couldn't stay still. He had this kind of automatic chant, 'Everything's going to be okay, okay, okay. Everything's going to be all right.' He'd say it not to tell her the truth—I had the feeling it was to keep her quiet. I'll never forget when the priest was giving her extreme unction—now they call it 'anointing of the sick.' The whole room got cool and smelled like candles and feminine hygiene deodorant.

" 'Am I going to die, Al?' she'd ask him, and he'd say, 'Why no, honey. Of course not. C'mon.'

"The priest who gave her the last rites, he came and talked to her—many times. They talked alone. He held her hand. Sometimes they prayed, and from the hall you could hear this low monotone duet. His visits would always give her some peace, they really would. If you could have seen that, you'd have thought, 'I don't *care* whether or not there's a God, get that guy back in there!'

"But my father—I could tell he wanted to be warm toward her, but something stopped him, the same thing that had stopped him since day one. She'd look right at him sometimes, all eyes, you know the way they get? She weighed about seventy-five pounds.

"Dad was the detail man, finding out what nurse was on duty, what doctor, holding the priest's oils, always away from her, back behind the candles, keeping busy. He was down the hall when she died.

"At the last, she was horror-struck—and what kills me is, I could tell she wasn't afraid out of pain or delirium or any of that but because she was seeing things *clearly.* She'd never be loved. She'd never have a love story. She was one little woman with this whole life behind her, nothing panning out, dying in a hospital where pulling the sheet over somebody was nothing—they did that *a few times* every day.

"Anyway, he was down the hall. I'd never seen anyone die. Have you? I guess I always thought that in hospitals they went in one of these slow, drugged-out swoons."

Rosie sighed, and I thought she might stop. But she went on.

"She kept saying in this loud, desperate whisper, 'If only he cared. If only he cared.'"

Rosie drank her beer down and clanked the bottle on the wrought-iron table. Then she folded her hands in her lap, staring down.

"I think about that. When Dad comes up on the train to visit so he can what he calls 'relate to' the kids."

When she looked down, her hair would fall forward. I had an impulse to put my arm around her, stayed where I was.

"We're probably the only ones not in bed," she said, wiping her nose, looking at her watch.

Her blouse fit loosely and casually around her. Her hands were large and expressive, not dainty. Her eyes could be hard just before these tears, and there was a scar intruding itself in the arrangement of her hair and the available light. Even in this discussion, I could pick out the aspects of Rosie that made it possible for her to deal in a business world, tough corners of herself she'd developed into tools of her trade.

"Well," I said after a while, "at least your mom had you. *You* were with her."

Rosie passed this off. In fact, her gesture seemed to deny it. "It wasn't even that simple," she said, dabbing at her eyes with this pink hanky she found in her handbag. "Sorry," she said as an aside. "I don't cry like this when I'm at home.

"Mom and I hadn't been friends for a long time. When I was sixteen, she caught me in bed with a boy. Walked in on me. My dad was out in New Mexico buying a ranch or something, and

Mom and I had this great admiration-and-trust thing going. She thought it was admiration and trust. I thought it was admiration and tacit permission—well, anyway, an opportunity—to be free. One afternoon she came home from shopping and caught me. I was in *her* bed with Michael Hannah. Truly, I don't think there's anything, at that angle, that she did not see in that short moment. She slammed the bedroom door and stomped down the hall. *Her* bed, isn't that a beaut?"

"Yikes," I said. It was the best I could do.

Rosie chuckled. "Michael Hannah's a lawyer in Florida now. I'll bet that scene replays with him from time to time." She brought her legs down and sat foward, pulling on a sandal. It was close to two-thirty. "I just want to say I didn't mean to be impolite when I said I wasn't listening."

"Not at all. I really got going. Sorry. I understand."

"And," she said. "I really enjoyed supper."

She was standing up. When she picked up her purse, I heard the clink of at least two more green bottles. 'I'm certain you enjoyed hearing about my dead mother and the great primal saga of Michael Hannah, right?"

She was taking my arm, whether out of affection or weariness I couldn't tell, and as we walked the sides of our legs would brush and bump and I could actually feel the curve of her thigh. She was talking in a low voice, but I wasn't listening. I was wondering about the next five minutes.

We had to walk across a dark patio that led through double doors into the bar, which was closed. In the dim of high-ceiling light, workers bent over the tables and stacked chairs, ran large barrel vacuums over the thick, royal-blue carpet. They were dressed in brown clothes, and the men wore hats stained through at the sweatband. They seemed to stoop so naturally, from the waist, like picking cotton; and their voices were low and sleepy. The room was still rank with the smell of stale barroom smoke. The door from the lounge led into the hotel lobby, where the lights were bright. Standing next to the column in the center of the room were two of my people, out of Dallas, and my first impulse was to duck. But they were just separating from a conversation, no doubt concerning prices at the pump, what's stored, and what we've still got in the ground.

"Here we go," I groaned to Rosie as Crazy Bob Price noticed us. He was coming.

"Oh no, this I don't believe!" Price shouted. "Harold!" he yelled back at his friend and mine, Harold Atwood. "Harold! Do you see this? Check this out, this company's only liberal meets Rose Targus, the Boston flash!" Harold disappeared on the elevator before Price finished getting this out. Bob and I worked closely and had had many talks. For him it was axiomatic that anyone who opposes human slaughter is liberal.

"I'm serious," Bob said, grinning, joining us for the short stroll down the corridor to the elevator for the west wing. "There should be media coverage of this. Movietone highlights, something. This is either a match made in heaven or the most unlikely combination I could summon myself to imagine in the whole company, coast to coast! I'm not kidding." Bob was one of those people who has known for twenty years that he can get by with this kind of talk because of the grin he has.

"Why aren't you in bed?" I asked him. I could see that he and Rosie knew each other, but, actually, everyone knew Bob Price. He seemed to have done all the groundwork for getting himself well promoted several years before, and even though the promotion never came, the groundwork remained. The promotion never came because of Bob's love of the night. The question was rhetorical.

He grinned. "I made a cardinal error, is why I'm not in bed. I

called someone I knew from the old days, who lives out in
Arlington. I received an invitation for supper—what could I
say? How was tonight's session?"
    We paused one count too long. "Never mind, never mind,
wrong question, forget I asked." He was winking at us, loosen-
ing his tie.
    "Hey," he said, a different tone now. "Was I as loud as I
think down there when I shouted to you just now? Seriously.
Was I?"
    "We understood," Rosie said, scoring back, and the elevator
was opening for Bob's floor. I was relieved that he would be
gone and I could say good-night to her in private, even though
I had no idea how.
    Bob was getting out. "Listen, Flash," he said, "good to see
you, no kidding. You too, big guy," he said to me, "but I see
you all the time anyway. Sorry if I was loud down there. I'm
working on that stuff. Even I get tired of being a buffoon."
    "No problem," I was saying, reassuring him, but then I
noticed something strange happening in the corner of my eye.
Rosie was getting off the elevator on the same floor.
    "This is my floor, too." She grinned at Bob. Then she half
turned to me, about to speak. Bob was holding the elevator
doors, just letting them go.
    "Amazing," he was saying. He was a little drunk, but there
was something warm and engaging about him, a kind of un-
abashedness-about-everything. It made him seem innocent of
business, even though he'd once done six months at Danforth
for a specialized piece of market research—he'd been caught in
the middle of the night microfilming abstracts of Sun's aerial
propane surveys.
    "Martin, is this amazing? Flash's room is on the same floor
as mine." The doors were almost closed.
    "For a hung-up old Catholic like myself, and a Texan, you

make good company," Rosie said to me through the narrowing gap, and she was gone.

"I'm not a Texan," I said.

"He's not a Texan," I heard Bob tell her as their voices dropped away below me. The elevator was taking me up to seventeen.

"I don't even sound like a Texan," I said, staring at the menu for the restaurant on the roof, posted on the wall of the elevator behind plexiglass. The bell dinged and I stepped off into a long hallway whose length and repetition of carpet pattern combined to upset my stomach.

"I don't like Texas very much, in fact," I said, trying to find my room key. "There's too much stress in Dallas. Too much rain in Houston."

The world is full of people, many of them at cross-purposes. When you encounter someone like Rosie and talk half the night, and you're on the open road, so to speak, and so is she, this business of saying good-night is such a problem, the whole business so futile, that veterans of the road hesitate to go through it at all.

I know many guys who have been on the road for years, and most of them eventually learn it's best to have one glass of wine, go to your room, turn on the Carson show, and lapse into sleep. For others, the puzzling game of instant intimacy goes on, banal, futile, sad. Everybody's married and everybody knows the problem, and yet the game occurs just enough beneath the surface of the things that are happening so that it keeps happening.

So I was thinking about the game and hating myself in my room, washing my face and brushing my teeth and avoiding the dresser mirror, trying to hang up my pants without dumping the change from the pockets. I confess that I felt some relief. In a way, I was glad she was gone. The good-bye in the elevator had been all wrong, yes, but I was going to make it to morning without the waftings of guilt. Lights out, I stretched out on the high double bed closest to the window and looked at the city. The amber lights on the expressways and bathing Capitol Hill gave an eerie cast to the night, with the low, thin haze seeming to dampen everything. I could see National Airport in the distance. I thought of my kids, how they reacted the first time we took a trip on a plane, something routine for me but seen through new eyes when I went with them. Thinking of them, as always, relaxed me. I closed my eyes and began my usual custom of stopping the room from its drunken spin by muttering the Lord's Prayer over and over unto sleep.

But the phone rang.

"Hello."

"Martin?"

"Hi."

"I wanted to tell you, it wasn't really my floor. It's just that goddamned Bob Price. Such a loudmouth. I know him from way back. I decided not to take any chances."

"Protecting your good name, as we say in Texas."

"Seems odd to you maybe."

"I'm not from Texas."

"That's what I hear. No, really, I never thought you were. I was just keeping the conversation rolling. You know?"

I didn't say anything.

"I acted like I was walking to my room, past his room, then doubled back. I'm too tired for intrigue, but I had to do it."

"Quick thinking," I said. You've come a long way since Michael Hannah, I was thinking, but luckily didn't say it.

"I guess, too, I wanted to thank you properly for the evening," she said. "Tolerating Mexican food and my crying." There was a long pause. "I just wanted to tell you that."

"That's real nice of you, Rosie. I enjoyed it, too. I am sorry about your mother. I got rolling with my old religion thing, and there you were, still in mourning for your mom."

"You didn't do anything wrong."

She was quiet then. I was elated she called, and could smell her perfume over the phone, but I couldn't get myself to start the whole process again. I flattened out on the bed and enjoyed simply listening to her breath over the phone line.

"Martin?" she said after a while. I was staring at the ceiling. It was stucco-looking, or was that stuff asbestos?

"Martin? Are you there?"

"Yes."

"You going to sleep?"

"Nope. Just resting."

"How's your view?"

"Well, I've got the Potomac. I've your Jefferson Monument, your Capitol dome. The two eerie red lights in windows on top of the Washington monument. How about you?"

"Foliage mostly. Treetops. Your deciduous and your native conifers. And there's a *very* tall tulip . . ." I could hear her moving, maybe stretching the phone cord. She was laughing. "Hold it, it's a flower box outside my window."

I laughed too.

"Martin?" she said to me then.

"Hmm?"

"Do you have pure blue ice in your veins, or what?"

She came to the door dressed in cut-off jeans, the same blouse, only not tucked in, and she carried a large plastic department store shopping bag which contained a robe and a few other things. We held each other by the window, her face against my chest.

I showed her all the sights through my window. I felt chatty. There was that feeling again that I always forget. The feeling that you've been out there alone all your life until now, and you want to explain to this woman how you've been feeling, go over all the stuff, the torment of work, the stress and the isolation. You want to thank her for being with you.

"Rosie . . ." I began.

"Don't start trying to talk about this," she said. "I'm only here to be held. And to hold you. I'm sleeping in the other bed—say so if you can't handle it."

I could feel the warm breath on my arm when she spoke. There was a desperate kind of trust she had, very sad. Under ordinary circumstances I'd have contrived to get past this little last-minute hesitation. I could handle the terms because of the vulnerable expressions of trust, but it wasn't easy. I didn't sleep much, but stared across the gap between the beds.

And then here I was, the sun on me and my headache—I was wide awake; and there was Rosie T., deep in blankets and still asleep, across the great divide. I couldn't see her face at all for her brown hair. I reached way over and spread it away so I could see the pretty brows and dark, shy lashes, the long straight nose. Recalling that encounter now, I find that I remember vividly the heat in the room that morning. I was fascinated by the little-girl wisps of hair at the scalp line, near her face, which I lightly touched with my fingers as she slept. I could hear her breathing, wonderful girl. In that skin and how those lips were, in the distinctive character of her hands, somewhere in there invisible to me was Rosie's mom, gone to her maker.

I looked at my watch on the table next to the bed. Outside the window and far away, a 727 rocked off the airport runway, plowed up into the capital sky and disappeared beyond the Capitol dome, conveying people like me, and wonderful people like Rosie T., home.

Geneseo

At dawn Jerome Slater came down the tall, chipping stairs of the carriage house apartment, down to the idling white Camaro in the drive. Behind the wheel, Janet messed with her gloves and he saw the frail blue-white skin of her hands. In the short time he'd known her, a few months, this was what he always noticed—her pallid, almost transparent color. The skin of a woman can make you wonder what you don't know about her.

Sometimes she would stay the night, and if she did she always dressed very early in the morning, and, thinking he was still asleep, she'd slide out the front door and soundlessly descend the rickety stairs. He would climb the ladder to the skylight and watch her as she hurried down the long back sidewalk through the trees, furtive and alone like a neighborhood cat.

He climbed into the car.

"Morning." He pulled the car door shut and slid down into the bucket seat.

"What's the matter?" she said. "You still up for this?"

"You've got rust on the back quarter-panel."

"You're speaking of the car?" She looked at him, smiled. "It's old, give me a break. Do you still want to go?"

"Tell you later," he said. She registered alarm, so he quickly leaned over and kissed her. "Yes, I still do."

They went down Scott Street, turned right onto Main, rumbled north past the college and into Tuscola's business district. The streets were brick and combined with the steel belts in Janet's radials to create a washboard effect. At the four-way stop downtown, Janet said, "Last call." She spoke staring straight ahead. "I'll whip a U-ey and you'll be home in sixty seconds."

"Don't make me keep reassuring you," he said. "I'm going."

Downtown was deserted except for a cluster of cars at the donut shop. She drove on.

Jerome had first met her at Gabby's, a tavern out on the township line. Out there they called her Geneseo because that's how she had introduced herself. He'd observed her from a distance then, as she charmed the construction crews and the guys from the chemical plant, the few professors from the college who ever went out there and, of course, the farmers' sons and all their country girlfriends. She told them long stories about rock and roll, and sometimes she'd even bring her twelve-string and sing old protest songs.

But also sometimes she would get too much to drink and she'd cry, her hair dragging in the water puddles left by her last four bottles of beer. Or halfway through the evening she would make a telltale switch to vodka, retreat to a corner. She had, it turned out, regrets about her former life—whether for having lived it or having lost it, Jerome was not always too clear.

Her former life: Janet had lived in what she called an "intentional community" for quite a number of years; within the past year, she had come to Tuscola to live, leaving her husband and daughter behind.

"Look at it like this," she had said, very good-naturedly. "Remember when communes were in? Back to nature, all that? Someone must have joined them, right?"

Fact was, Jerome knew several people out of New York who'd joined Virginia and Tennessee communes.

"The place was called Geneseo," she said. "On that land the

women were all called places. I was an early one there and was named after that very place. Make sense?"

When he first met her, Jerome probably didn't believe half the things she said. Yet she sort of grew on him over the months. She was so soft and likable, and so feisty. Who knew where she'd been in her forty years, or who she'd been with? Who knew where her stories ended and the truth began, as she rambled on about things? Her clothes betrayed an obsession with her life many years ago, beads and shawls, jeans and workshirts. She held him with a kind of desperate, childlike "help me" stare, very level because of the sharp, even browline against the pale skin. He knew someday he was going to draw those sparse lines of hers and remember her forever.

Now, Janet was heading back to Geneseo to reclaim her daughter, Barbara, and she seemed reassured that Jerome was willing to go, too, and they were heading north out of town. At the hardroad she turned left—the gates were down at the Illinois Central crossing. In a few moments a slick chrome Amtrak flew by.

"That's the famous City of New Orleans," she said. "Steve Goodman's dead, did you know that?"

"No," Jerome said.

"Don't you like music?" Janet turned onto Highway 45. She handed him the map. "You're the co-pilot—get me there. It's along the river."

Jerome wasn't used to getting up this early. "What river would that be?" he said.

Janet laughed, slammed a Beatles tape into the tape player. *Abbey Road*, pretty loud. Jerome pulled it out again. "What river?"

"The Mississippi, dorkus. Maybe *I* better navigate."

He put the cassette in its case, the case in its holder on the console, and went back to scanning the map. For a while they

were quiet, and Janet put the first miles behind them at sixty-
five.

"How about Steppenwolf—I've got everything they ever did
in that box."

The vent window on his side whistled, and Jerome tried
tightening it. Then he found himself forgetting the map and
watching the barns fly past. Each barn was a different weathered color and bent shape, bent into its surroundings. Janet
slammed in a Richie Havens tape. *Alarm Clock*. Here comes
the sun. Recently Jerome had taught a summer class in painting at the college. "Don't bring me pictures of barns," he told
them.

"Goddamn," he muttered.

"What's wrong?"

"I forgot the thermos. I had it ready. Walked off without it."

"Big hairy deal. Who needs it," she said, reaching behind
Jerome's seat, "when we have each other." She pulled two
cans of Stroh's out of a Styrofoam cooler, set his on the console, opened hers. "Cheers, my friend! We're on the road!"

It was a good state, Illinois: the middle. Here was the future
population of California, Bimini, New England, Alaska, the
cities of Texas, being nurtured up in these little farming
towns: Strawn, Forrest, Neoga, Watseka, Kankakee, Urbana,
Rockford, Plainfield. In the city Jerome had known many artists and Soho-dwellers who'd come from towns like these in
the middle states. In fact, his ex-wife, a New York architect,
had been raised in Waverly, Iowa.

"There's a picnic table on the spot. Find Galesburg . . ."
Janet was reaching over and pointing at the map, trying to
hold her beer and drive with the other hand. They swerved a
little. "Then find a little town named Joy—it's west of Joy—
and don't say 'Aren't we all,' because I've heard all possible
Joy jokes. Find the picnic table."

"I found Geneseo."

"That's Geneseo the town, not the commune. The commune isn't on the map. Look for a picnic table on the river."

"Now we have three Geneseos?"

"It's a bitch, right? Can you handle it?" She laughed.

He traced the river north from Hannibal with his index finger. "I fixed that damned thermos and then forgot it."

"You're unusual, all right," she said, turning up the music.

The plan was to bring Janet's little girl back to Tuscola to live with her. There were unknowns. For instance, Janet didn't know how things were going at Geneseo these days.

"When I think of places like this, I keep thinking of Jonestown—the congressman's films and all that," he said.

"Of course, you do," Janet said. "How 'bout the commune in *Easy Rider*, remember it? That was a *real* beaut."

She sipped her beer. "The CIA has a plot going with the news media to make these pinko communities look pinko." She laughed. "I love this. You're gonna learn so much." She was smiling and gestured big, a joyful arm-wave that let the car swerve again.

"So tell me about it," he said, reaching back to locate the seat belt. He fastened it.

"My husband, Will . . . I've told you about him, right? He's something. I just hope he's sensible about this. God, that just reminded me of my dream last night." She was staring straight ahead.

"Wonderful."

"You think I talk too much, right?" She smiled right at him. "Tell you what, this was a strange dream. I woke up to a knocking on the door downstairs. Three or four raps, then a pause. Three or four more, pause. No telling how long it had been going on while I was asleep. So l woke up then—I wasn't

really awake, just in the dream—and I went to Barbara's room
and woke her up. I said, 'Barbara, someone's knocking at the
door in the middle of the night.' And she sat up. There she
was, except she was about fourteen. I saw what my little
eight-year-old will look like when she's a teenager—this is
weird."

"No kidding."

"Barbara was sleeping in this guest room in this strange
part of the apartment I've never been in—it doesn't exist, actually. She wasn't wearing any clothes." Janet stared ahead as
though she were back in the dream. "Amazing."

"Incest," Jerome said, jokingly. He turned down the music.

She looked over at him but then she went back to it. She
had her forearms resting over the top of the steering wheel,
leaning forward. "She was under a blanket or bedspread or
something. I was glad that she was with me again, even
though so much time had gone by and she was older and I'd
missed—you know—a time in her life."

"Guilt," Jerome said.

She gave him another look.

"Sorry."

"I said, 'Someone's knocking on the door and it's the middle
of the night.' Her bed had a window right above it. We could
look out and see down in the front yard, but we couldn't see
the porch because the porch roof hid who was down there
knocking. A couple of more times the knocking came, and we
lay on the bed together, real low, watching out the window.
Then the knocking stopped and we saw this young woman.
She was dressed like—I don't know—like Florence Night-
ingale or something, that kind of era—the bonnet, you
know?—and all in black? She was hurrying away, I mean
walking real fast, through the shadows and stuff—where
could she have been going?—so fast I almost couldn't see her

in the dark, almost couldn't focus on her, but I saw that she was carrying these flowers and they were black. Black flowers."

Janet was quiet for a while. She stared up the road. Finally, Jerome said, "Guilt. And death."

She punched him on the leg good-naturedly, then opened her window and chucked the can, rolled the window back up, and opened another beer.

He looked up the highway, trying to think of a way to change the subject. "Why didn't you bring Barbara with you when you left the place?"

"I didn't know what in hell I was doing—I was just getting out." Janet ran her fingers through her hair, shook her head. "I don't know. Don't ask me that. I was nuts."

The road was narrow, the old kind. The grass grew right up to the edge. The land was fairly flat, so the road was straight. In his mind, Jerome sketched it, stick and ink, the very subtle contours of the retreating tree lines and pastures, the clusters of houses, the receding road in the flatness. He wrestled with the colors in his mind, trying to paint it. In this season, the values were close, tans and grays, blacks and browns. In art school he'd drawn and painted a lot of landscapes, efforts he had long ago ditched.

Janet cut back the heat. She reached up on the dashboard and found a picture, which she handed to him. It was a wrinkled-up Polaroid of a little blond girl next to a tire swing. "I need this little girl in my life." Now there were tears. "Anyway," she said, wiping them, "Geneseo's an anarchist community, founded by libertarians. That was the name of the game in 1969 or whenever. The main guy's still there—Stephen Boyce."

Jerome was still looking at the picture.

"These communities, if you're wondering, aren't all drugs

and free love like the CIA says. They often turn out to be more rigid than ordinary society or whatever. Believe that?"

Someone passed them in a van, honking. She stared into the cab as they went by. "Speed on, hell ain't half full." She toasted them with her beer. "Sometimes we'd get kids from Chicago or St. Louis, and they'd think they wanted to join. But they wouldn't work. We'd always split over what to do about it. One side believed that if these creeps wouldn't work they should be gone. And you had these other people over here who believed in the 'process' of anarchism. Very big idea. They believed the kids should be allowed to stay and that the process of community would convert them to work and the cooperative life."

They went on up the road a while. They were coming into the west side of Champaign. Jerome said, "So tell me about Stephen Boyce."

"He's like . . . the main person."

They shot under a sign for Interstate 74, and Jerome pointed her onto the cloverleaf. The van ahead of them was gone. Janet rolled down her window and chucked the can.

"As he gets older, he settles down more and more. He's a father figure there now. Beard's getting gray, that sort of thing." She smiled. "He's a literature buff, however, and big on Kafka, so anything can happen. He makes money for us by giving speeches about community and communes and stuff."

They were passing an enormous salvage yard with piles of old cars.

"I have a friend there named Clay City. Forgot her real name. May seem odd to you, but she's just Clay City to me, plain as day. She runs the school. Has a son there about Barbara's age. She and I were tight—she used to be a teacher, in the world."

Jerome put the picture of Barbara back on the dashboard. "A

very pretty little girl," he said. He reached to cut the heat, discovered she'd already done it, and cracked his window. He heard her pop another Stroh's.

"She had been a teacher—out in Kansas somewhere. A terrible thing happened to her."

"Isn't that usually the deal? Something terrible has happened, so people join a commune?"

"You're so smart," she said, raising her can in a toast, smiling at him. "You're going to learn so much."

"Will I learn how the old hippie rationalizes throwing these cans out on the highway?"

She looked over at him. "Sorry," she said. She took a deep breath. *"Anyway."* She smiled at him. "So anyway, Clay City was living with her sister, both of them teaching. But Clay City was dating someone, and one day she found out she was pregnant. And listen, this wasn't any of that sexual revolution 1960's shit—it's just something that happened, you know? Like it happens?" She stared at Jerome. The car swerved again. "Men don't understand this stuff, and I'm not kidding. Why do I bother? Anyway, she was ashamed, and you can bet she was never going to get an abortion, and so she headed back to her parents' home—somewhere, I forget—leaving her sister in Kansas to teach. She'd be back when the baby was born. Well, it's incredible, but while she was home having her baby, her sister, alone back in Kansas, twenty-seven years old, something like that, died. Believe it?"

Janet looked over at Jerome. "She just died in bed. Do you believe it? What kind of luck is that? Very rare virus, the doctor said." Janet wiped the rim of her beer can with the elbow of her jacket. "Well, of course, Clay City had a theory that God was getting her for her sin. A sort of divine scarlet letter, only hardball." She gulped down some beer. "I'd think it myself, and I'm not Catholic, never been to church a day in my life. Anyway, she reacts by following some extreme religious guys, a bunch of movements and groups. She was up in Winnipeg for a while, following some wise man named Murray. Then she heard about Geneseo and it sounded a little broader in scope, but was still shelter. So she packed up the kid and came. Stay there 'til she dies, too."

Jerome stared up the highway.

"The community group is very logical for some people," she said.

"You didn't find that, though."

She gulped her beer. "Actually, I did for a while. But like Will says, 'Some folks don't fit nowhere.' I kinda stopped fitting."

They drove north and west. Sometimes they were quiet for a while, and it seemed to Jerome like Janet was averaging ten minutes per beer. A couple of more times she swerved, so he suggested they stop at a Burger Chef for coffee. They arrived about the same time as a chartered bus loaded with Illinois State University students. Feeling rowdy, Janet exchanged one-liners with some of the boys. While she went to the bathroom, Jerome carried their coffee to the car, splashing it on his hand and shirt. He decided he would do the driving unless she argued against it, and sat behind the wheel. He dabbed at the spilled coffee with napkins. Traveling with Janet made him feel married to her. Jerome's ex-wife, Erica, still lived in the city with their little boy, and for some reason now he was missing them both terribly. He wondered how anyone in his generation ever stayed married.

He watched Janet come across the Burger Chef driveway. She knew he was watching, and it changed something in how she held her shoulders, the expression at the corners of her mouth.

The warmth of the coffee seemed to refresh Jerome, but

Janet leaned her head back against the headrest, looking out the window away from him. Finally, she was asleep. The day had become warmer with the last warm weather of the year. He tried to imagine what to expect when they arrived and to prepare for it. After a while she was awake again, but still they said nothing for nearly an hour. Then they were coming through the town of Joy. Hovering just above the town's business district was a large steel ball propped atop four legs—the water tower. "Joy" was painted on it in big black block-type letters which loomed over an IGA, post office, drugstore, and police station. They parked in front of a Rexall drugstore, and Janet ran inside for aspirin. Outside, leaning against the car, Jerome watched the pantomime of Janet in the drugstore through the front window.

When she came out, she wanted to drive. They pulled away from the curb and in a moment they were back in the country. "Will's a good person," she said after a while. "He'll let her come with us."

They turned onto a country road and white gravel dust flew up behind them. The land was now very hilly. They plunged into a parklike area, deep in beech trees and shade, with ravines first on one side of the road, then the other. They crossed ravines on old iron bridges. Old farmhouses were decaying in every hollow.

"There's your picnic table, from the map," she told him when they came into a picnic ground. "Geneseo community maintains this for the state. Pretty good job, eh?"

Soon they came up out of the trees. There was a gate and a simple handpainted sign: "Geneseo, Intentional Community, founded 1968." Several kids came running to the gate. Jerome was now leaning forward in his seat, watching. Two swung it open and the others clamored up around the car, smiling and shouting at Janet.

"Hi, Mick," Janet said to one of them. "Is Stephen here today?" The air felt so good coming in through Janet's window that Jerome rolled his own down. As he did so, he heard the gate swinging and craned his neck just in time to see it latch shut again behind them.

The little boy pointed toward several barns clustered in the distance, off to the right across the grassy field. "At the dairy barn," he said.

"Thank you. You're getting very big," she told him. "Where's Barbara?" she asked, and the boy gestured back in a different direction. "Thanks, Mick," she said to him.

All the buildings seemed scaled down. There was something new about most of them. They were made of rough-sawn wood on the outside, stained dark, with decorative detail that seemed almost nineteenth century in style. Janet was driving across the large field toward the barns on a two-rutted grass path, grasshoppers jumping on the hood and butterflies scattering. The grass was brushing hard underneath the car. It was nearly noon and the sun was warm, the sky blue as crystal. For a distance the children chased along behind them, laughing loudly. Jerome could hear a bell ringing, like the yard bells they used to have on farms.

Presently Janet pulled up to one of the barns and stopped the car. She stared at the big double doors, closed, and took a deep breath. "He's in there," she said. "I'll be back in a minute."

She climbed out, disappeared into the cool, abrupt shade of the building. The sunlight on the windshield and dash was so bright Jerome couldn't look toward the barn. He stared off to his right, to a stand of trees in the distance.

After a few moments, a tall clean-shaven man came out with Janet. He seemed very friendly to her, chatting as they walked toward the car, laughing warmly at one point, his hand on her shoulder, her arm around his waist. He came to Jerome's side of the car and leaned down.

"Hi. I'm Stephen. Brought Janet back to us, looks like."

They shook hands. Jerome didn't say anything, but smiled cordially at him. "Maybe you'd like to come in and get some water or something, look around? We've got to head over and find Barbara and her dad."

"I'd like him to come along," Janet said.

"Look," Stephen said to Janet, speaking over the roof of the car, "this is a family thing, Geneseo. There's no problem with Barbara leaving. But it's Will—we should be sensitive to how he feels about this."

For a moment everyone was still, saying nothing and not moving. Then Stephen opened Jerome's door, and Jerome found himself almost automatically climbing out of the car, Stephen sliding in. He looked up at Jerome. "Half an hour, give us. We won't be long."

Over the top of the car, Janet told Jerome, "I'll be right back." He was looking for some signal from her. Nothing came. She was absorbed now.

He stood outside the barn. Stephen looked large in the passenger seat, next to a very thin and frail Janet. He leaned back, his arm reaching all the way behind her on the back of the seat. The white Camaro slowly turned around in deep grass and headed off the way it had come, the exhaust rising up out of the grass behind it.

Jerome went into the barn. Inside were several cows, and on the other side it was open to a large pasture where many more dairy cattle were grazing. There was a pump and a tin cup like he hadn't seen for years. He pumped himself a drink of cold water, then a second one, washing away the sour taste of the morning beer and coffee. The cows watched him as he looked around. After a while he went outside. The south side of the barn had a painting of John Lennon on it, painted in dots like a Lichtenstein, only in black and white. "In Memoriam" was printed at the lower edge. Each dot was the size of a silver dollar. Jerome needed to get off a ways in order to really see the picture. He decided to head toward the clump of trees. The sun was warm on his back as he walked. Erica, his ex-wife, came into his mind. If they had lived in a situation like this, maybe they'd have survived. No, he thought, she depended on the city, and, really, so had he back then. Judging from the amount of work he was getting done these days, maybe he still did. He thought of the painting he had going right now, felt a wave of discouragement about it. Right now it felt a little irrelevant.

At the edge of the clump of trees he looked back at the Lennon painting on the barn. It was a close-up of the last Lennon we knew, gaunt, amazed at being forty, wire rims on the long bony nose, singing into the microphone, eyes half shut.

Looking into the woods, Jerome spotted a small pond among the trees and a house on the other side. The house seemed large and peculiarly modern, but sunken in among the foliage as though it too had grown there from roots. He sat in tall grass at the edge of the pond, in a large square of sunlight blazing down, high noon. He watched the house and occasionally looked back toward the barn, half a mile behind him, to see if the car had returned. He thought about little Barbara. This was what she knew, had always known. It was sad to be a part of showing her the larger world. It was bound to disappoint.

Presently Jerome heard the bell again, ringing off beyond the barns, and soon after that two men came out of the house and hurried along a path that led right toward him. He couldn't tell whether they had seen him or not. His heart sped up, and he bent farther down until he thought he might be completely obscured by the tan grass. The two men passed him, heading out across the field. They seemed like monks, their hair short, their work clothes ill-fitting. And there was something about their silence as they walked fast, side by side, first among the tall trees, then out into the sunlight, crossing the field toward the distant rise.

He walked closer to the house. It was a large cottage, older than the other buildings. As he approached, a woman came out. Right away he thought he might know who she was. She was wearing an old dress that was long.

"Hello," Jerome said, going to meet her. "I'm here with Janet."

"I know," the woman said. "I can see the gate from the other side of the lodge. Her famous white car." A smile. The two of them were standing under gray beeches, oaks red and brown. Jerome could sense their branches arching high above him.

"Am I trespassing? That bell rang and I thought . . ."

"The bell is how we put out word if someone is needed," she said. "You aren't trespassing. I love the sound of it, don't you? You can hear it for miles. Stephen got it from a school that was being torn down in Rockford. It was made in the Netherlands. The new school probably uses buzzers." She looked at him. "Did you find Stephen?" Maybe there was some tension in the question.

A woman appeared in shadows on the steps of the cottage, another at the window. Jerome felt as though he'd come into a herd of deer, gentle, wary. Any sudden move might cause them to leap away.

"Well . . ." He gestured back toward the dairy barn. "Stephen and Janet went off that way somewhere, to find Janet's husband, I think. Stephen was at the barn—they went off that way." Jerome pointed again. "They wanted me to wait."

"We all know to find Stephen at the dairy barn if it's a workday," she said.

"Why's that?"

"It's just true. The cattle are his project. Will's not well, I assume they told you." She extended her hand to him. "My name is Madeline Eisley. I'm called Clay City here." She smiled. "It's so your old boyfriends won't ever find you. That's what we always say among ourselves."

"Like Sister Mary Fatima?"

"Exactly," she said. She looked around. She gestured toward the other women, watching from the cottage. "We almost never get visitors. Can you tell?" She tried to wave them out into the yard, but they wouldn't come. "Janet's name here was Geneseo. Somehow it fit. You get used to things."

In the awkward pauses, Jerome looked out over the pond. Clay City looked back toward the cottage, where her friends continued to watch.

"We know you're here for Barbara," she said. "Is that right?"

Jerome nodded. "Yes."

"It took Janet longer to come for her than we thought it would."

"Yes," Jerome said. "She misses you all."

"She was unhappy here. What's your name?" This directness was much like the assuming way Stephen Boyce had taken Jerome's seat in Janet's car. When Jerome paused a beat too long, she went on. "I don't know what all Janet's told you . . ."

"I'm Jerome. She's talked about her daughter—and, of course, her husband. She talks a lot about the old days, this place. She misses this life, I think."

Clay City looked over her shoulder to the women watching. She stared out at the pond.

"Don't let me keep you from anything," Jerome said. "Maybe I'll walk back to the barn. I'd have stayed but the cows made me self-conscious. Those big brown eyes." They both laughed.

"Will's been having trouble lately. I don't know how much you know."

There was no telling what this lady meant or what she was assuming. Jerome watched her eyes, and what he saw was that she was watching his. After a while he pointed out over the pond, down a long slope to a cluster of rough shacks. "What's that?" The ground around the shacks had been cut up, bulldozed.

"We've been doing some clearing down there," she said. "When visitors come—or 'temporaries,' we call them, somebody who might want to join—they stay there. Might end up down there several weeks before they're allowed to come up and stay in the lodge." She indicated the house. "That's the lodge. A lot of kinds of people used to think they wanted to live here . . ." She smiled again. "And we, of course, would never know if we wanted them. Now nobody's coming at all," she added after a moment. "Mostly, we're losing people." She avoided his eyes. "Some of them, when they leave it's in the middle of the night. Like they feel they've failed." The pond whipped up a little in an afternoon breeze. She led him down to the edge of the water, where there was a sort of log bench. "Mostly we would get the young ones. They would always be disappointed that certain things here were about the same as in the world."

"Such as?"

"Such as the raggedy ways people relate."

The woods were very quiet except for the gentle wind. He checked back toward the barn.

"You go through times when this life out here is all you need." She shyly laughed at herself.

"I can understand why someone might want to come here to live," he said.

"We're awfully isolated."

"Isolation can be good sometimes, can't it?" He realized as he said it that he'd never lived in any real isolation in his life.

"Stephen thinks we're almost gone. He compares us to an endangered species—he says that at some point the animal gets the hint and begins to aid in the process of its own extinction." She stood up. "Want to look at the river?"

"Maybe I'll walk back to the barn," he said. "I think we should stay close."

"It *is* close," she said.

A cat came out of some bushes nearby, a small gray cat, carrying in its mouth a baby rabbit. The rabbit was kicking. The cat found some soft grass and sat holding the rabbit tight until finally the kicking stopped and it stretched out softly in a bent U-shape hanging from the cat's mouth.

"C'mon. It'll pass the time," she said, and she turned to the women who were still watching from the lodge. "I'm going to the gazebo," she called to them. She kicked off her leather sandals and tossed them toward the porch. The women disappeared inside.

The path arched around the pond and deeper into the woods. "The pond is quite important here at Geneseo," Clay City was saying. She was walking ahead of Jerome, her soft old dress flowing off her hips and down almost to the ground. It dragged among the burrs and scrub, and when something caught on the skirt it pulled away, revealing for a moment her bare feet, reddish and rough.

"Little places like this depend heavily on symbols, and the pond is one of ours. So's the bell, I guess. The pond is spring-fed. The spring is back there in the trees somewhere. Stephen and some of the other early ones used to give talks at the pond. The idea was to inspire the group to the ideas that founded us. One guy taped most of the pond talks and typed them up. Some have actually been published in magazines.

I've never read them, but so they say. This is the cemetery."
She indicated off to the left of the path. "We don't mark the
graves. One man got sick or something, way back when.
There's two babies, and some others. We buried a soldier out
here in 1974. He arrived in one of those aluminum cans. Nobody knows who he was. They had an extra body, I think."

As he listened, Jerome thought of the sad story of Clay City
which Janet had told him. He sensed that the immediacy of
the death of her sister was gone. He looked back into the
woods. The dead mouldered under this ancient stand of trees.

"Owl," she said. A big bird lifted up out of the treetops to
their right. Its shadow passed over. She was talking straight
ahead of her. They came into an area of birches, a wonderland
of white and yellow amazingly different from the part of the
woods they'd just been in. The birchwood, she called it. Then
they came out of the trees high above the river. The gazebo
was a round, porchlike structure, covered, enclosed at the
back. The walls were a gleaming white wood lattice letting
the light through in small diamond shapes which gleamed on
the green floor.

"We just repainted it last week. Isn't it stunning?" she said.
"I wanted to show it to you because Will built it. He's our best
builder. He has all the best ideas." From the gazebo platform,
she pointed out over the river to the village of New Boston,
and the other way toward what she called Lock 17, a dam.

Jerome sat on the bench in the gazebo and looked out on
the river.

"Did you see the sign?" she said. There was a small handpainted plaque over the threshold of the gazebo, on the inside.
It said "Save the Earth." "Seems a little dated now. When he
came, he was one of these big ecology people. You can about
estimate the date of his arrival knowing that—1972, right?
He had T-shirts with that green ecology flag, remember?

Turned out he was more complicated than that. But we're
glad he came to us. For a long time he and Geneseo were very
close—but he got worse. He beat her up." She looked at
Jerome. "Janet—when things started coming apart with Will
and all, so did she. She's an alcoholic. Has she told you all
this?"

"No," he said.

"Maybe I should shut up. I'm sorry—I keep wondering how
you fit in."

Good question, Jerome thought but didn't say.

She laughed. "You're friends with Janet? That's all?"

Jerome shrugged, feeling a little helpless. "I don't mean to
be coy, but isn't being friends enough?"

"Yes." She said it quietly. "I mean," she said, "I guess. We'll
see."

"I paint," he said. "I've been teaching some out at the college, in Tuscola. And I do a little carpentry with a local construction crew, to pay the rent. I'm not a craftsman like this
guy, though." He indicated the gazebo.

"Well, you must have noticed that Janet drinks a lot. People
die of it when they have it like she does."

Jerome stared out across the river from the bluff where they
were standing. Iowa.

"Tell me," she said. "Do you think she's stable enough for
Barbara to be with her?"

Jerome sat there. He did not answer her. He wondered if
they hadn't now struck upon the whole reason for this walk.

"What's Janet doing to eat? Does she have a job?"

Again he said nothing.

"Look," Clay City said, "we love this little girl. She's frail,
like her mother. She has a lot of friends here who are as close
as brothers and sisters. We can take care of her. Don't take her
if Janet isn't ready yet." When he didn't say anything, she

pressed on. "I'm trying to talk sense with you. We love Barbara very much. We don't know where she's going."

"I understand you," he said. He held up his hand for her to stop. She stepped away from the gazebo and stood looking out on the river. He wanted her to trust him, and he knew she didn't at all. He felt accused of being a party to Janet's problems. He had to think about that one. He realized he would like to have been a friend of Clay City, wouldn't ever be.

"There are only twenty-seven on this land now," Clay City said. "Nine children. There are eleven men and seven women. We've lost eight in two years. We're definitely the whooping crane."

Jerome looked at her. He tried to imagine her, how she'd look and what she'd be like if this commune had not been part of her life.

"A couple of the originals are here. Stephen is the main one. He says he'll be the one to close the door and turn off the lights." She smiled, perhaps having noted that Jerome's guard was up and trying to relax him. "Well, anyway, that's the Mississippi. There are other pretty places I could show you if you had the time. A painter could love this area. I suspect you don't have time, right?" Her tone was cooler now.

Down below, the river stretched before them. At that distance there was no sense of the water flowing, although in the sunlight it gleamed and flashed between colors of blue and brown. She was leading him back toward the lodge, a different route. For some distance, they were climbing uphill. At one point, she passed between Jerome and the sun. He caught a flash of her brown hair in the wind and saw the silhouette of her legs through the veil of thin cotton she wore around her. From the top of the high bank they had climbed, he saw that the Camaro had pulled up to the edge of the trees. Stephen and Janet were sitting on the log next to the pond. Standing off from them, along the edge of the pond, was Barbara. On the hood of the car was a large cloth bag.

When they got to the pond, Clay City hugged Janet, held her a long time. Janet had been crying, and now she was again. Her hair was messed. She was utterly apart from Jerome—it was clear that he didn't belong there at all.

"They'll be taking Barbara," Stephen said.

Clay City looked at him. "Of course they will," she said.

She took Janet's arm gently and they walked together toward the lodge, the other women coming into the yard to meet them. Janet's blue jeans were a contrast to the long old dresses. Jerome was standing several feet from Stephen, and neither of them said anything. Barbara was on the bench, her arms folded tightly around herself. She was taller than in the picture Jerome had seen, and her nose was sunburned and peeled. Some of the other children had gathered there, too. Jerome could see Janet talking with people in the lodge. All he could hear was the wind.

When they came out of the house, Janet and Clay City were arm-in-arm, walking close, talking quietly. They went down to the edge of the pond and bent down over Barbara.

"How did it go?" Jerome asked Stephen.

"This is his daughter."

Jerome tried to hear friendliness in the tone, but he wasn't sure there was any.

"Will knows it's better this way. He's been confused for days, you know. Not because of this. He had a bad war." Stephen bent down, pulled a long blade of grass. "Janet's terrified of him. He's in a room and won't come out. She tried to talk to him. Forget it. It's a bad time, everything at once." Stephen paused a moment. Then he said, "You're an artist, didn't Janet say?"

Jerome nodded.

"We have several here, artists. Quite a number through the years. One older gentleman here helps the whole community financially with his work. He sells through a gallery on the near northside, New Town, in Chicago."

"Is he the one who did the Lennon on the barn?"

"Nah, one of our people put that up there when John was shot." He turned so that he could see it, and Jerome looked back that way, too. "I always think of the eye-doctor billboard in *Gatsby*. The way it stares out across the field. 'In Memoriam.' I guess I haven't really looked at it for a long time. We aren't ordinarily grim around here. Listen," he said then, talking straight at Jerome but not looking at him, speaking quieter to keep from being heard by anyone else. "We want this girl taken care of. If Janet has problems, you let us know, will you? We can come down and get Barbara. We can come and get them both, although I don't think Janet wants to come back. This little girl—she's part of us almost as much as she's part of Janet. We care about her, I'm trying to say. You must let us know. Call me—I'll send money—anything."

"I understand," Jerome said. Again, as with Clay City, he had the impulse to show Stephen that he could fit in here, that he was likable in the terms of this community. But it was a futile notion. He watched the women at the edge of the pond.

Stephen spoke in a southern accent, strong and steady. "They call this an anarchist community." Now he was looking right at Jerome, smiling. "To my way of thinking, you got most of the anarchy out where you live."

"No argument on that," Jerome said. He and Stephen shook hands.

The women walked back up to them, bringing Barbara along, their hands on her shoulders. Barbara had the same kind of wide-open face and level stare, but she also had that pale, frail blue-white skin, blue veins in her forehead and temples, at the corners of her eyes.

"I'll be coming back, won't I?" she was asking her mom.

"Maybe so," Janet said.

"No," Stephen said, and he squatted down to her. "You stay with your mother. We love you, but you stay with your mom, Barbara. Okay?" She was crying, and Stephen hugged her. The bell, far off, was ringing again. "I've got to go," Stephen said, standing up and turning to Janet. He embraced her, saying something to her no one else could hear. Then he waved again and jogged toward the barns, heading for where the tolling sound of the bell had come from.

"Will I see Daddy anymore?" the little girl said.

Janet put Barbara's cloth bag in the front seat of the car. "You will," she said. "Of course you will." She and Barbara both got in the back seat. Jerome started the car and slowly, driving on dry leaves, pulled out from under the oaks. In the rearview mirror there was Clay City waving. Barbara was waving, too, through the back window.

Suddenly Jerome was thinking about where they were going. A time or two he'd stayed the night at Janet's rented trailer when they'd dragged in late from Gabby's. The feeling was desperate and temporary. The trailer was dark inside, and damp—so damp that the borrowed couch smelled and the dark walnut-print contact paper on the bathroom wall was peeling off in a sheet. The little grass that might have separated Janet's from the next trailer down had long ago been fried away by the sun.

"What did Stephen say to you?" Jerome asked

"He said good-bye. He said Geneseo's going down. It was like he was apologizing. He said it isn't a failure just because it doesn't last forever."

Clay City came forward out of the shade into the afternoon

sun. As they went down the long two-rutted grassy path toward the gate, Jerome could see her, still waving. The children
had taken a shortcut and met the car near the gate. One of the
older boys swung it open wide. He said "See you, Barbara" as
the car went by him.

Barbara was crying quietly, her head down in her mother's
lap. Once on the road just beyond Geneseo's gate, Jerome
looked back toward the clump of trees, and now he could see
where the lodge was, and down the hill to the shacks where the
visitors stayed, and deep in the trees he saw Clay City one last
time, watching them drive away toward the main highway.

Wilbur Gray Falls in Love
with an Idea

For my friend Craig Sanderson

When I run, like now, I head down Court Street because of its grassy boulevard. I turn west on Prairie so that I approach the University Park fountain bronze dancing girls with the sun behind them, a vast and holy prism of spray breathing out toward me. Then I face the dark welling up in the north, orange setting sun to my left, and do intervals, fast and slow, two miles uphill to Patterson Springs, the old chautauqua ground.

I've been battling depression this whole summer. It's the price I pay in middle life for living lies and harboring secrets. I've waged the battle with daydreams (I conjure, for instance, Skidmore, waving as he drives by, 1963, in the old Ford Victoria his dad had saved for him). When daydreams don't work, I lapse into the mindless, subvocal recitation of memorized prayers, or I surrender to music. Mainly, though, I've learned to depend on the faddish but nevertheless helpful practice of running six miles a day, rain or shine.

In running, I set my mind to the rhythm of my stride and think of things positive and hopeful. I remember, for instance, Ann Hollander, in church nearly twenty years ago (Father Casey in the pulpit lecturing in gravelly Irish on the topic of fund-raising for the new school)—Ann sat in the stained-glass shadows of her father, his mind on God and democracy, her eyes trained on the statue of the Virgin, his shoulders slouched toughly forward, her back straight, her body new and lovely beneath a pretty cotton dress. This was a sweet, sweet girl— she'd slip away through moonlit backyards to love the neighbor boy, she'd dance through dry shadows, across the driveways of sleeping doctors, lawyers, dentists, through the sleeping flowers of their sleeping wives (I'd see her coming, through speckles of light). Through dry grass and cicadas buzzing she came.

My best memories are from this neighborhood, and the exhaustion from running seems cleansing, but even so, the fear and regret, the wrenching isolation of secrets, they stalk me, and sometimes they prevail over me like the lightning in a hot summer thunderstorm once prevailed over the large belfry crucifix here at St. Paul's, our neighborhood parish.

My friends suggest I marry again, or seek absolution. When I pass this church, I always think of that. Absolution—they're on to something there. In 1957, jerking off was the moral equivalent of murder in the dim light of the confessional. Casey's voice, from behind the plastic mesh screen, made the whole empty church vibrate with his priestly authority. Absolution was grudgingly granted to frightened children whose mistakes were limited to the scale of childhood and whose problems were gloriously solvable—even then none of us ever felt completely forgiven.

I think sometimes of form: raise the knees higher and the speed increases, lengthen the stride to heel-toe and feel the therapy in the hamstring.

I remember 1957 as a clean, well-mothered time, and I wonder sometimes what went wrong later. I remember that year as one long baseball summer—textures of wood and leather, grass stains in cotton; the science of raking the infield dry and raking it wet, waiting for the dew to evaporate, learning to spit and other initiations—watching clouds billow up and get black, checking the sun for lunchtime. Establishing a reputation: good arm, good glove, good power to right; vaulting the fence, good form.

That was years before the nights of parking spots like Black River Road and the Hanging Tree, time-honored lovers' lanes deep in the hills left when the glacier melted. I guess I love this day, red and waning; I guess I love this town, falling down. After the fire at St. Paul's we attended mass for what seemed like years in a forest of gray, towering scaffolding inside the church. These old houses, I know them like familiar faces. These streets, I know where they lead. (Skidmore goes by again—he wants to stop, offer me condolences on my poems, show me his latest metafiction, razz me about my knee.) This town and I have deep, dark confidentialities. I twisted my knee in the steering wheel, 1962, in a glen on the Black River Road while missing basketball practice on an earnest, determined mission to discover what made Carol Canfield tick. Even now I think of 1962 as the long vibrato whine of a car horn echoing through the glacier hills on a cold autumn evening. No regrets. They told me she became a nurse in later life.

I'd left the car to pee and when I got back she wasn't wearing anything. She just sat there, the girl of my dreams, smiling, enjoying my embarrassment—her, a tall feisty senior cheerleader—me, a tangled-up, over-anxious second-string forward, Dad's car. Until the day he died, my dad thought I hurt the knee going to the hoop.

J. Richard Peck Hollander, rest his soul, was president of the draft board, and he told my dad no twisted knee nor allegation of color blindness would defer this doctor's son from his duty.

"If doctors' sons don't serve, then why should anyone else?" he asked, my question precisely, but my dad was insulted—of course I would serve. I went and talked to them myself. I asked, "How is this thing in Asia a threat to our security?"

J. Richard said, "You won't wonder that when the communists come up Scott Street and rape your sister."

"But these guys, they don't even have a boat. How they going to get to central Illinois? How they going to get past the Pennsylvania National Guard, the Indianapolis police department?" Forget it. I was drafted.

One afternoon right after I got back, I climbed those steps at St. Paul's and caught Casey just at the end of confessions when no one else was there. He opened the little window and waited. I could see his dim shadow, his profile, waiting. I could see the Roman collar and the ceremonial stole. I tried to think how to begin. I was trying to separate sins from duty. He waited several minutes, neither of us saying anything. Finally, he slid the window closed.

I note my knee almost twenty years later—in recent years the ankle has twisted several times. Maybe, after the steering wheel thing, the alignment never got quite right again, hip to toe. No regrets. I turned the ankle pretty bad in basic training; then I broke it pretty good in Vietnam in a fall off a personnel carrier when the dumb shit driving it drove through a small mine crater at forty miles an hour. A lot of guys were hurt more than me.

I've learned from experience that it takes me a mile and a quarter to break a sweat in reasonable weather, eighty degrees or less. I can feel myself operate, or I can disengage my mind from it, closing around the usual daydreams or some comfortable mantra. Tell you this: I'd never remarry.

I've known people who develop a cold view of things. They find their passion in a few close friends and come to expect

nothing from the larger world—except blockage and thwartment, puzzlement and consternation. Close to the ground they
huddle. Instinctively they limit themselves, away from wind,
experience, people, other natural currents. For them the world
is an animation viewed through windows, a home movie run at
too slow a speed, existential HBO, silent life except for the
clicking projector and the occasional comment from the dark.
But I know the world is too complicated to relate to on a part-
time basis—we spring from it, we're part of it, it's inside us,
any separation from it is artificial and doomed. I know what
Skidmore means when he says he's sorry he missed the war.
Ann Hollander became an example of those insulated people.
She became Sister Ann Rene Hollander, even more deeply con-
ditioned to guilt than I am, shrouded under starch, living in the
dark linoleum cloister of the most conservative order of mo-
nastic housewives of Christ that J. Richard Peck Hollander
could find in a new age.

You hear rumors of those who see auras, ghostly hues like
halos around people, suggesting their character and destiny.
Sister Ann Rene claimed to see a violet aura over the body of
her dead father, J. Richard, gaunt like Lincoln, resting on the
coroner's slab. Ann dressed him for the grave in the quiet back
room of the Waddington Funeral Home down the street. She
wrote notes to him and put them in his casket. That's where I
got the idea.

Patterson Springs is my halfway point, a place of solitude
these days. It's familiar to me from when I was little—I used
to play there, and later Skidmore and I would camp there. I
rejoice at the wonderful existence of this forest. I take it per-
sonally. I marvel at the patience of these oaks. You imagine
their roots, reaching down, holding tight. They are my reward
for making it this far—the rich fragrance of hickory, white

oak, their rotting leaves and cracking acorns, renewal of sprouts.

The old chautauqua ground is located where a deep-running network of pure-water springs suddenly wells up out of the earth. The pioneer Virgil Patterson built his place among these oaks and so honored the blessing of cold, pure water that he built a shrine, now dank and moss-covered, back in the trees where the water presents with a deep rippling sound coming straight up out of the black loam.

The hush of the wind here, blended with the windy brushing sound of my footfalls in bent grass, momentarily absolves me from, rids me of, my depression, even though I know this absolution is nothing but the arrival of my second wind, the sudden alignment of energy, circulation, and chemistry that produces a moment of strength and optimism. I've learned from experience it arrives at three and one-half miles, deep in this forest on the path that leads to the fresh-water springs and, beyond that, the chautauqua ground. During this fleeting moment I can hallucinate God and Peace, I can envision my own reincarnation, I can summon a sense of relative innocence and well-being. In this moment I realize that this moment is the whole reason I'm running.

As I come across the flat here, the trees arch high above me and through them I see the navy-blue sky. I'm running in the last light. By fall I'll have to start earlier or change the route; scrub bushes and abrupt gullies occupy this tract without pattern. But now as I run I can see the burr oak, sixty meters to my right across the flat. Struck by lightning one night in July of 1959, its top is shattered and its trunk is split but it still lives. Its arms reach wide and have old men's elbows, and at the ends the limbs suddenly plunge upward into the sky.

Several years ago I got the idea to bury a time capsule under the burr oak. It was a strange notion, I admit, and I thought about it a long time, years, before I actually went through with it, this summer. It was a project that occupied me for several weeks. Already a bed of weeds, dense and yellow, obscures the spot.

Roger. Lost a hand in Vietnam. And I remember him squinting through smoke and green beer, St. Patrick's Day, Pat's Pub, Charlottesville, 1974, complaining about his life and prying into mine. Twelve years ago. Even though Roger has always worked hard at pissing me off, I keep him as a friend because he's the only person I can talk to who has been ambushed and knows how it feels. Sometimes I have to find him and talk about being ambushed, or just talk about anything, knowing he's been ambushed, too. I watch his pulse beat a rhythm in his neck—he's alive and I can see that; therefore we both are.

"How've you been?" he's asking me. He knows I'm in the middle of a divorce, that my wife took the kids and headed south to be a potter, rolled the VW bus outside of Oklahoma City and sent me the bill.

"Fine."

Up at the bar there's a St. Patrick's Day party going on. We talk louder to get above it.

"Good," he says. "That's good." He moves his beer mug between us with his hook. I call it a hook. Really it's more like a steel clamp.

"What's good?" I say.

He stares at me. "Actually," he says after a while, "I hear you're bonkers."

"Then why'd you ask how I am?"

He doesn't answer me, leans back in his chair.

I say to him, "Do I ask, 'So, how's your hand?'"

We're both laughing, but we're pissed.

"So, how've you been?" I ask him after a while.

"Great," he says. Roger says he remembers a marine who could drink more than anyone he's ever seen, says he heard the guy recently barged into a newspaper office in Anderson, Indiana, and held the whole place hostage at shotgun point until he started crying and gave up.

"I know how he felt," Roger says to me. "I was in a hardware store buying some wire. The clerk, an old guy, was showing me where it was, and we walked by this bin with big wrenches in it. For no reason it hit me that I could kill this old guy, I could smash this guy's skull. I pictured myself doing it. I knew what it would look like. I got out of there."

I recognize that feeling. It makes my stomach roll to hear Roger give it words. It comes from knowing how close death can be, an old ambush lesson. I tell Roger that J. Richard Peck Hollander died, president of the draft board back when we were ushered out of town in the dead of night on a Greyhound bus, the modern equivalent of marching off to war. Roger says he's sorry to hear it, he really is.

He says his dad was a veteran of Guadalcanal, and now every year veterans of Guadalcanal come to some great hotel in Dallas or Denver and have a reunion. He says even the Japanese come. "Now goddamn it, Wilbur, I'm telling you that is proof positive that the world has gone completely crazy." His beer spills. Quietly he mops at it.

He says he'll miss J. Richard at our reunion, when we get in the mood to have one.

"Forget it," I say.

"Forget what?" he says, and we laugh.

"What a pitiful son of a bitch you are," he says to me at the end of the laughing, and we laugh again, guzzle a little green beer, and toast the party at the bar. "The worst is over," he says after a while, and then we say nothing, watch the party.

"Gotta girl?" I say. He looks down, keeps looking down. I try to think of something hilarious to say. Can't.

"C'mon," I tell him. "You're a great-looking guy. There's somebody out there for . . . godDAMN it, don't hold that thing up. That's not the reason . . . that thing's sexy . . ."

Roger laughs, there's relief in the air. "Seriously," I tell him, "you gotta find some other excuse, not that. Women love a good war wound. Signals a hero."

He's retreating. He's being cordial, but he wants no part of that talk. He'll be out the door in another few seconds. Fast, I try to tell him our conversations never turn out the way I hope they will but I can never think of how to improve them. I tell him I want to be real close friends, confidants, and tell him some of these terrible secrets and shit that give me the clangs when I'm trying to sleep. He's sliding his chair back— he's angling for his jacket on the back of it. He doesn't want that stuff. I think of maybe grabbing him to try to keep him there. His face flushes up in the cheeks—his eyes water. He's afraid, he doesn't know what might be said or if he can handle it, he's running. He doesn't want all that warm friendship and frank talk.

And, getting up to leave, he says, "Wilbur, you know what you need? You need a sophisticated shrink."

And I knew this woman, Erica—my wife. For many years we lived alone together and had children whom she wanted to consider gifts from her to me. Whether she has night terrors like mine, I wouldn't know. For me, marriage is under the burr oak, and fatherhood. With them I buried this poster I had of the mushroom cloud over Hiroshima—I had framed it with the caption "The Baby Boom." It hung in our various rented living rooms, later our various rented bathrooms.

That's us, Ann, Skidmore, Roger, Erica—the baby boom. It took us until about 1958 to realize what was happening. For a long time in the fifties we thought we were in the clear because we'd managed to dodge polio.

At this point, I complete a mile loop through the Patterson Springs acreage and am back on the road headed south. I already know I won't sleep well this evening, with Roger and Erica and Skidmore haunting me, with guilt scratching at me inside my chest and stomach. I think I miss my kids. I can see, perhaps a mile ahead, the first lights of the University Park, and I focus right on them, set it to automatic, and move through the dark down the asphalt at 60 percent. I can hear the wind in the drying corn husks in the fields on both sides of me. I try to take my mind into the hush of the drying corn.

Tomorrow we shall die. Or at least we could if we didn't already, not that dying is the enemy necessarily. I guess I didn't like the bomb tests much, the ones on TV in the early fifties, Sunday mornings. Right after mass you got to come home and watch while they showed in slow motion what the hydrogen bomb would do to your house if it was made of straw, if it was made of sticks, and if it was made of brick. It blew harder than the big bad wolf, you figured out, age five.

The time capsule was made from an old and very large footlocker I got at a garage sale. I mixed concrete in a wheelbarrow after I dug the hole, set the footlocker in a foot of wet concrete and pushed it down in it. I had chicken wire in the concrete for reinforcement. I filled the locker with all the stuff, closed it, folded the chicken wire over the top of it, and then poured in the rest of the concrete. I waited a couple of days to be sure there were no cracks. In a few years I'll check on it again. Two thousand years hence, some other life form will bulldoze it up, crack it open, and put it in a museum. Or maybe, a monument to my terror and secrets, it will remain

there in the dark for all time, undisturbed, unrevealed, uncon-
fessed, steeping inside the drawn-out ravages of the long haul.
Or maybe the doom I've been taught to expect will occur, and
that odd rock will hurtle through space as one of the frag-
ments, holding together even though the brick houses did
not. Or maybe it too will be emulsified—but at least I tried.

So, what else did I bury? Old newspaper clippings I'd kept in
a space behind a false wall in the house I grew up in—a picture of Jackie on the car trunk and Clint Hill jumping aboard,
somebody's shoe sticking straight up from the back seat,
speaking of ambushes; a picture of Musial, speaking of hero
worship, standing on second after his three-thousandth hit; a
picture of Laika, the Russian space dog, in a space suit—poor
furry little corpse may still be in orbit for all I know; a picture
of J. Richard Peck Hollander and his daughter Ann getting a
trophy for winning the Kaskaskia Father-Daughter golf tour-
nament; a clipping from the newspaper about the destruction
by fire of St. Paul's, struck by lightning—I still remember how
high the flames soared, and the helpless flitting through the
trees of the red lights of the local volunteers, running and
shouting in their red helmets and yellow raincoats, neighborhood dogs howling in the red shower of sparks.

I also buried a photograph of my dad, a doctor, giving TB
tests at school, his hands on someone's little white arm. I
buried a portable TV, believe it or not—every time capsule
should have one. I buried my chess set, from back in the days
when I could concentrate, my Selective Service card which I
won't be needing anymore, my dad's twelve-gauge automatic
(broken into its two principal parts) and a box of shells. I buried some poems I never want to see again; two defunct suicide
notes, 1969 and 1974; a dozen eggs in the Styrofoam egg
holder (seemed funny at the time); a fading photo of Roger
when he was in high school, shooting me the bird, taken in

one of those K Mart foto-booths—he's using the doomed
hand; drawings rendered by my boy, of a boat, bike, house
with yellow sun. I buried all my Vietnam photographs, the
friends living and dead, toasting the camera with Miller's
High Life in steel cans, standing next to dark green helicop-
ters whose motors I can hear the thump of this moment; and
a plain old white towel—unbelievable story, but I ran a marathon in Louisville several years ago and the route went past
the convent, and wouldn't you know, the nuns all came down
to watch, and, I swear this happened, there she was, doing
what marathon watchers do, holding out drinks and towels
for the runners—I took the towel, Veronica Wipes the Face of
Jesus—Jesus, I loved that girl.

Maybe it wasn't her, I don't know. Never in one million
years would I discuss my life with a shrink.

I buried my briefcase from when I was working, without
even checking what was in it. I buried the sad letters my
mother received from my dad during Korea—he never got
over that one either, and damn sure never went to any conventions—and the manic letters my mother received from me in
Vietnam. Naturally I buried the explanatory letters from the
VA about the defoliants. Buried in the ground forever.

Sometimes I try to neutralize my thoughts by reciting
poems to myself, like "Fern Hill." I feel that people pass
through me, through my life, and through their own, like
water, like different temperatures of water mixing.

Lately I've been thinking that maybe by burying my past,
my lies and secrets and the enormous collection of mun-
danities and froth I've amassed, maybe instead of escaping
from these things, I've preserved them. I guess it was only
meant to be ritual anyway—there is no real-life absolution for
the frightened and faithless, no grace, no way at all to explain
it, or find relief, or to get away.

I also buried my ball glove and my bat, leather and wood all cracked from years of playing in the dew followed by years of no play at all. And, of course, I buried the series of pictures I'd taken of the wonderful center bronze-and-dancing nymphet of the University Park fountain—here she comes now.

When I was working, I would come over to the park at noon to eat. I was unhappy and sleepless, this was 1972 or so, and I couldn't understand anything that was happening to me, so there's no wonder I fell in love with a statue. It reduced the number of variables in love remarkably. Whoever the sculptor was, he loved this one, too. While the others, all of them dancing arm in arm in the center of the falling water, seemed blurred, this one was smiling like stars and like children smile, staring down into Fountain Circle through cascades and spray and attentive pigeons setting their wings to land. Her eyes would always seem to be looking at me. She was perpetually a little girl, as, face it, I'm perpetually a little boy—I never have wanted any of this shit about being grown-up. I'd gladly play an afternoon of Indian ball on one of the overgrown-in-weeds ball diamonds in the park or at the school. I have no illusions about getting ahead. I'd rather have it the way it was: a dancing nymphet forgetting the world, coming across the dark green lawns, and why? To love the neighbor boy, happy and fun.

But Erica had always been nice to me, and we'd had days happy and fun, be sure of that. When the life went out of it, however, it went all the way out and all of it went. You know about marriage, sometimes, especially among children of my generation, whose notion that "happiness must happen today for tomorrow we shall die" is tatooed to the back wall of their brain. How she rolled the bus without hurting anybody, I'll never know.

This would be called the homestretch. I'm now in the neighborhood of my boyhood again, and every front porch along here has had me under it and I've climbed every maple and chestnut, been in the attic of every garage, buried birds and cats in Ball jars and shoe boxes, and secret concoctions in plastic bowls, all along the alleyway. In crannies in the old foundations of all these houses, perhaps there are still notes and secret pocketknives. In this dark, I feel the presence of my past on either side of me—I sense the ghosts of the neighbors long gone and the neighborhood dogs, good companions then and two generations gone by now, the low voices of moms and dads in yard chairs who later grew old and withdrew inside—I see their amber lights in the windows now, and sometimes their shadows moving; I sense the echoes of the wheeting and tooting of little kids, parading down the sidewalk on roller skates and pulling wagons full of kids littler yet, or hiding in the bushes and laughing loud.

An ambush takes about one minute sometimes. The people on both sides of you get killed. They go down like a bale of hay, then maybe they roll around, dead but still terrified. Sometimes the bodies get hit so many times they start to dissolve. The air is electric with the ripping, the snapping, ripping sound of automatic weapons and rounds popping everywhere, and everybody firing wild, branches falling out of the trees. Adrenalin makes you think you can't die—you feel your nerves and blood jump the thin line between your hand and the plastic rifle stock and your actual being goes right down into the weapon to do its business. There's boys yelling and branches falling and the air is black and hot, and there's the ripping, the ripping sound, the cushioned ripping of people and air around you, it's all the same, forget it. Then it's over. You aren't finished—"ambush interruptus," Roger calls it. You're pumped up but there's nothing left to shoot at and it's over to the extent anything like that ever gets over.

I had a daughter born with an open spine. I got a letter from the VA that explained that a bunch of government lawyers had proven in a court of government law that the defoliants aren't why. There were some good doctors in Chicago, and we got her there early. But I don't know. The past is never quite gone, it seems. Steeps inside, for the long haul. I buried, as I said, the VA letters, and my peace-sign belt buckle and my green, nylon-mesh jungle boots. I buried Skidmore's letters, including a fairly recent one:

Dear Wilbur,

I read some of the poems you sent me, and I want you to know they are the most worthless, pitiable utterances I've ever known to be authored by an adult. I get embarrassed just thinking about them. They're abstract and escapist and have very little to do with you. All I want to know about is your pain, Wilbur, and if you can't write about it, then hang it up. I'm telling you pain is all that motivates and everything you write should be an extended paraphrase of the word "Ouch." Stop mulling over abstractions and keep running, is my advice. If it hurts, run faster.

Here's my latest effort at metafiction—"Wilbur Gray Falls in Love with an Idea"—and who knows, you might see a little of yourself in it! I know it's contrived and shitty, so don't send comments. I think I agree with Roger (down here we call him Lefty): You're a real downer. I know it's been rough, but like Lefty says, the worst is over. You know what you need? You need Carol Canfield. Maybe you could catch her between husbands, take a hot bath with her, get her to give you a back rub, hit the road. You need to hit the road, Wilbur. That town will make you nuts. Keep in touch.

Your pal,
Skidmore

It would be nice, I think, to be a little boy again and to see my parents in patio chairs in shadows on the lawn, my mom talking in low tones about the choir, smiling and hoping for the best, my dad just spotting me now and rising up, arm extended, the hand reaching to touch mine. I imagine sometimes that I would talk with them better, given another chance, knowing what I know, discuss for instance Oedipus and why my own dad wouldn't do anything to get me out of what I went through if he was really my dad, and why his didn't either. But Dad and Mom were never any better at talking than I am, and maybe it wouldn't work. I had music, the Stones, the Doors, Joe Cocker; my parents had phrases representing what they believed, and prayers to speak aloud in church in unison with the community of the faithful. They had their war and childhood, I had mine.

The grass boulevard along Court Street here, it's a blessing to the knees. I see the gables on my house in the distance. The job I had, back when I had it, was quite interesting. I was hired by the culture to have and carry a briefcase, wear a dark three-piece suit, and have my hair razor-cut, to rush up and down the street (briefcase in hand), across the mall, to occupy the sidewalks, to have an office and use the phone energetically, carry a busy calendar of meetings and to participate in those meetings to the fullest, to state the obvious emphatically and as often as possible, and in as many ways, all in an effort to give the illusion of quality, productivity, upward movement, the rightness and nonfutility of democratic life in a guns-and-butter economy, action and activity, creativity and motion, motivation and, of course, obedience, go, go, go. I would buy a paper and read the editorials. I would catch the news and read *Time* magazine. I would watch the market, even daydream of buying stocks. I would think of good ideas and route them up the organization. I would make wind and then piss into it.

The lines in my forehead get deeper, I brood without control sometimes, sleepless, like a child in tears, and like all the hard-handed workers, smug patriots, and ordinary men on the street I've known in my life, for whom money, work, women, and the church are all there is and whose hearts these crazy days are breaking.

I have a new pair of running shoes. They cost sixty dollars because of the wing-shaped stripe they have on the side. They are my Sunday best. Hard to believe, but Skidmore and I were camping in the old chautauqua ground the night the burr oak was split by lightning. You could smell the ozone and the heat even after the rain.

THE FLANNERY O'CONNOR AWARD FOR SHORT FICTION

David Walton, *Evening Out*
Leigh Allison Wilson, *From the Bottom Up*
Sandra Thompson, *Close-Ups*
Susan Neville, *The Invention of Flight*
Mary Hood, *How Far She Went*
François Camoin, *Why Men Are Afraid of Women*
Molly Giles, *Rough Translations*
Daniel Curley, *Living with Snakes*
Peter Meinke, *The Piano Tuner*
Tony Ardizzone, *The Evening News*
Salvatore La Puma, *The Boys of Bensonhurst*
Melissa Pritchard, *Spirit Seizures*
Philip F. Deaver, *Silent Retreats*
Gail Galloway Adams, *The Purchase of Order*
Carole L. Glickfeld, *Useful Gifts*
Antonya Nelson, *The Expendables*
Nancy Zafris, *The People I Know*
Debra Monroe, *The Source of Trouble*
Robert H. Abel, *Ghost Traps*
T. M. McNally, *Low Flying Aircraft*
Alfred DePew, *The Melancholy of Departure*
Dennis Hathaway, *The Consequences of Desire*
Rita Ciresi, *Mother Rocket*
Dianne Nelson, *A Brief History of Male Nudes in America*
Christopher McIlroy, *All My Relations*
Alyce Miller, *The Nature of Longing*

CPSIA information can be obtained at www.ICGtesting.com
Printed in the USA
BVOW030119180412

287903BV00001B/26/P